SPIDER-MAN

SECRET IDENTITY

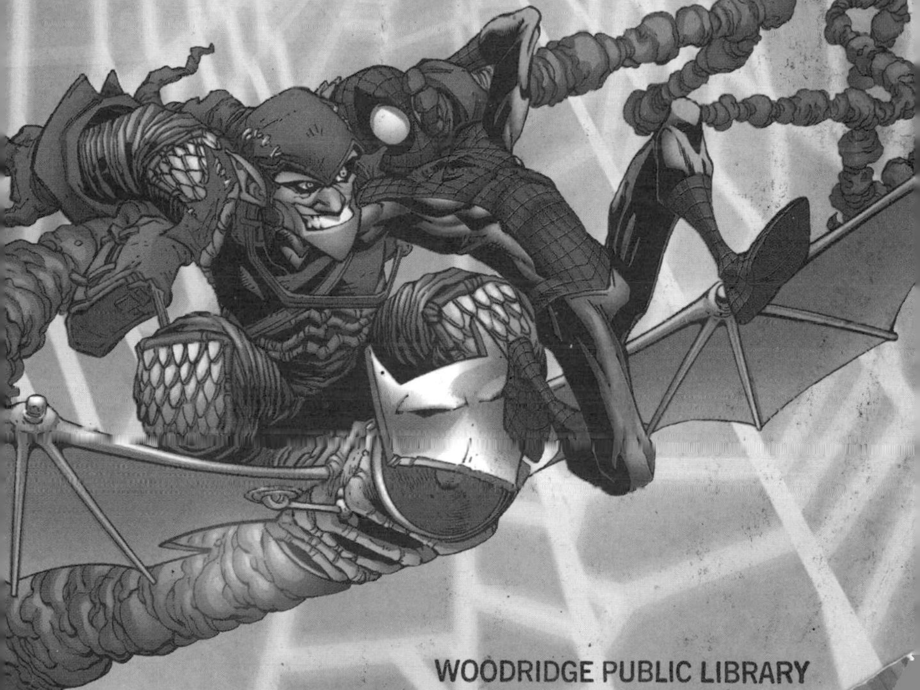

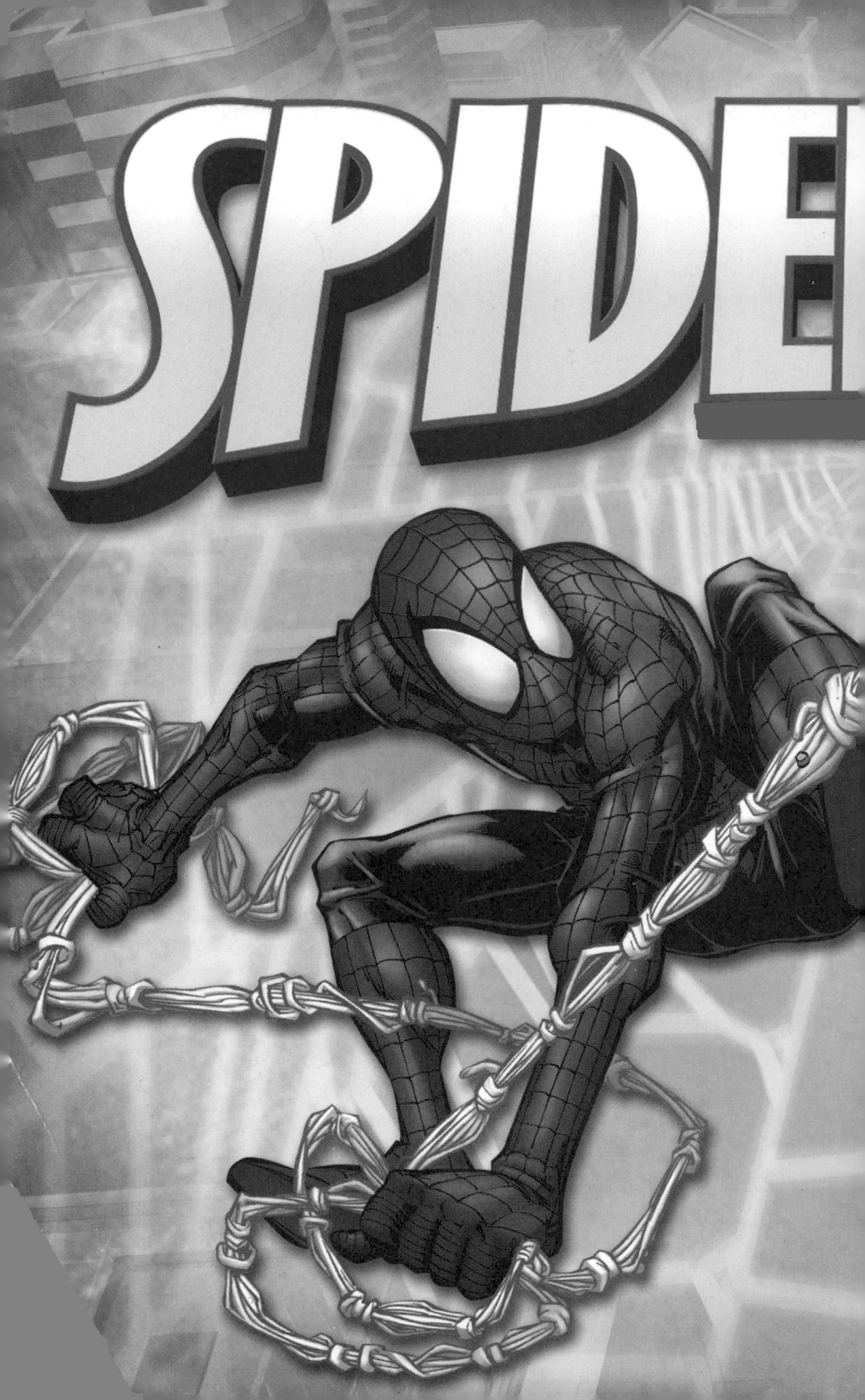
SPIDE

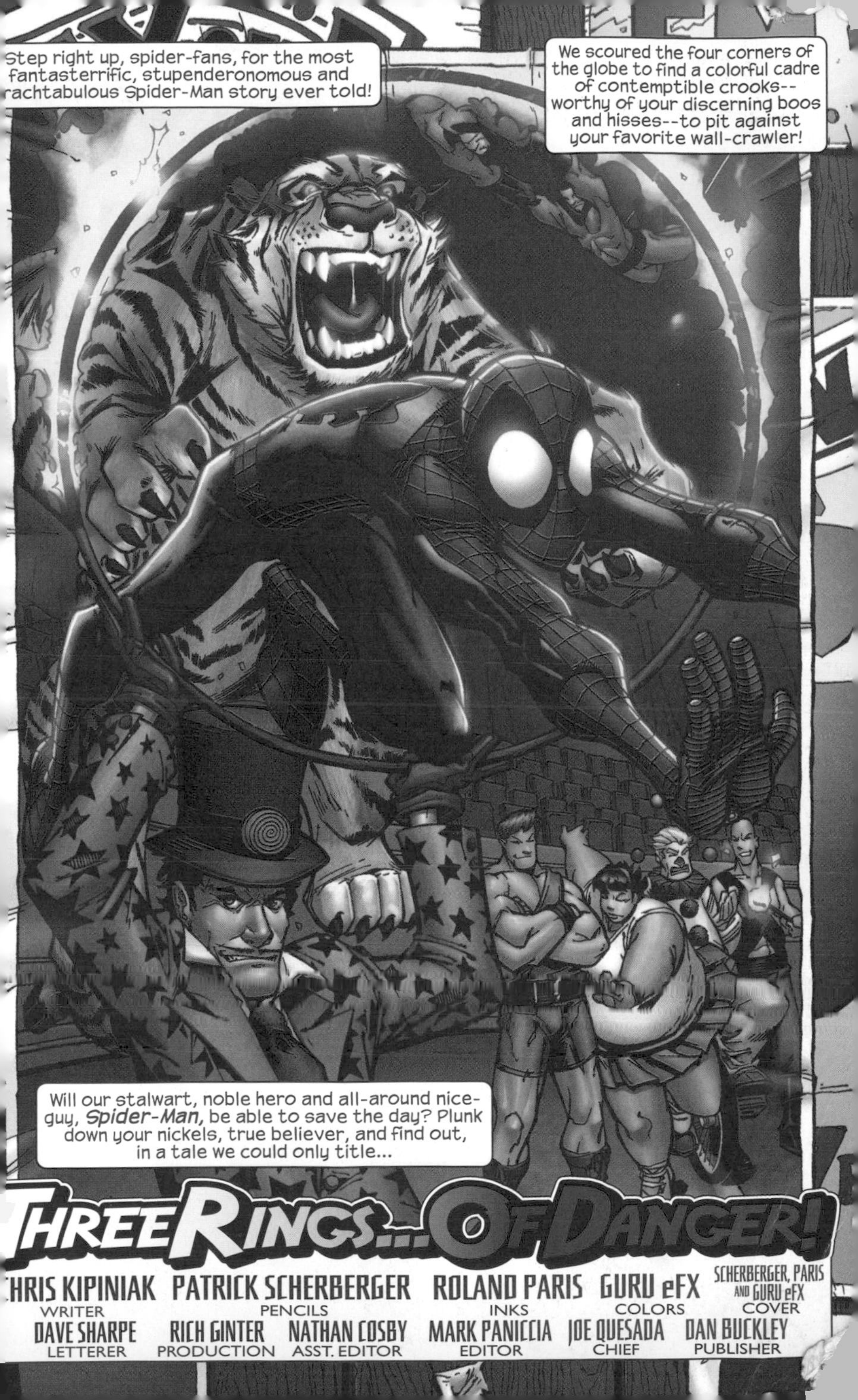
Step right up, spider-fans, for the most fantasterrific, stupenderonomous and rachtabulous Spider-Man story ever told!
We scoured the four corners of the globe to find a colorful cadre of contemptible crooks--worthy of your discerning boos and hisses--to pit against your favorite wall-crawler!
Will our stalwart, noble hero and all-around nice-guy, Spider-Man, be able to save the day? Plunk down your nickels, true believer, and find out, in a tale we could only title...
THREE RINGS...OF DANGER!
HRIS KIPINIAK WRITER
PATRICK SCHERBERGER PENCILS
ROLAND PARIS INKS
GURU eFX COLORS
SCHERBERGER, PARIS AND GURU eFX COVER
DAVE SHARPE LETTERER
RICH GINTER PRODUCTION
NATHAN COSBY ASST. EDITOR
MARK PANICCIA EDITOR
JOE QUESADA CHIEF
DAN BUCKLEY PUBLISHER

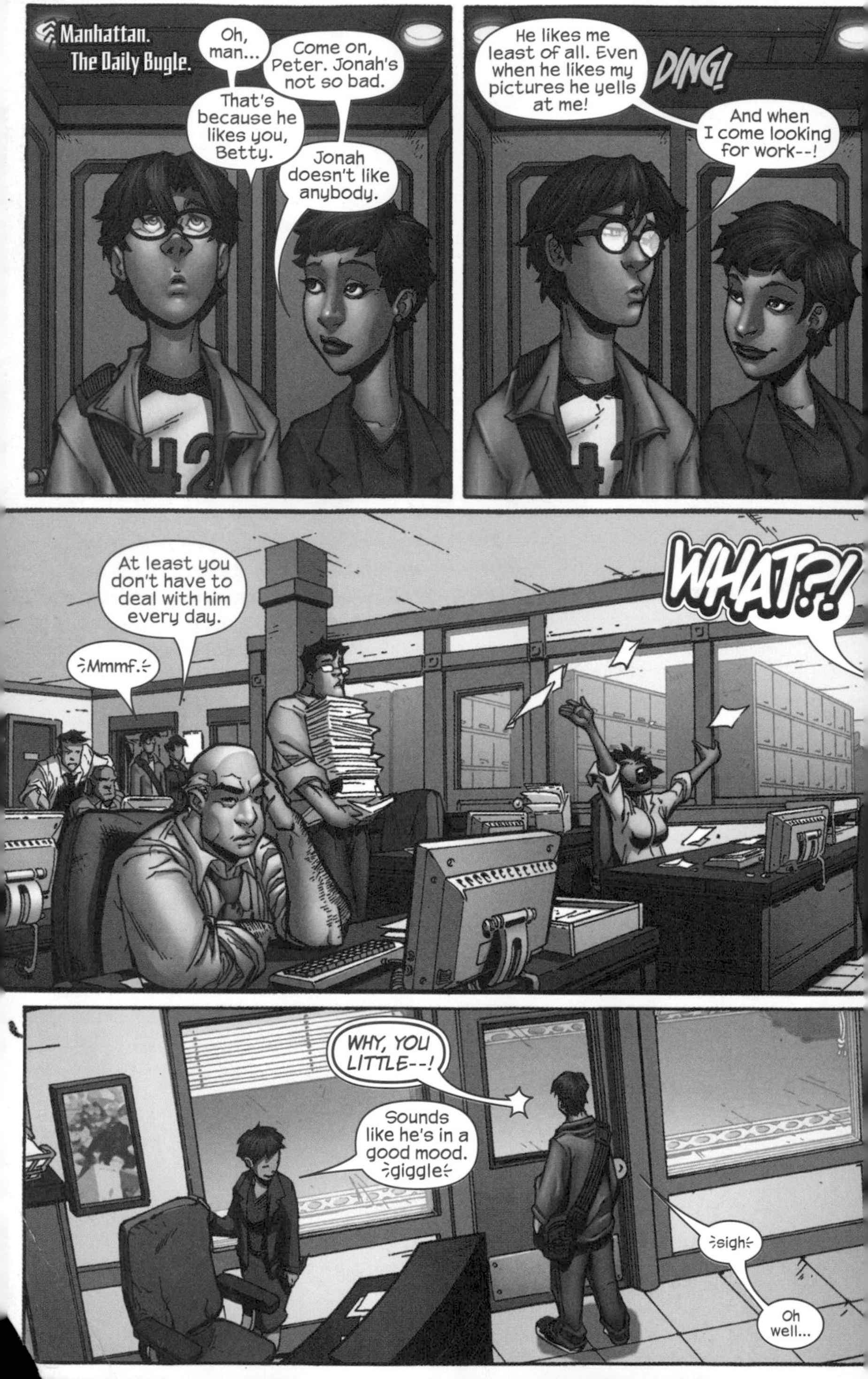
Manhattan. The Daily Bugle.
Oh, man...
That's because he likes you, Betty.
Come on, Peter. Jonah's not so bad.
Jonah doesn't like anybody.
He likes me least of all. Even when he likes my pictures he yells at me!
DING!
And when I come looking for work--!
At least you don't have to deal with him every day.
Mmmf.
WHAT?!
WHY, YOU LITTLE--!
Sounds like he's in a good mood. giggle
sigh
Oh well...

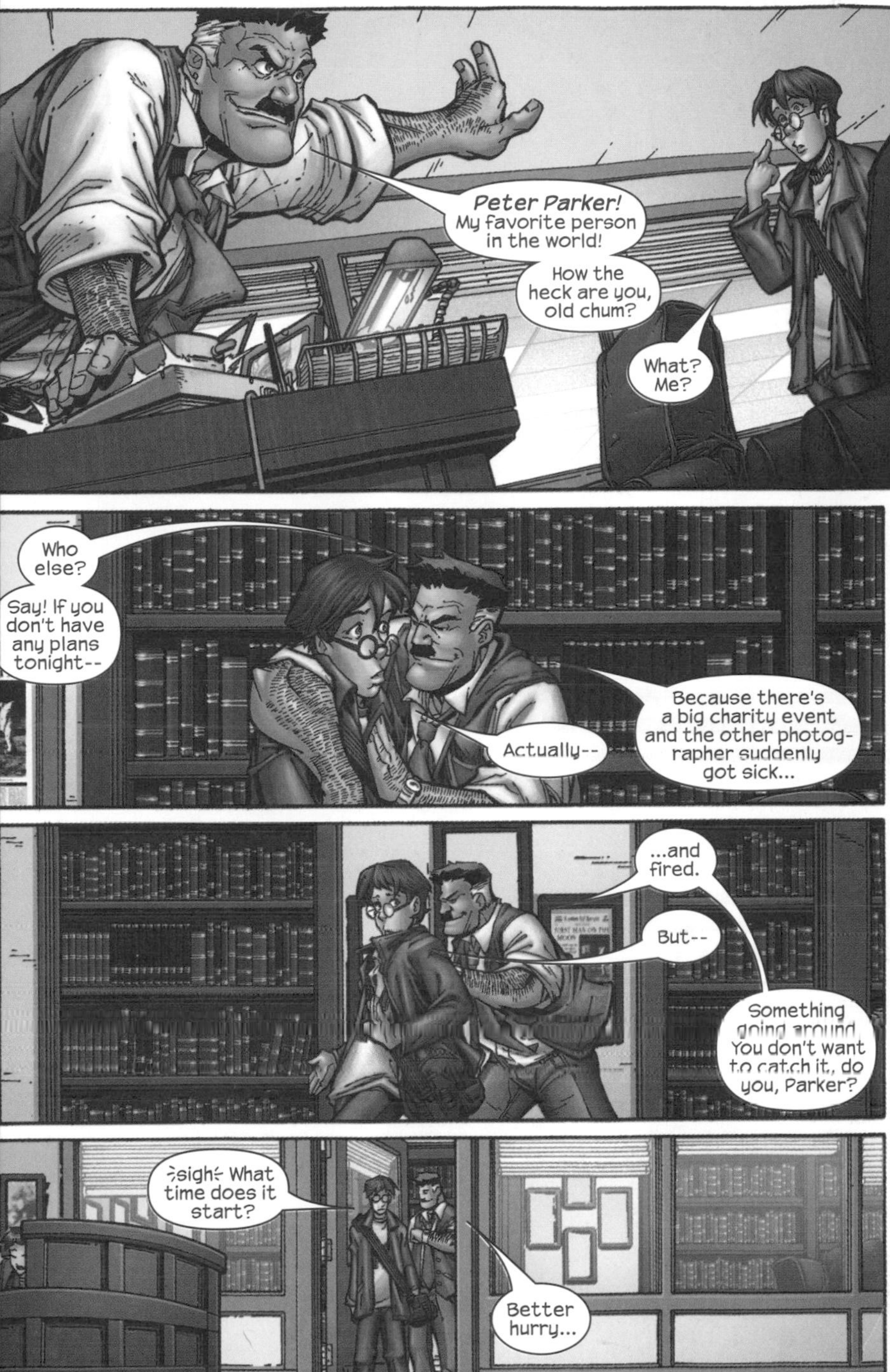
Peter Parker! My favorite person in the world!
How the heck are you, old chum?
What? Me?
Who else?
Say! If you don't have any plans tonight--
Actually--
Because there's a big charity event and the other photographer suddenly got sick...
...and fired.
But--
Something going around. You don't want to catch it, do you, Parker?
=sigh= What time does it start?
Better hurry...

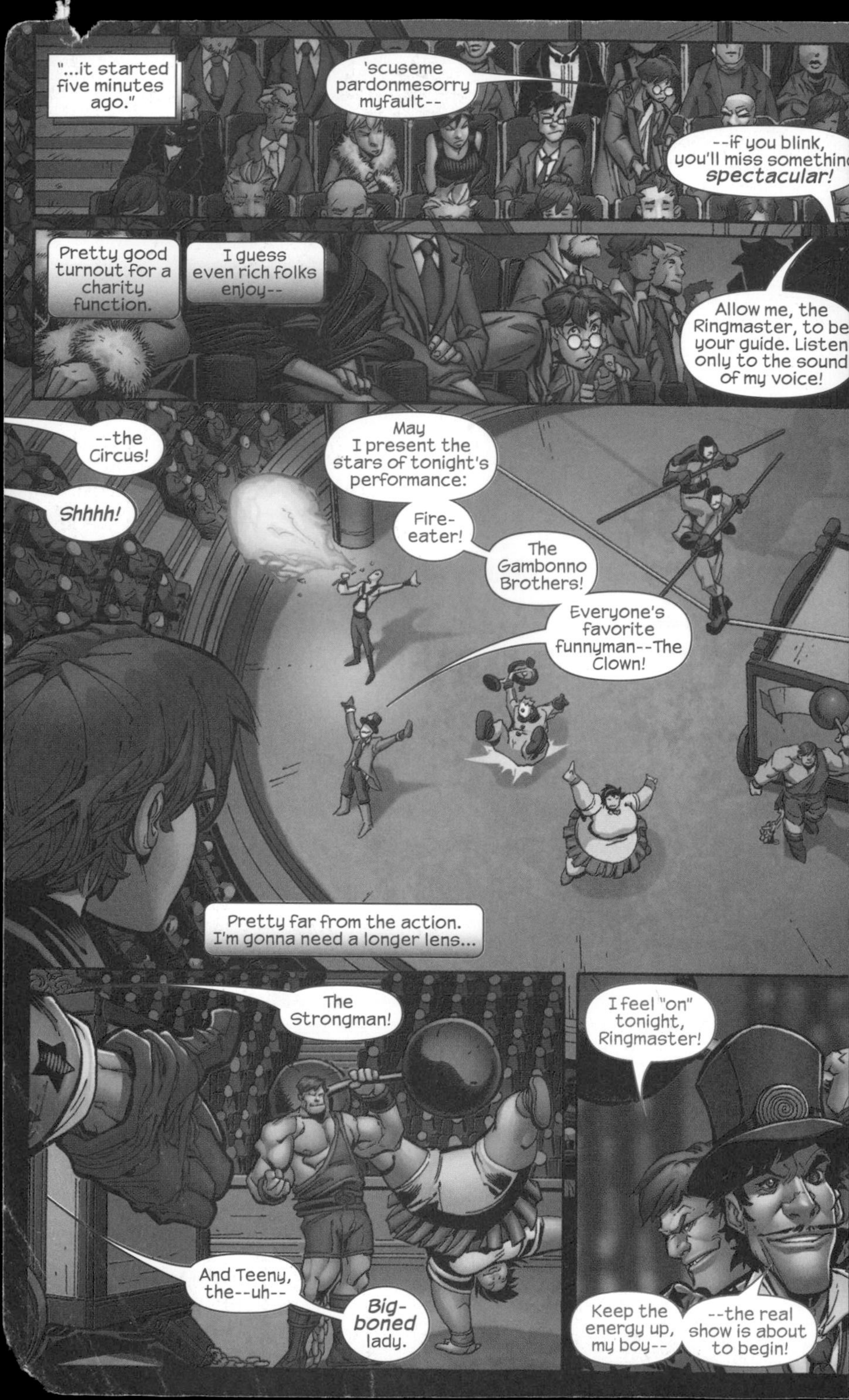
"...it started five minutes ago."
'scuseme pardonmesorry myfault--
--if you blink, you'll miss something spectacular!
Pretty good turnout for a charity function.
I guess even rich folks enjoy--
Allow me, the Ringmaster, to be your guide. Listen only to the sound of my voice!
--the Circus!
Shhhh!
May I present the stars of tonight's performance:
Fire-eater!
The Gambonno Brothers!
Everyone's favorite funnyman--The Clown!
Pretty far from the action. I'm gonna need a longer lens...
The Strongman!
And Teeny, the--uh--
Big-boned lady.
I feel "on" tonight, Ringmaster!
Keep the energy up, my boy--
--the real show is about to begin!

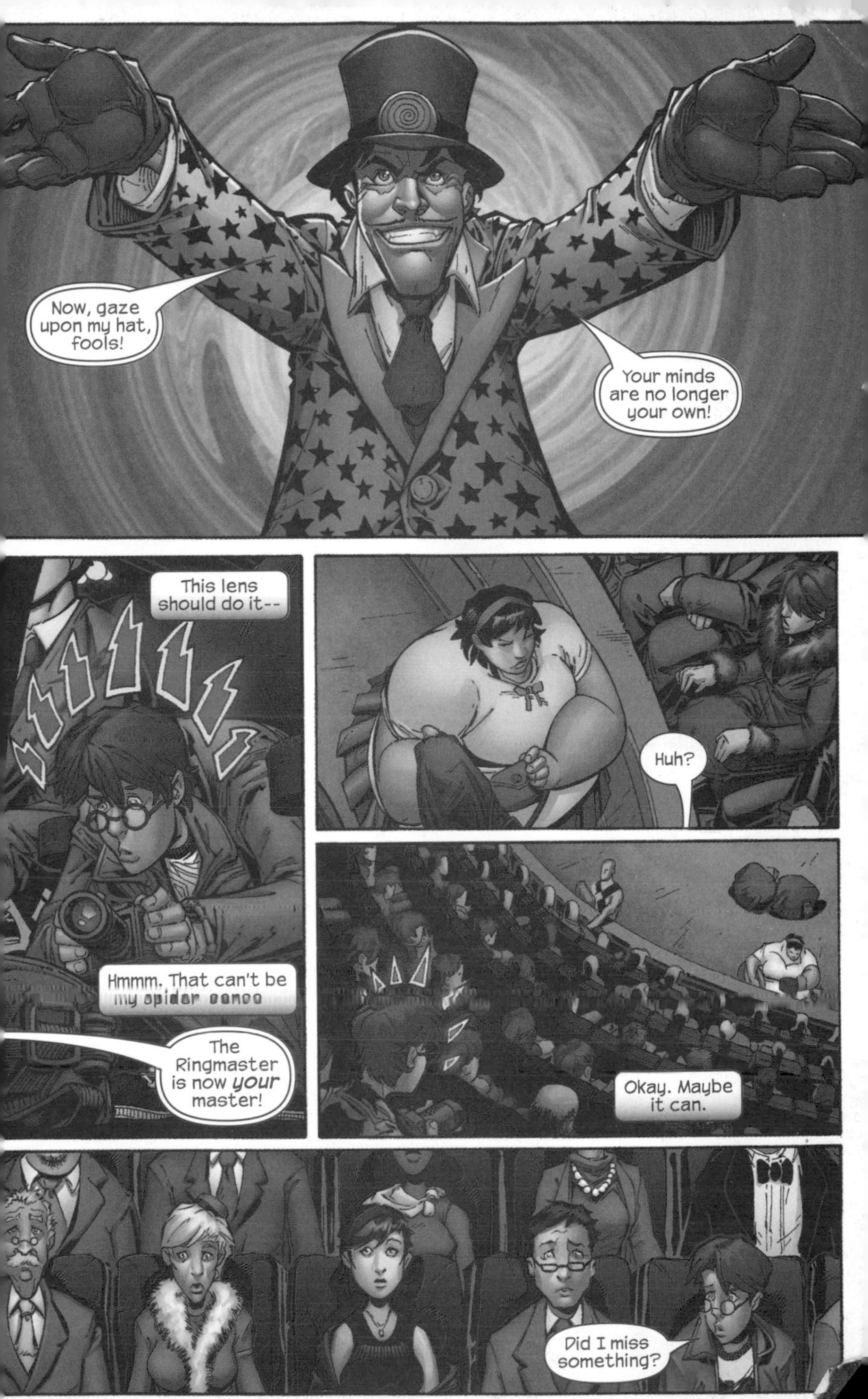
Now, gaze upon my hat, fools!
Your minds are no longer your own!
This lens should do it--
Huh?
Hmmm. That can't be my spider sense
The Ringmaster is now *your* master!
Okay. Maybe it can.
Did I miss something?

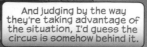

And judging by the way they're taking advantage of the situation, I'd guess the circus is somehow behind it.

The audience is in some kind of trance!

Better get out of sight before they reach my ro

Oh well. Guess I'm not gonna get to see the monkeys.

Rats.

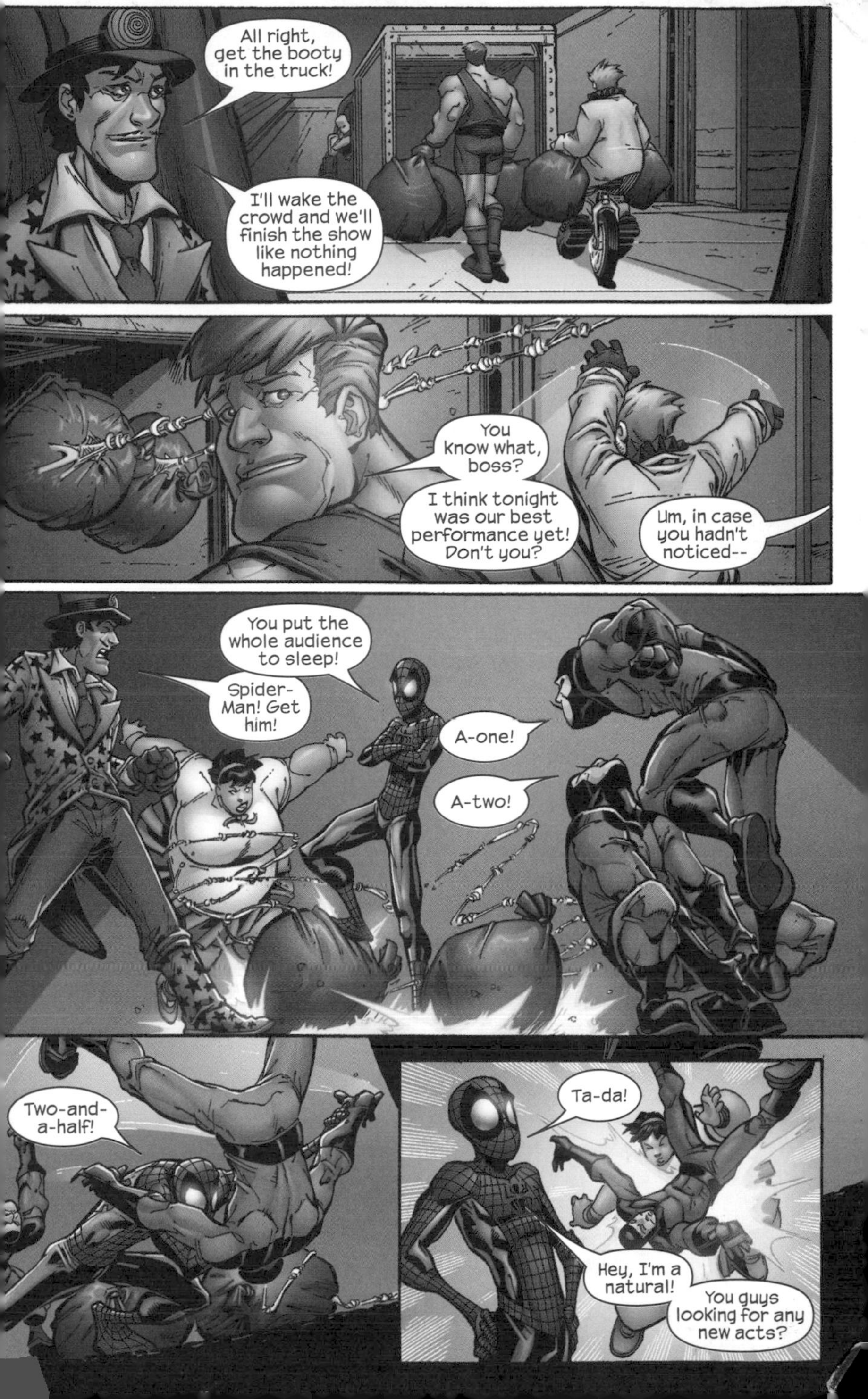
All right, get the booty in the truck!
I'll wake the crowd and we'll finish the show like nothing happened!
You know what, boss?
I think tonight was our best performance yet! Don't you?
Um, in case you hadn't noticed--
You put the whole audience to sleep!
Spider-Man! Get him!
A-one!
A-two!
Two-and-a-half!
Ta-da!
Hey, I'm a natural!
You guys looking for any new acts?

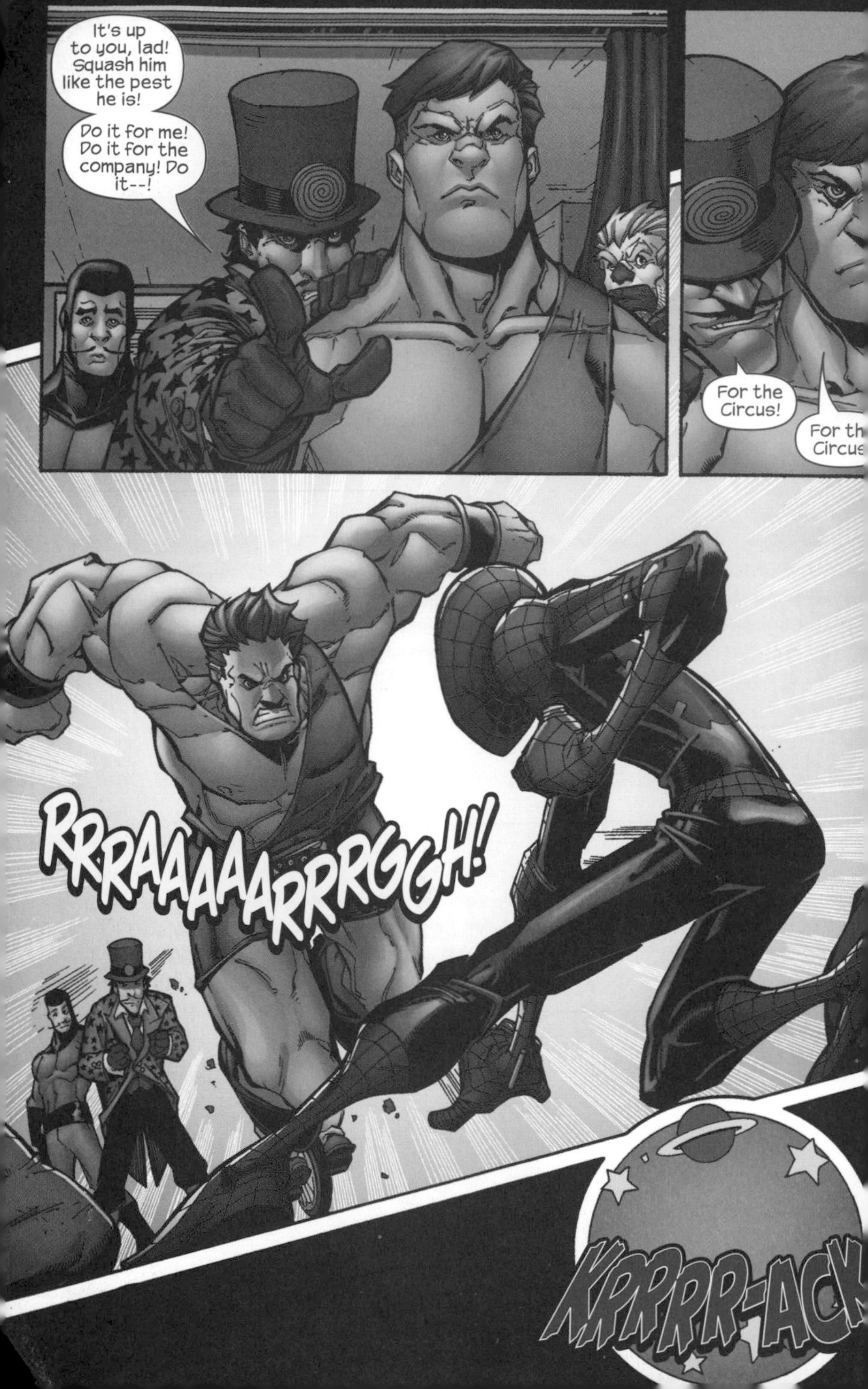

It's up to you, lad! Squash him like the pest he is!
Do it for me! Do it for the company! Do it--!
For the Circus!
For th Circus
RRRAAAAAARRRGGH!
KRRRR-ACK

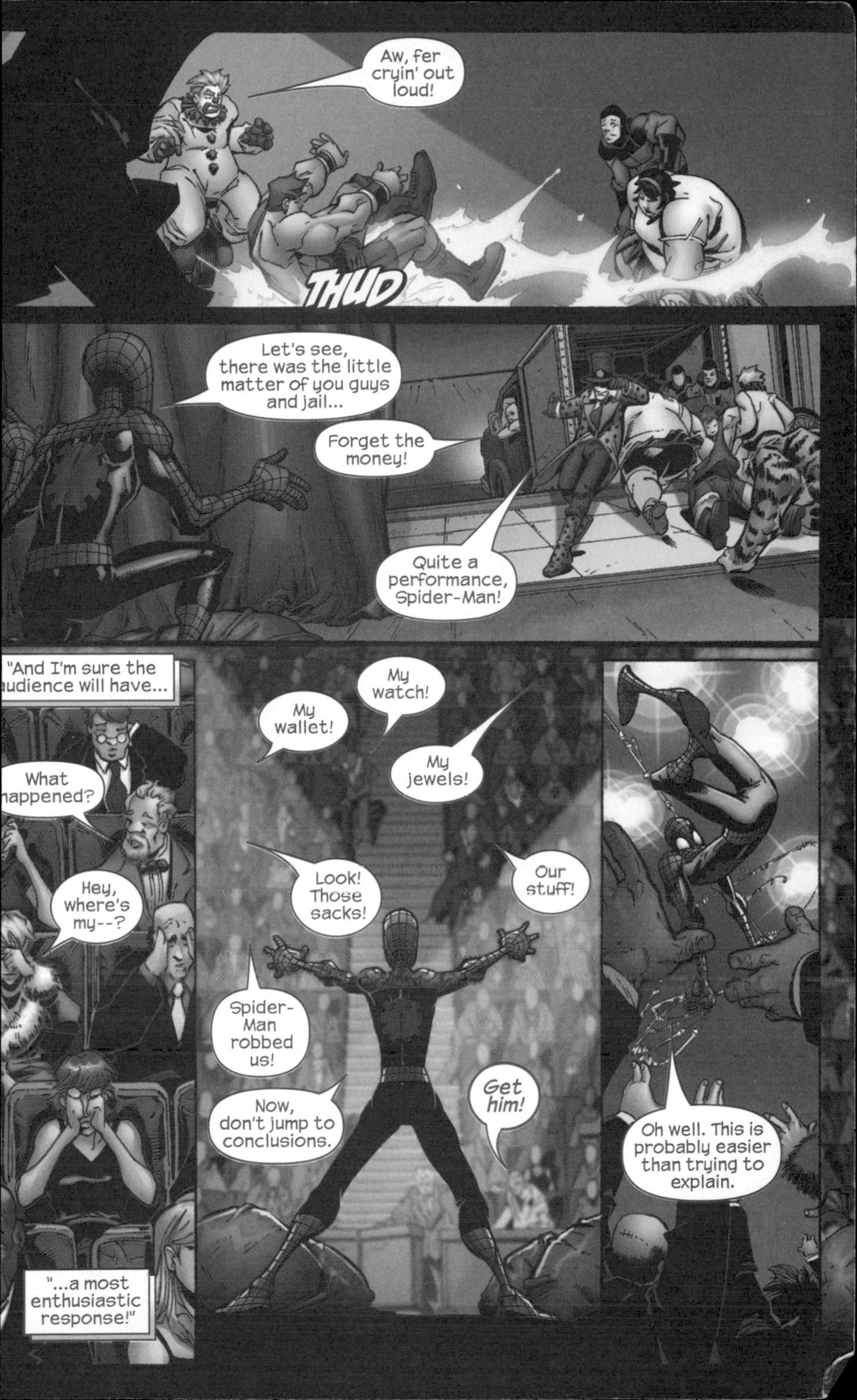
Aw, fer cryin' out loud!
THUD
Let's see, there was the little matter of you guys and jail...
Forget the money!
Quite a performance, Spider-Man!
"And I'm sure the audience will have...
What happened?
Hey, where's my--?
"...a most enthusiastic response!"
My wallet!
My watch!
My jewels!
Look! Those sacks!
Our stuff!
Spider-Man robbed us!
Now, don't jump to conclusions.
Get him!
Oh well. This is probably easier than trying to explain.

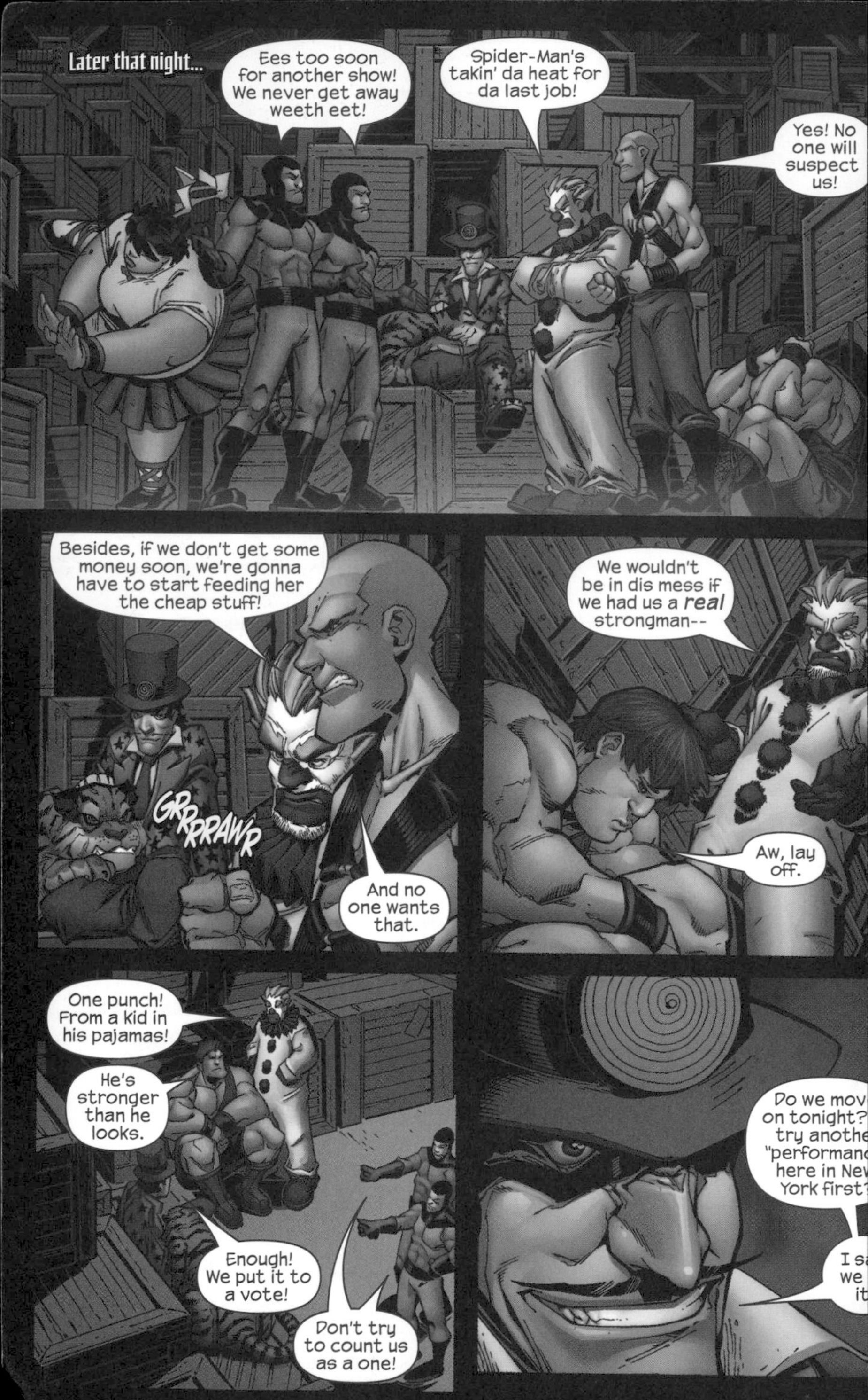

Later that night...
Ees too soon for another show! We never get away weeth eet!
Spider-Man's takin' da heat for da last job!
Yes! No one will suspect us!
Besides, if we don't get some money soon, we're gonna have to start feeding her the cheap stuff!
GRRRRAWR
And no one wants that.
We wouldn't be in dis mess if we had us a *real* strongman--
Aw, lay off.
One punch! From a kid in his pajamas!
He's stronger than he looks.
Enough! We put it to a vote!
Don't try to count us as a one!

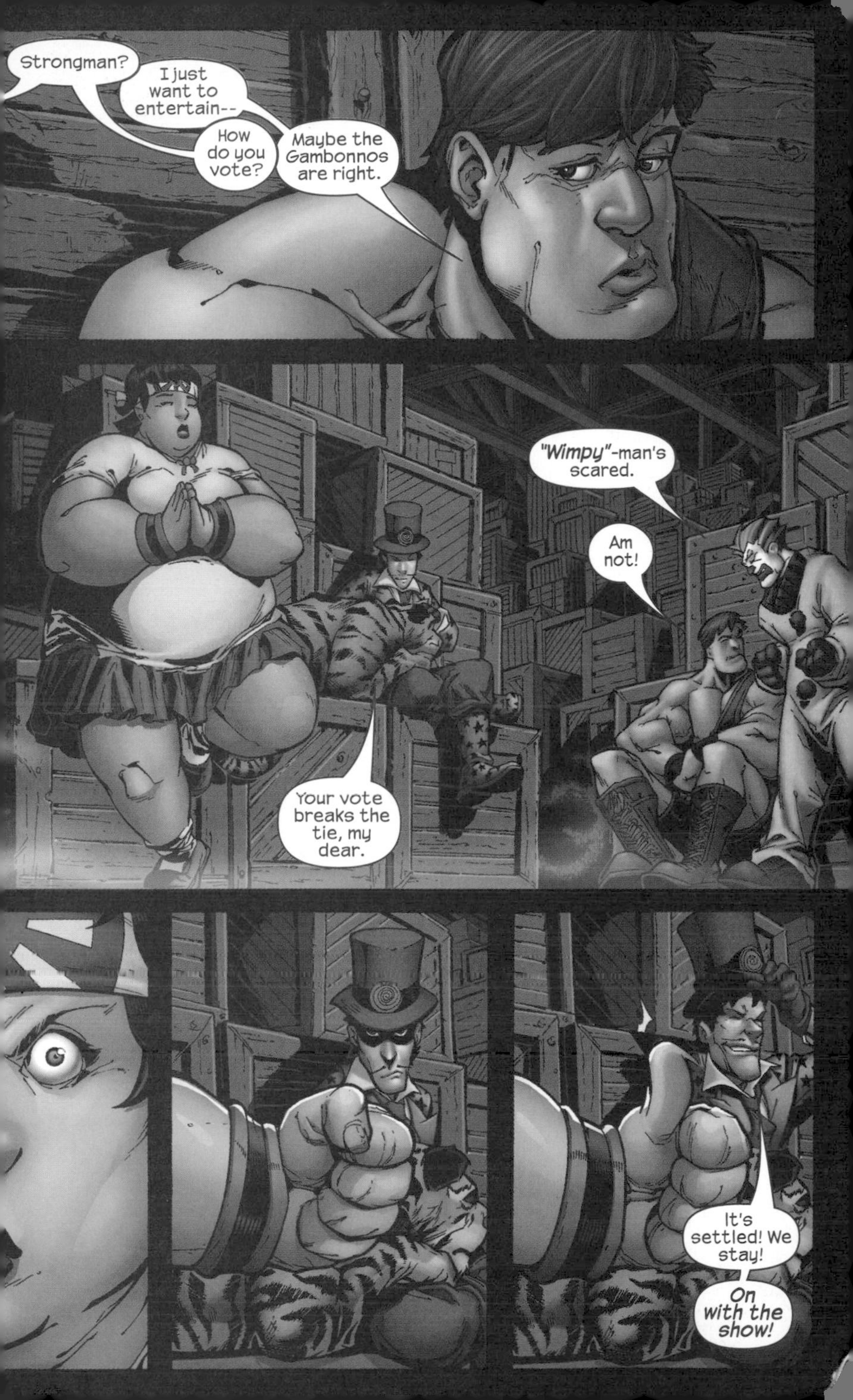
Strongman?
I just want to entertain--
How do you vote?
Maybe the Gambonnos are right.
"Wimpy"-man's scared.
Am not!
Your vote breaks the tie, my dear.
It's settled! We stay!
On with the show!

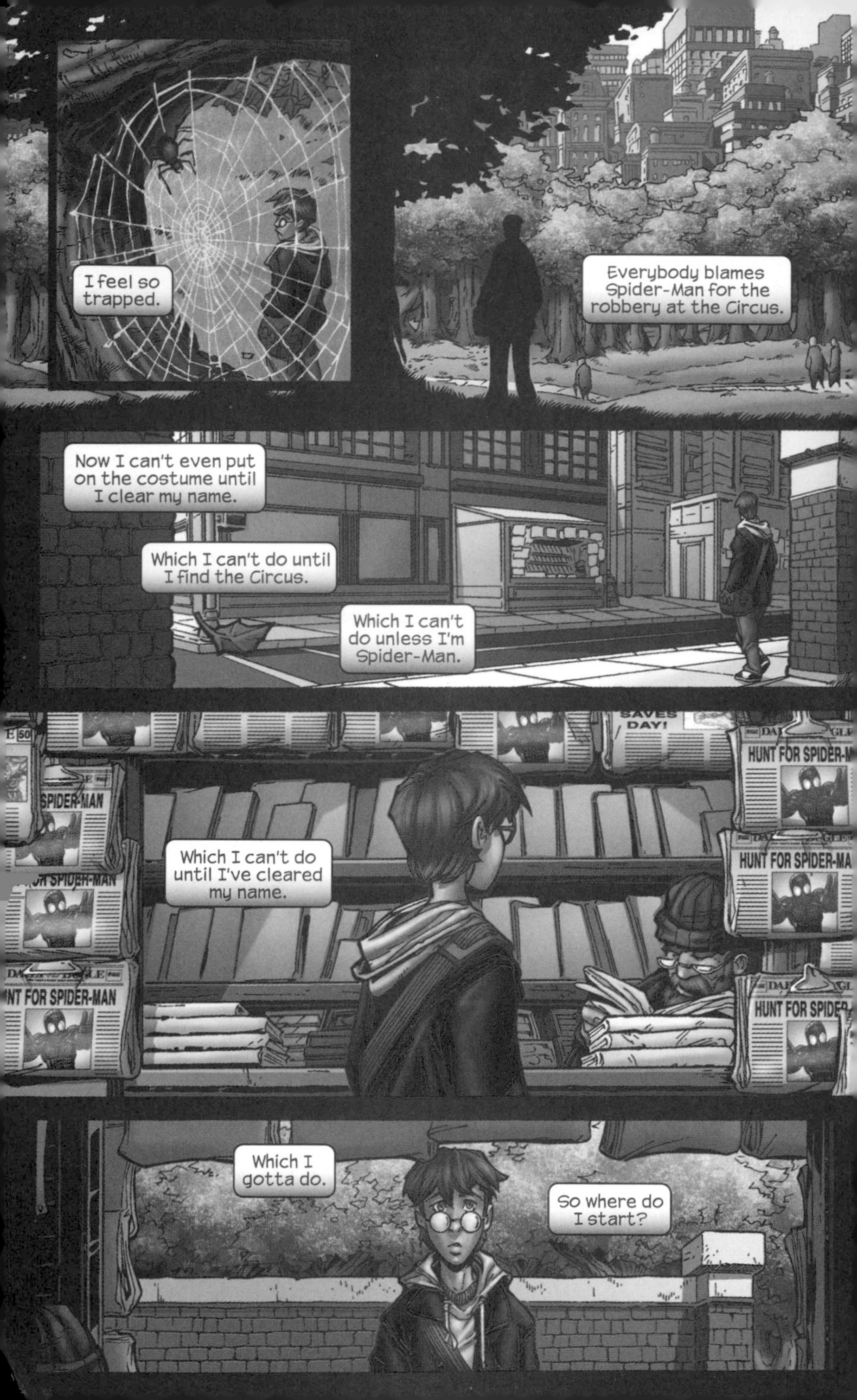

I feel so trapped.
Everybody blames Spider-Man for the robbery at the Circus.
Now I can't even put on the costume until I clear my name.
Which I can't do until I find the Circus.
Which I can't do unless I'm Spider-Man.
SAVES DAY!
SPIDER-MAN
Which I can't do until I've cleared my name.
Which I gotta do.
So where do I start?

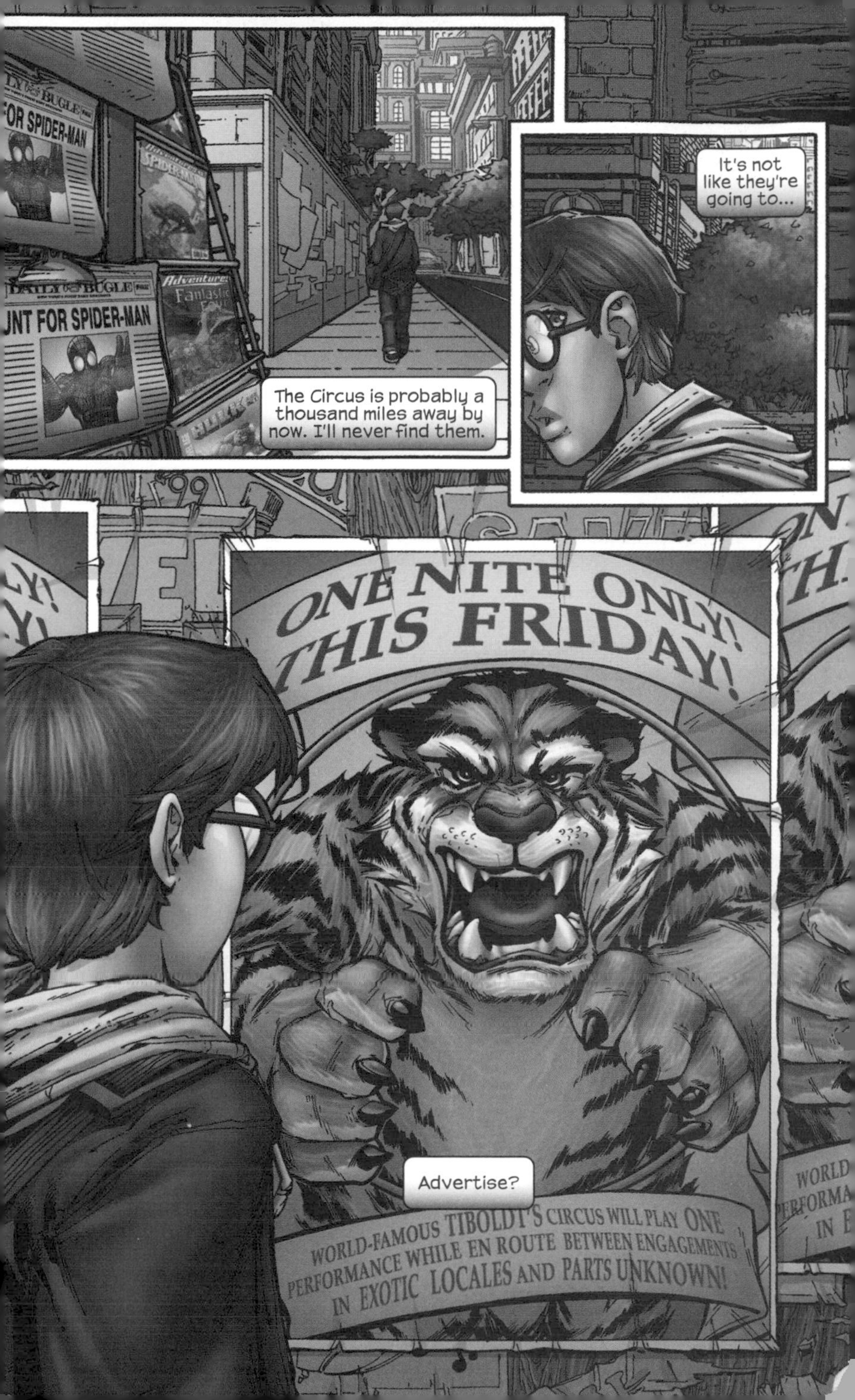
FOR SPIDER-MAN
UNT FOR SPIDER-MAN
The Circus is probably a thousand miles away by now. I'll never find them.
It's not like they're going to...
ONE NITE ONLY! THIS FRIDAY!
Advertise?
WORLD-FAMOUS TIBOLDT'S CIRCUS WILL PLAY ONE PERFORMANCE WHILE EN ROUTE BETWEEN ENGAGEMENTS IN EXOTIC LOCALES AND PARTS UNKNOWN!

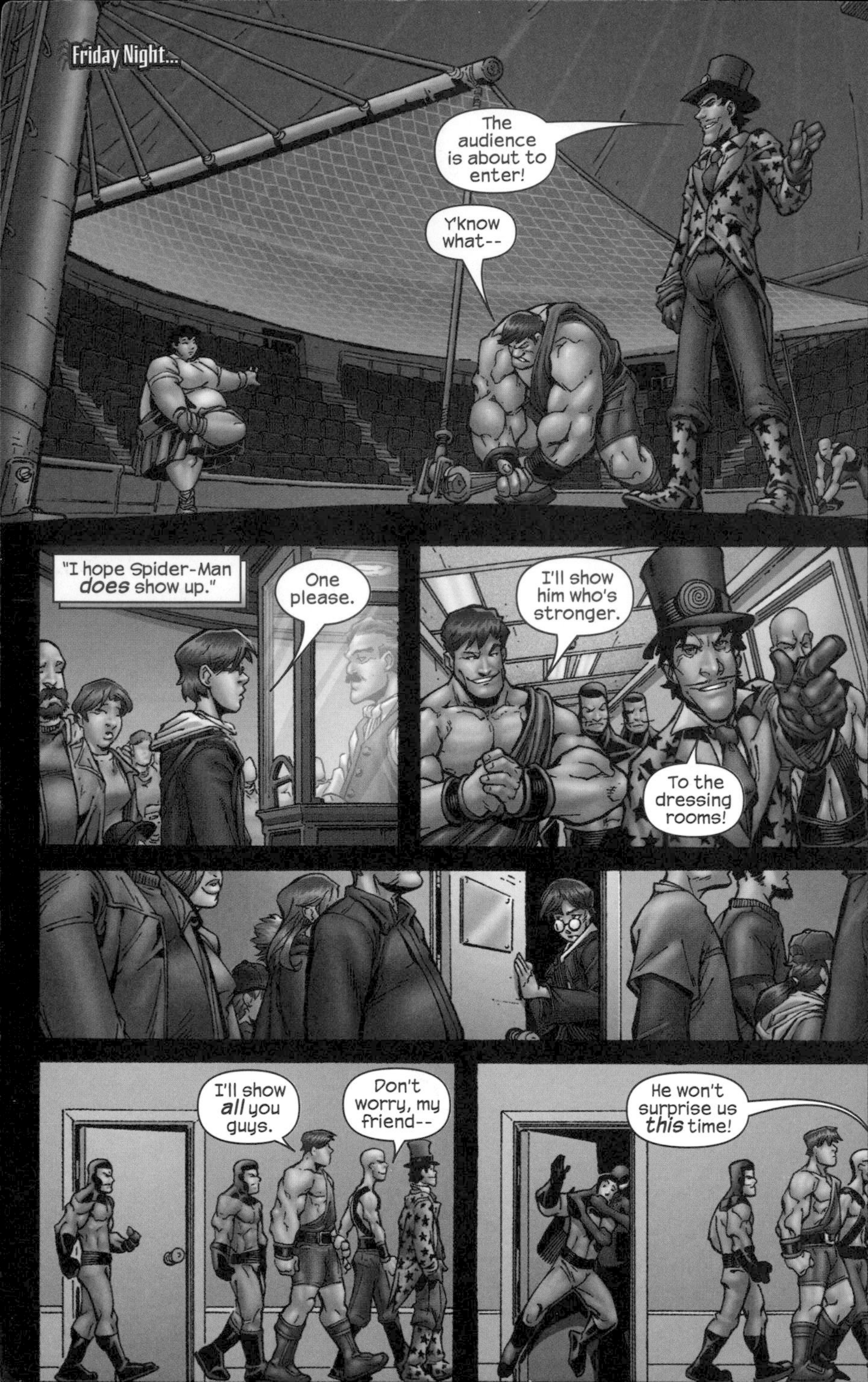
Friday Night...
The audience is about to enter!
Y'know what--
"I hope Spider-Man does show up."
One please.
I'll show him who's stronger.
To the dressing rooms!
I'll show all you guys.
Don't worry, my friend--
He won't surprise us this time!

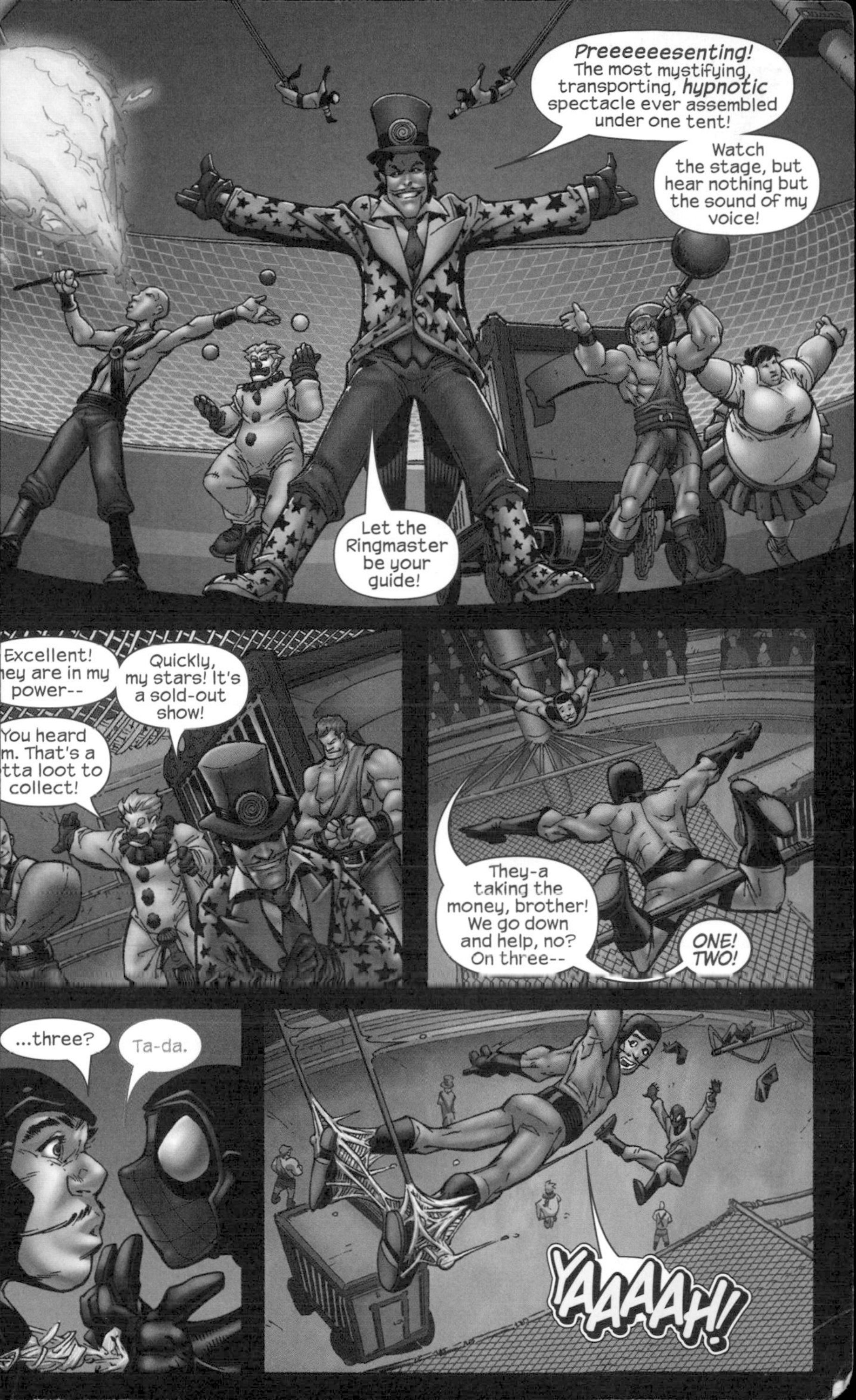
Preeeeeeesenting! The most mystifying, transporting, hypnotic spectacle ever assembled under one tent!
Watch the stage, but hear nothing but the sound of my voice!
Let the Ringmaster be your guide!
Excellent! ...ey are in my power--
Quickly, my stars! It's a sold-out show!
You heard ...m. That's a ...tta loot to collect!
They-a taking the money, brother! We go down and help, no? On three--
ONE! TWO!
...three?
Ta-da.
YAAAAH!

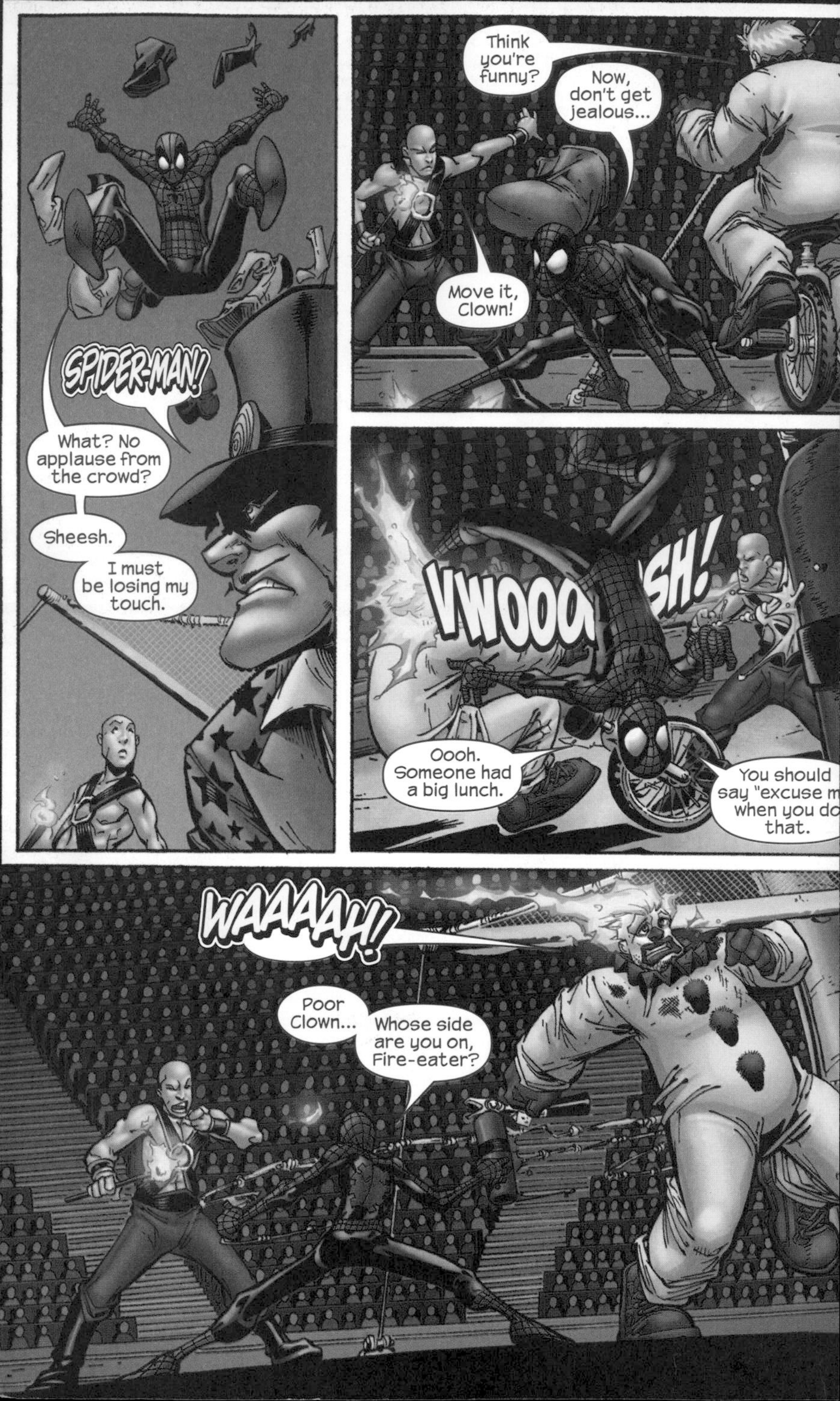
SPIDER-MAN!
What? No applause from the crowd?
Sheesh.
I must be losing my touch.
Think you're funny?
Now, don't get jealous...
Move it, Clown!
VWOOO SH!
Oooh. Someone had a big lunch.
You should say "excuse m when you do that.
WAAAAH!!
Poor Clown...
Whose side are you on, Fire-eater?

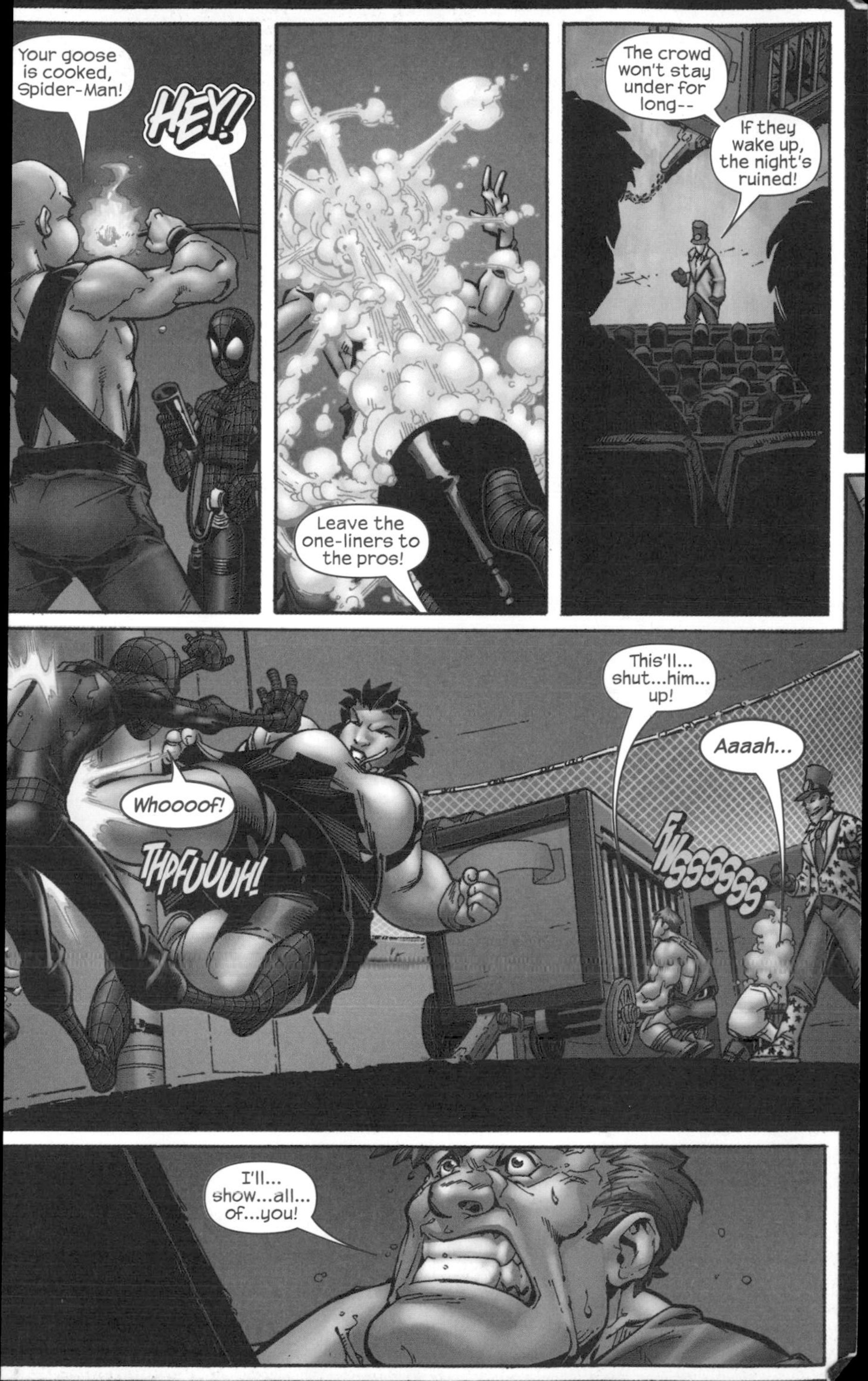

Your goose is cooked, Spider-Man!
HEY!
Leave the one-liners to the pros!
The crowd won't stay under for long--
If they wake up, the night's ruined!
Whoooof!
THPFUUUH!
This'll... shut...him... up!
FWSSSSSS
Aaaah...
I'll... show...all... of...you!

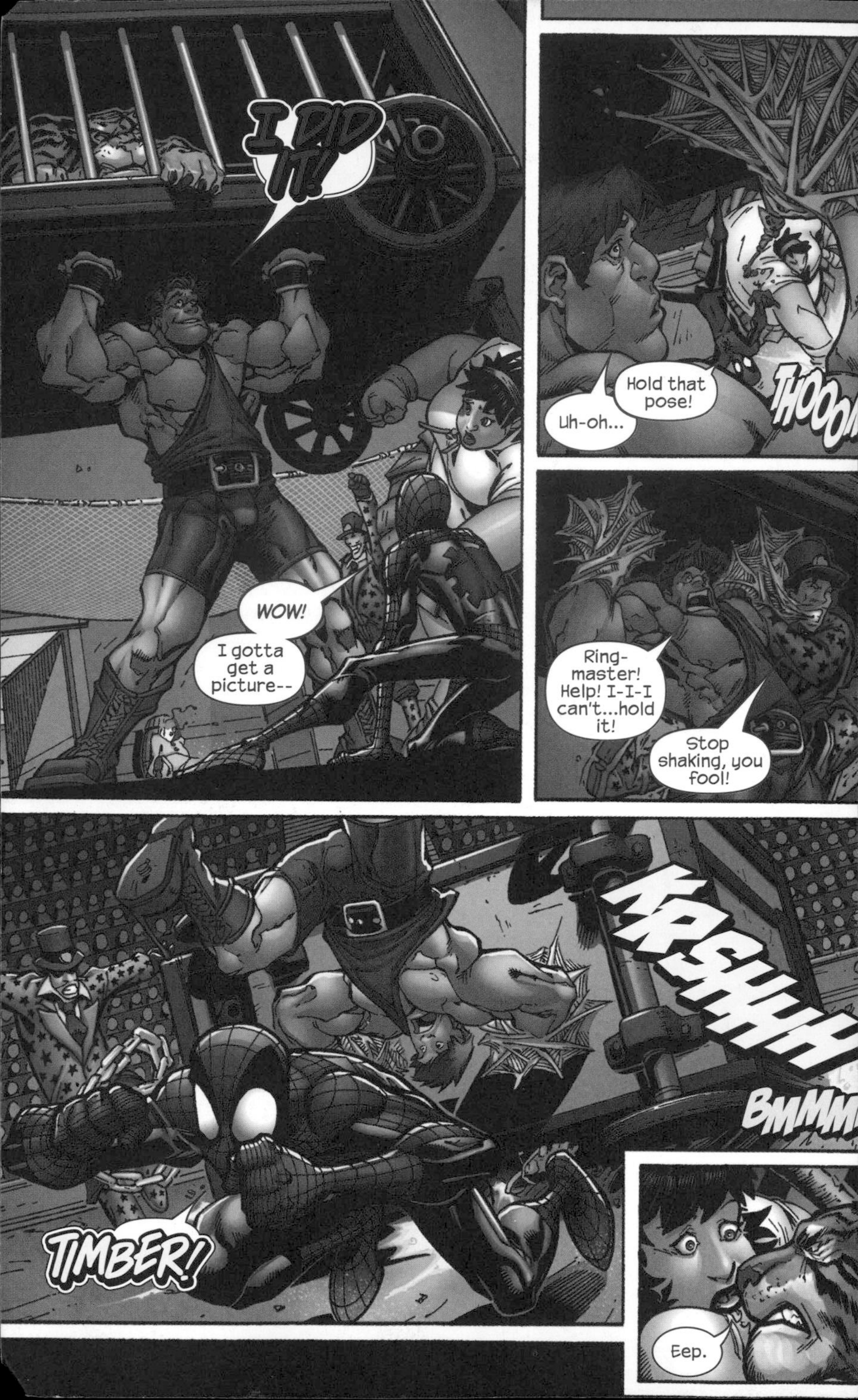
I DID IT!
WOW!
I gotta get a picture--
Uh-oh...
Hold that pose!
THOOOM
Ring-master! Help! I-I-I can't...hold it!
Stop shaking, you fool!
KRSHHH
BMMM
TIMBER!
Eep.

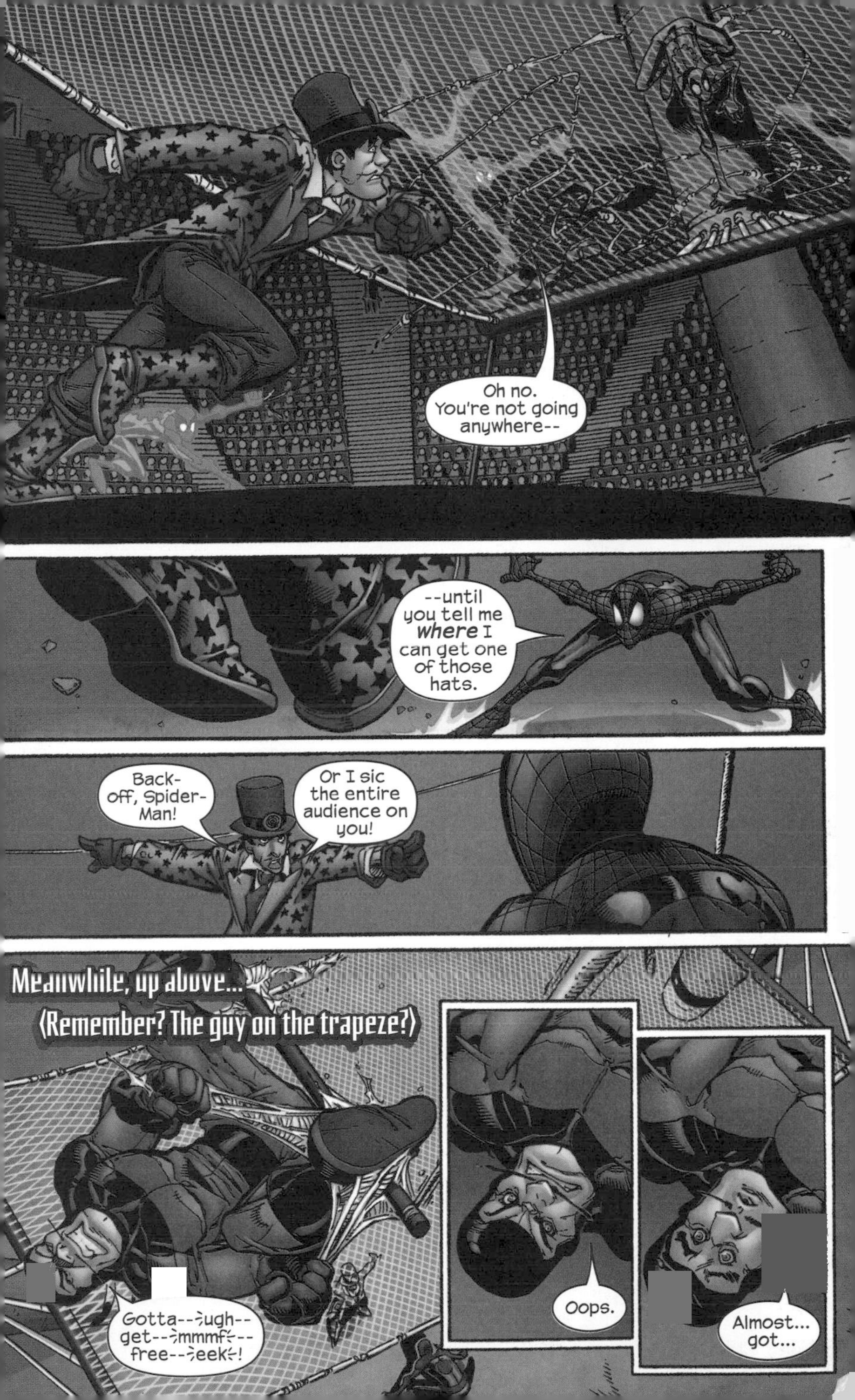

Oh no. You're not going anywhere--
--until you tell me *where* I can get one of those hats.
Back-off, Spider-Man!
Or I sic the entire audience on you!
Meanwhile, up above...
(Remember? The guy on the trapeze?)
Gotta--ugh--get--mmmf--free--eek!
Oops.
Almost... got...

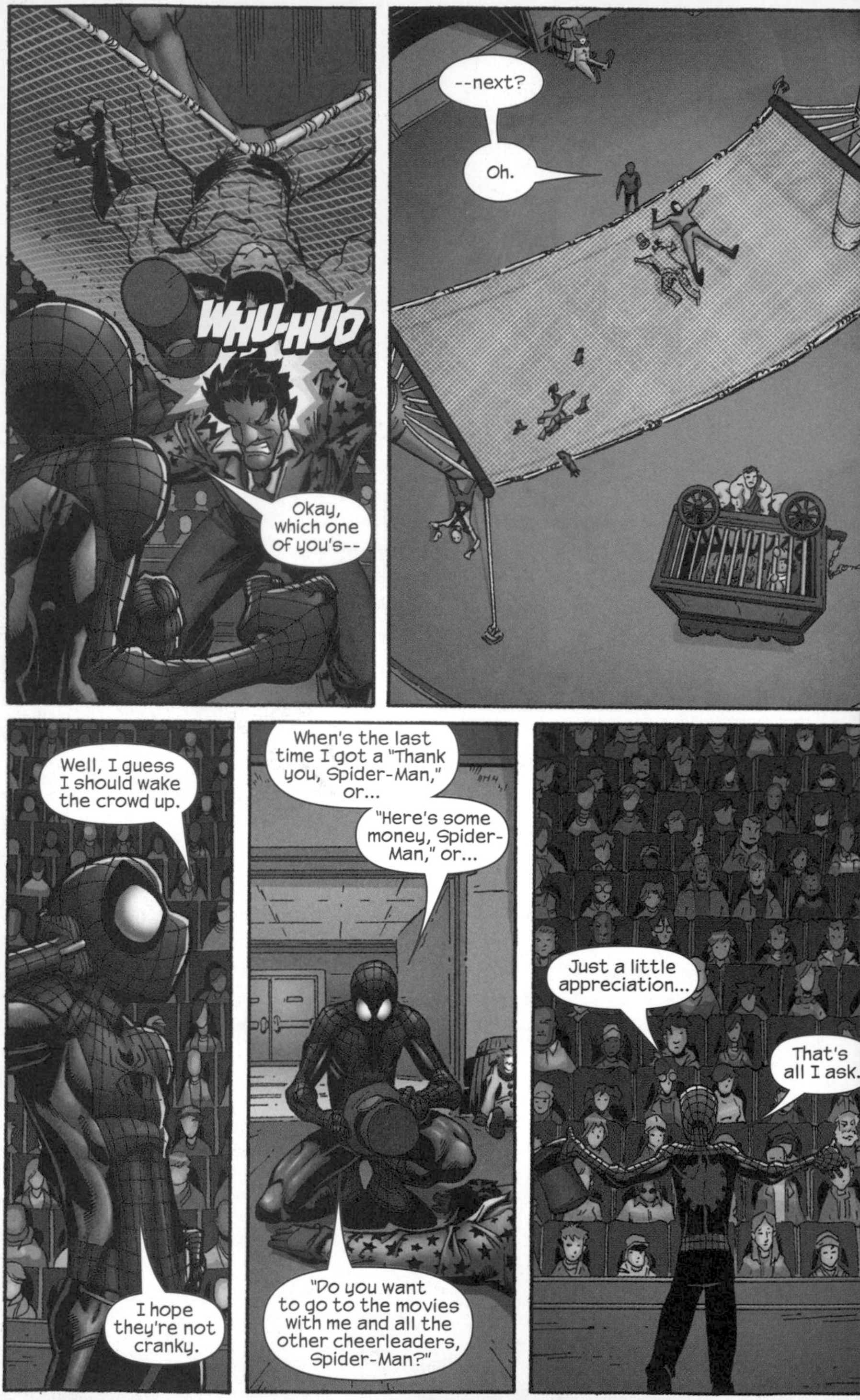
WHU-HUD
Okay, which one of you's--
--next?
Oh.
Well, I guess I should wake the crowd up.
I hope they're not cranky.
When's the last time I got a "Thank you, Spider-Man," or...
"Here's some money, Spider-Man," or...
"Do you want to go to the movies with me and all the other cheerleaders, Spider-Man?"
Just a little appreciation...
That's all I ask.

I suppose I could...

I mean, it wouldn't be that--

No. Definitely not.

But...

Before I release the audience from its trance...

There is one thing I gotta do.

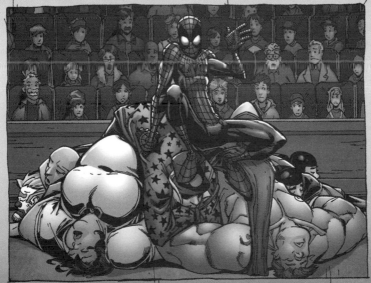

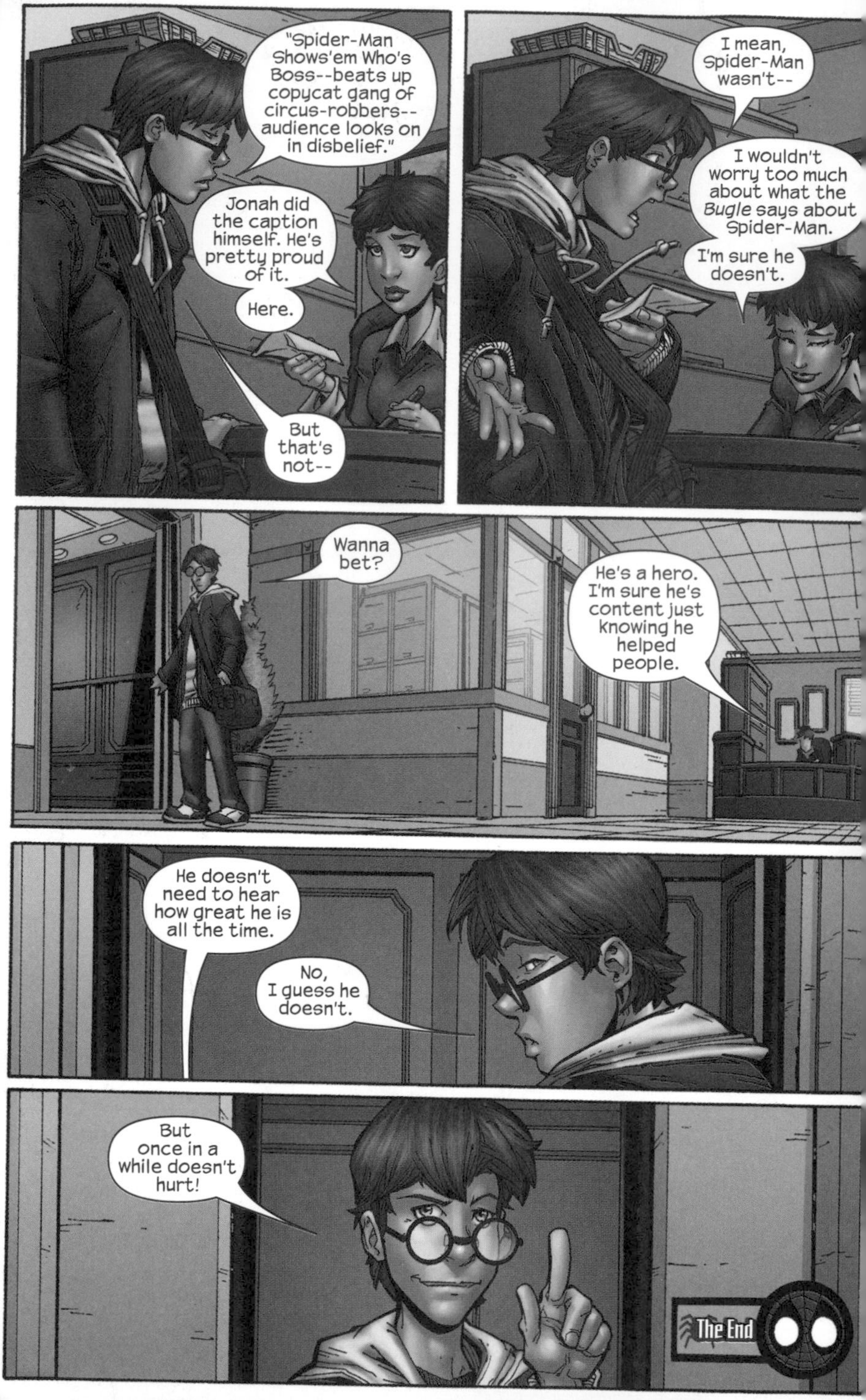
"Spider-Man Shows'em Who's Boss--beats up copycat gang of circus-robbers--audience looks on in disbelief."
Jonah did the caption himself. He's pretty proud of it.
Here.
But that's not--
I mean, Spider-Man wasn't--
I wouldn't worry too much about what the *Bugle* says about Spider-Man.
I'm sure he doesn't.
Wanna bet?
He's a hero. I'm sure he's content just knowing he helped people.
He doesn't need to hear how great he is all the time.
No, I guess he doesn't.
But once in a while doesn't hurt!
The End

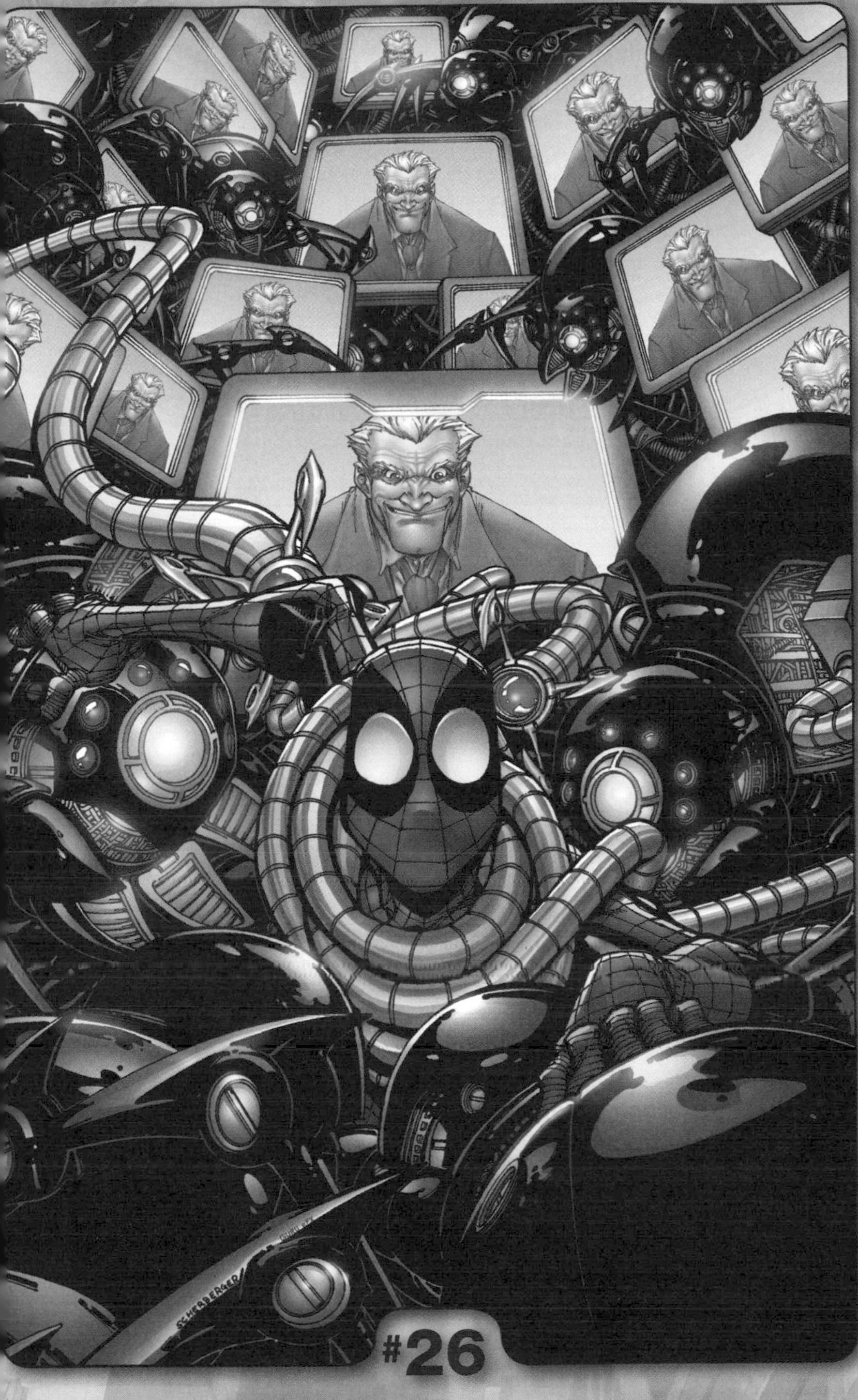
SCHERBERGER
#26

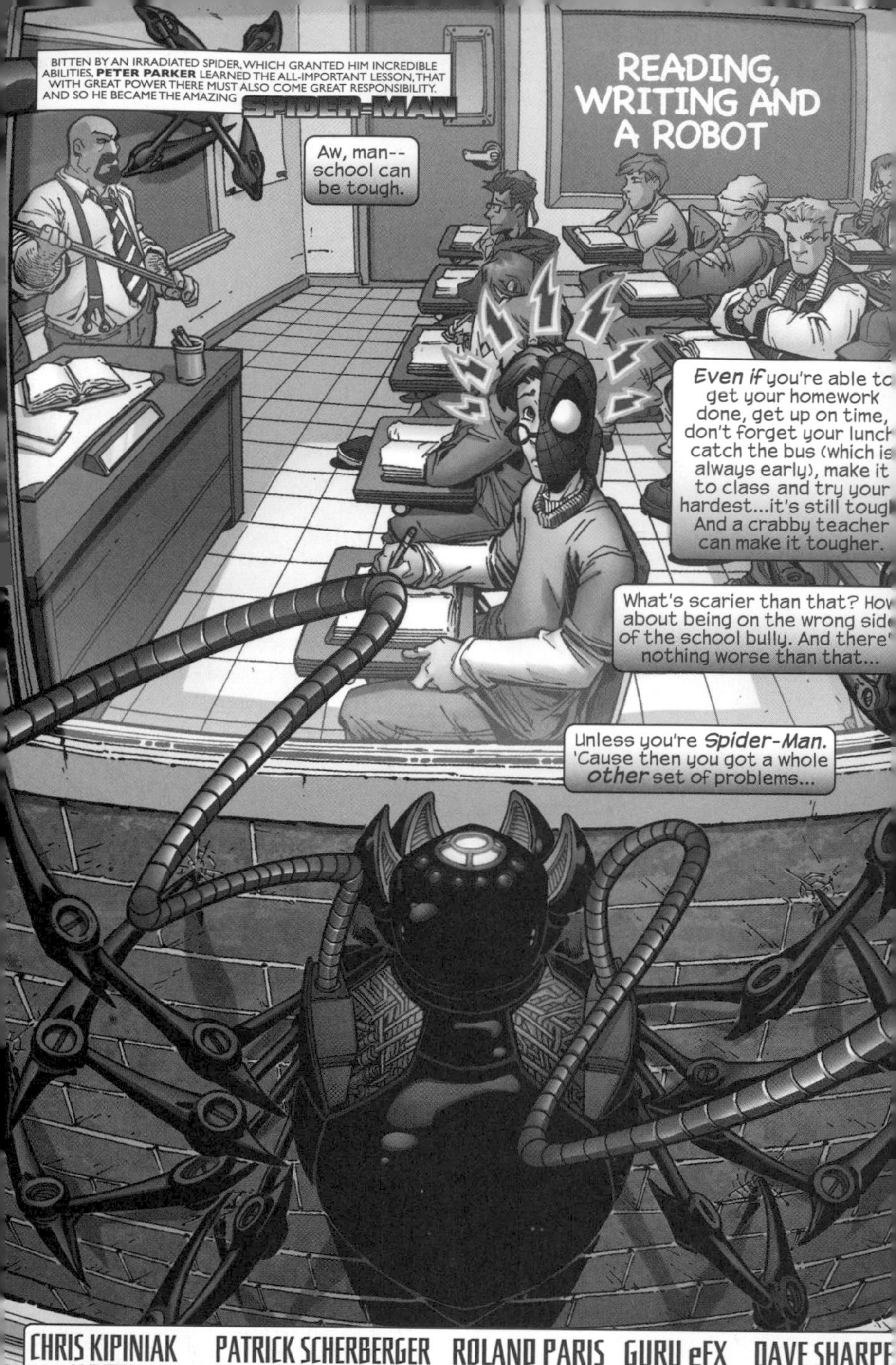
BITTEN BY AN IRRADIATED SPIDER, WHICH GRANTED HIM INCREDIBLE ABILITIES, PETER PARKER LEARNED THE ALL-IMPORTANT LESSON, THAT WITH GREAT POWER THERE MUST ALSO COME GREAT RESPONSIBILITY. AND SO HE BECAME THE AMAZING
SPIDER-MAN
READING, WRITING AND A ROBOT
Aw, man-- school can be tough.
Even if you're able t get your homework done, get up on time, don't forget your lunc catch the bus (which i always early), make it to class and try your hardest...it's still toug And a crabby teacher can make it tougher.
What's scarier than that? Ho about being on the wrong sid of the school bully. And there nothing worse than that...
Unless you're Spider-Man. 'Cause then you got a whole other set of problems...

CHRIS KIPINIAK WRITER
PATRICK SCHERBERGER PENCILER
ROLAND PARIS INKER
GURU eFX COLORISTS
DAVE SHARPE LETTERER
SCHERBERGER, PARIS et GURU eFX COVER
ANTHONY DIAL PRODUCTION
NATHAN COSBY ASSISTANT EDITOR
MARK PANICCIA EDITOR
JOE QUESADA EDITOR IN CHIEF
DAN BUCKLEY PUBLISHER

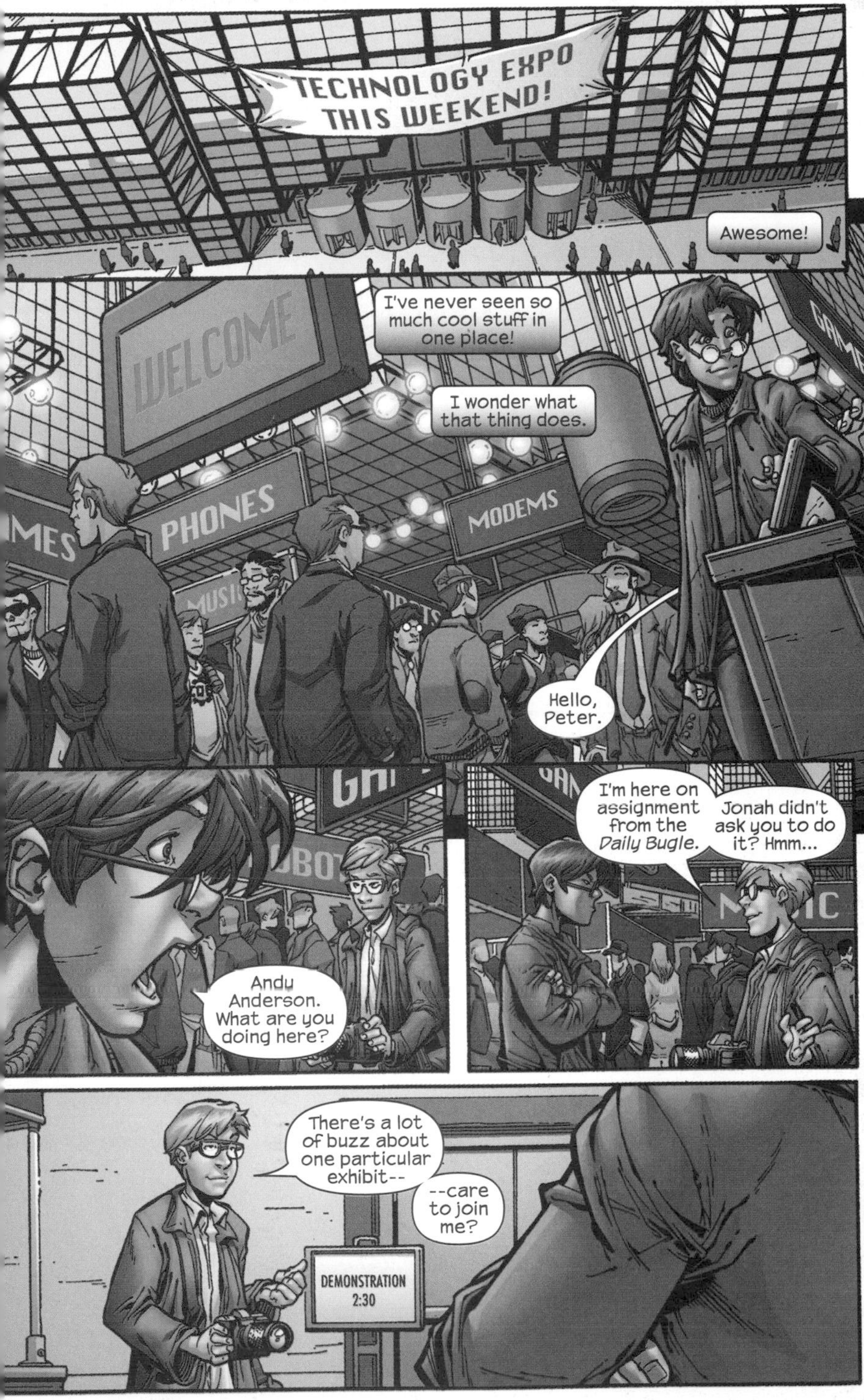
TECHNOLOGY EXPO THIS WEEKEND!
Awesome!
WELCOME
I've never seen so much cool stuff in one place!
I wonder what that thing does.
PHONES
MODEMS
Hello, Peter.
Andy Anderson. What are you doing here?
I'm here on assignment from the *Daily Bugle*.
Jonah didn't ask you to do it? Hmm...
There's a lot of buzz about one particular exhibit--
--care to join me?
DEMONSTRATION
2:30

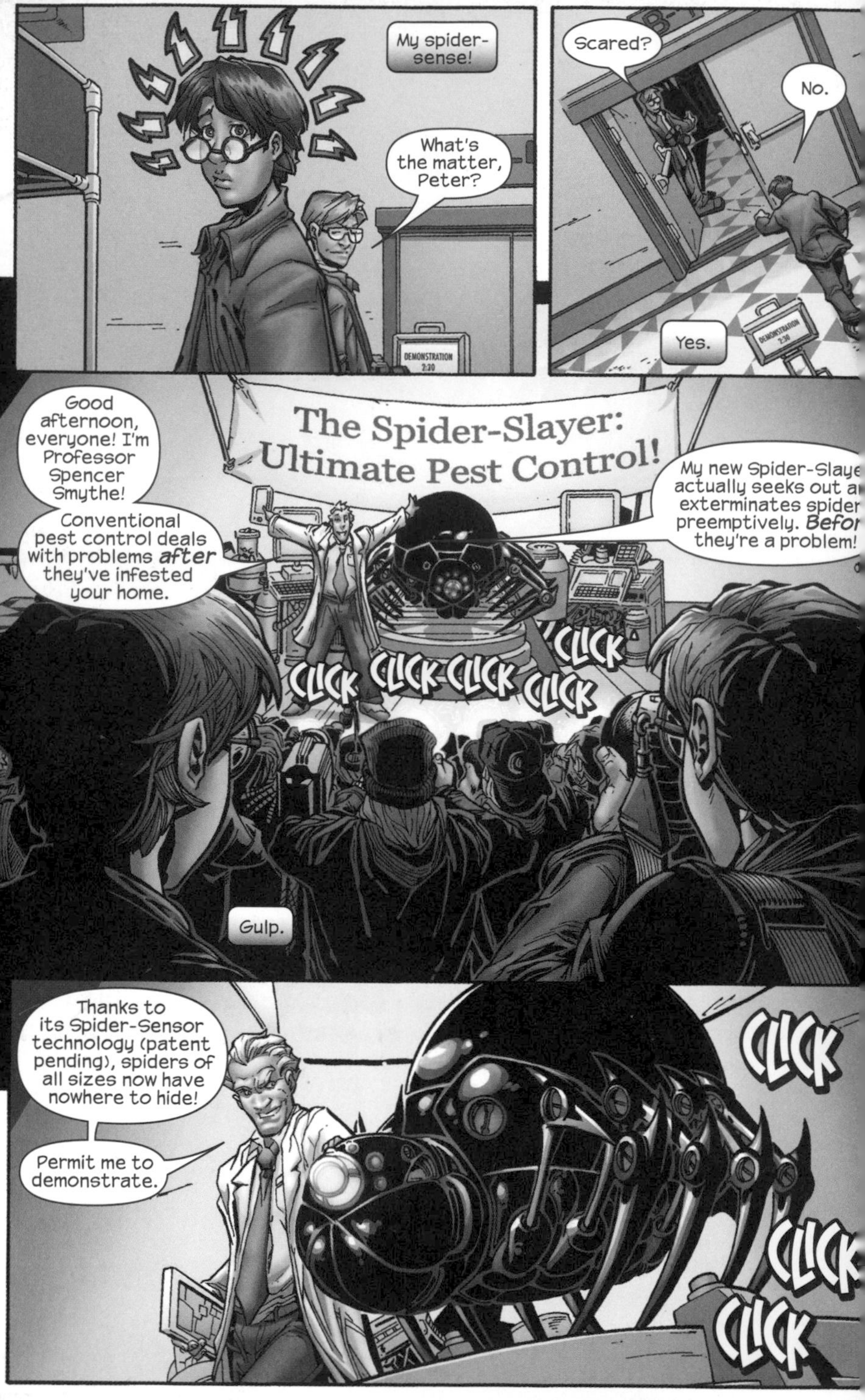
My spider-sense!
What's the matter, Peter?
DEMONSTRATION 2:30
Scared?
No.
Yes.
DEMONSTRATION 2:30
The Spider-Slayer: Ultimate Pest Control!
Good afternoon, everyone! I'm Professor Spencer Smythe!
Conventional pest control deals with problems *after* they've infested your home.
My new Spider-Slaye actually seeks out a exterminates spider preemptively. *Befor* they're a problem!
CLICK CLICK CLICK CLICK CLICK
Gulp.
Thanks to its Spider-Sensor technology (patent pending), spiders of all sizes now have nowhere to hide!
Permit me to demonstrate.
CLICK
CLICK
CLICK

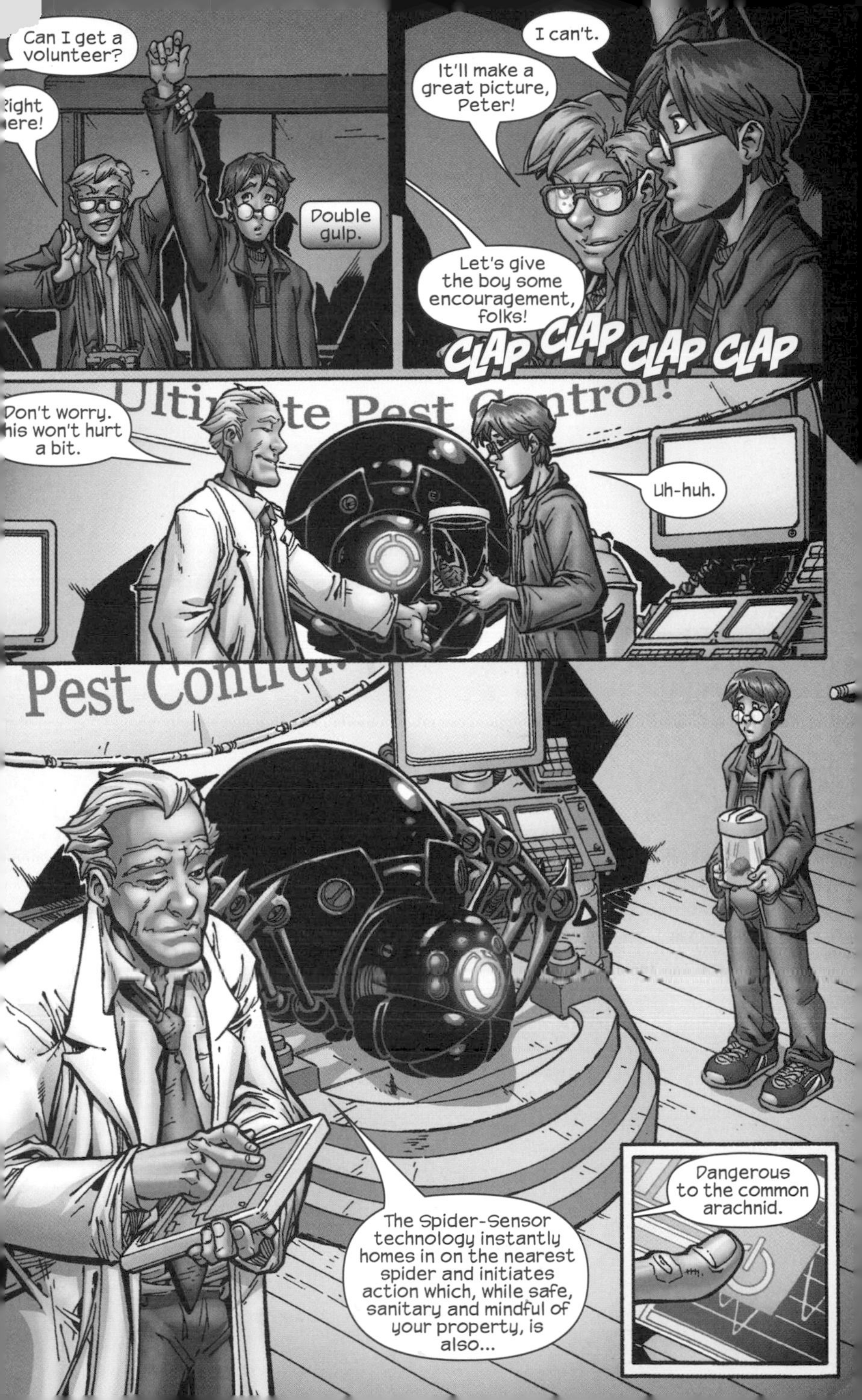
Can I get a volunteer?
Right here!
Double gulp.
I can't.
It'll make a great picture, Peter!
Let's give the boy some encouragement, folks!
CLAP CLAP CLAP CLAP
Ultimate Pest Control!
Don't worry. This won't hurt a bit.
Uh-huh.
Pest Control
The Spider-Sensor technology instantly homes in on the nearest spider and initiates action which, while safe, sanitary and mindful of your property, is also...
Dangerous to the common arachnid.

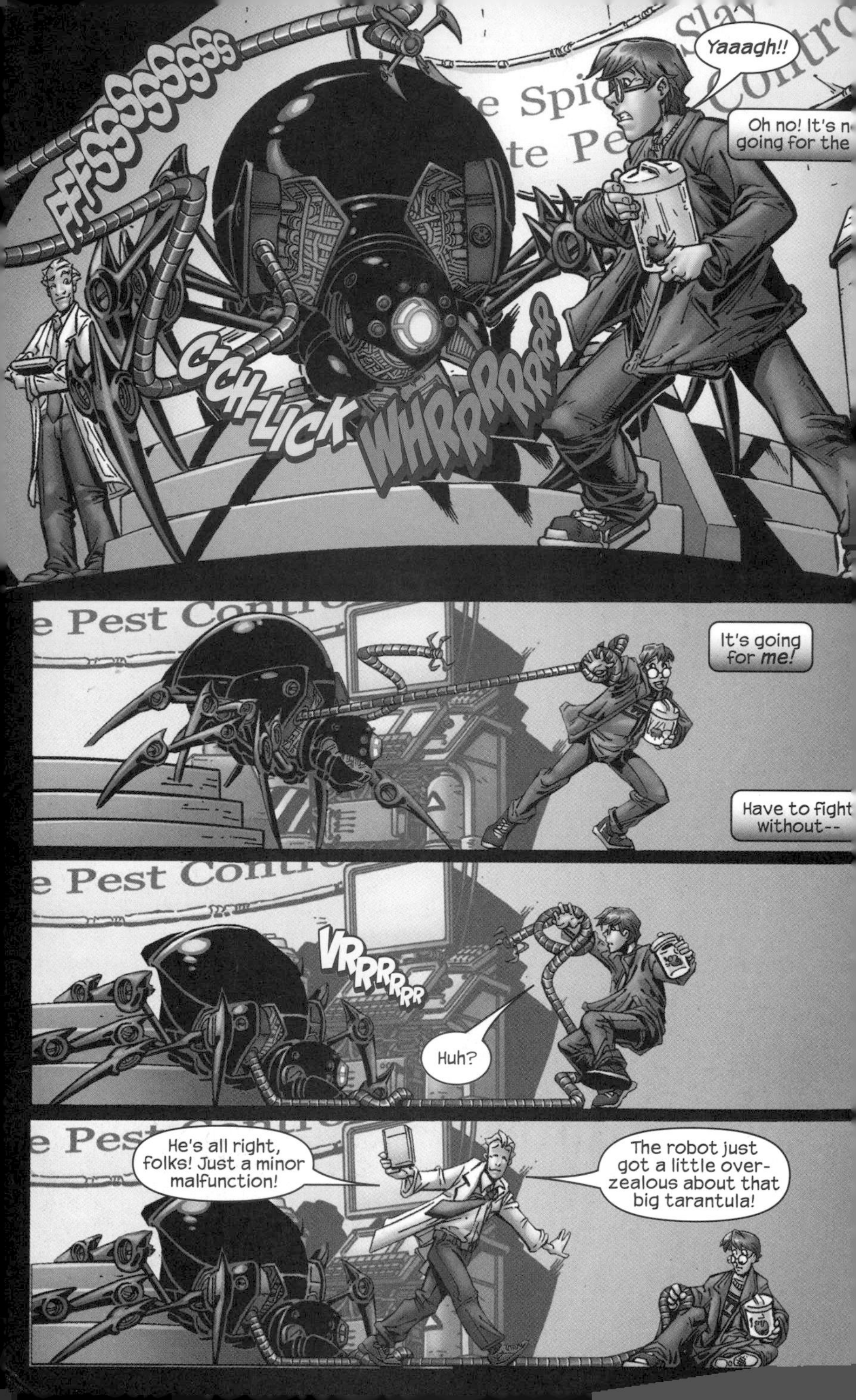
FFSSSSSSSSS
Yaaagh!!
Oh no! It's n
going for the
C-CH-LICK
WHRRRRRRR
It's going
for me!
Have to fight
without--
VRRRRRR
Huh?
He's all right,
folks! Just a minor
malfunction!
The robot just
got a little over-
zealous about that
big tarantula!

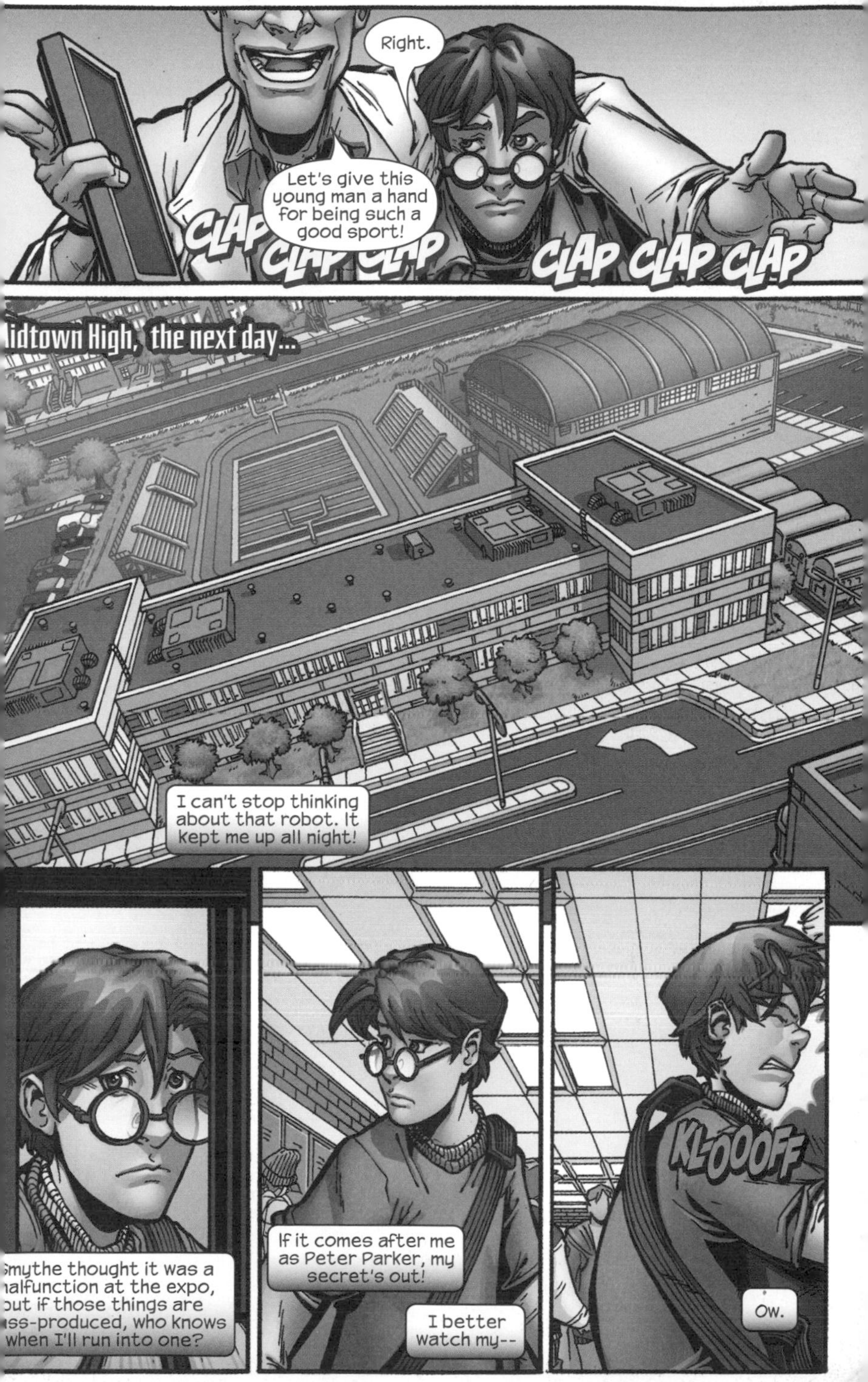
Right.
Let's give this young man a hand for being such a good sport!
CLAP CLAP CLAP
CLAP CLAP CLAP
idtown High, the next day...
I can't stop thinking about that robot. It kept me up all night!
mythe thought it was a alfunction at the expo, out if those things are ss-produced, who knows when I'll run into one?
If it comes after me as Peter Parker, my secret's out!
I better watch my--
KL-OOOFF
Ow.

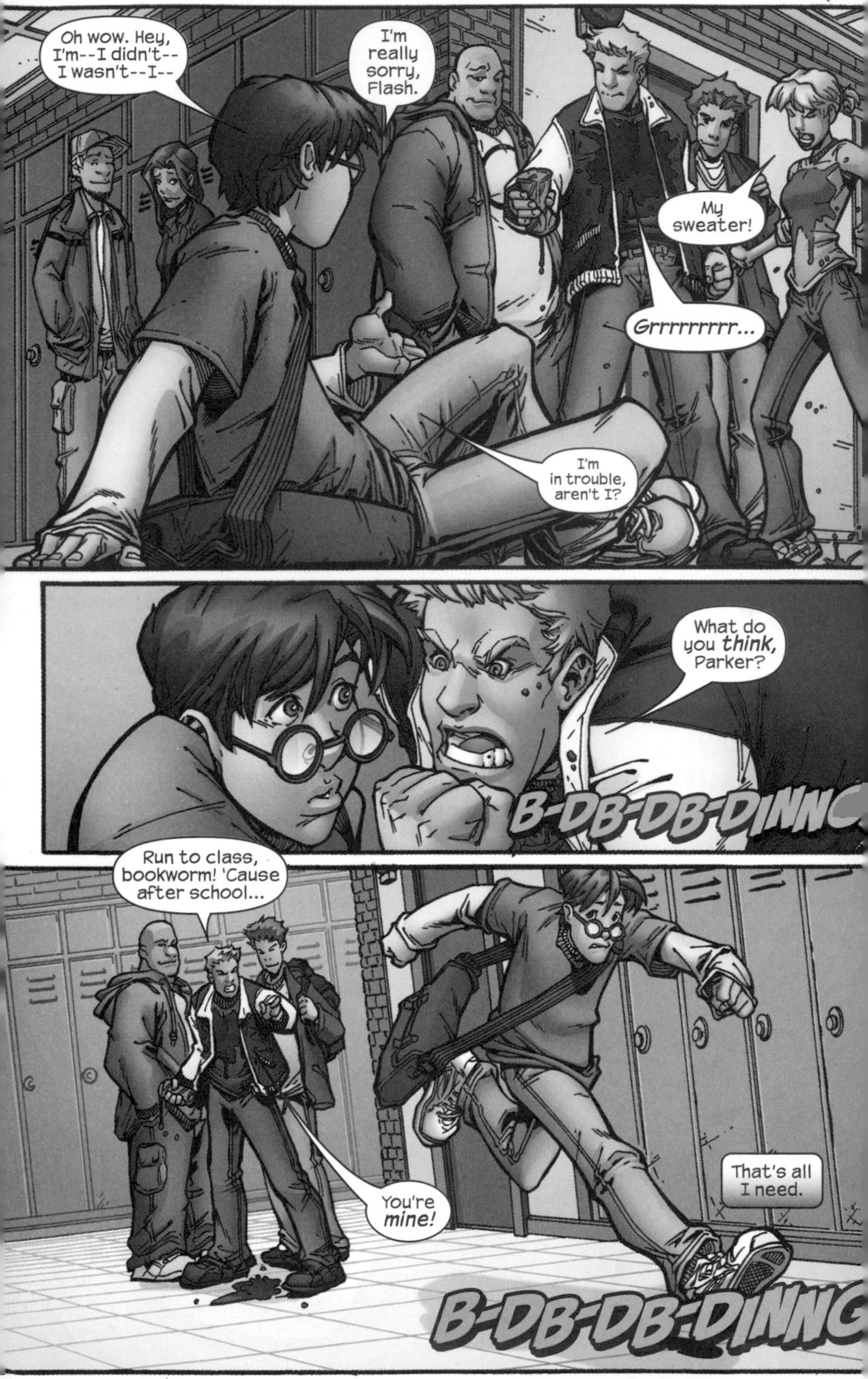
Oh wow. Hey, I'm--I didn't--I wasn't--I--
I'm really sorry, Flash.
My sweater!
Grrrrrrrrr...
I'm in trouble, aren't I?
What do you *think*, Parker?
B-DB-DB-DINNG
Run to class, bookworm! 'Cause after school...
You're *mine!*
That's all I need.
B-DB-DB-DINNG

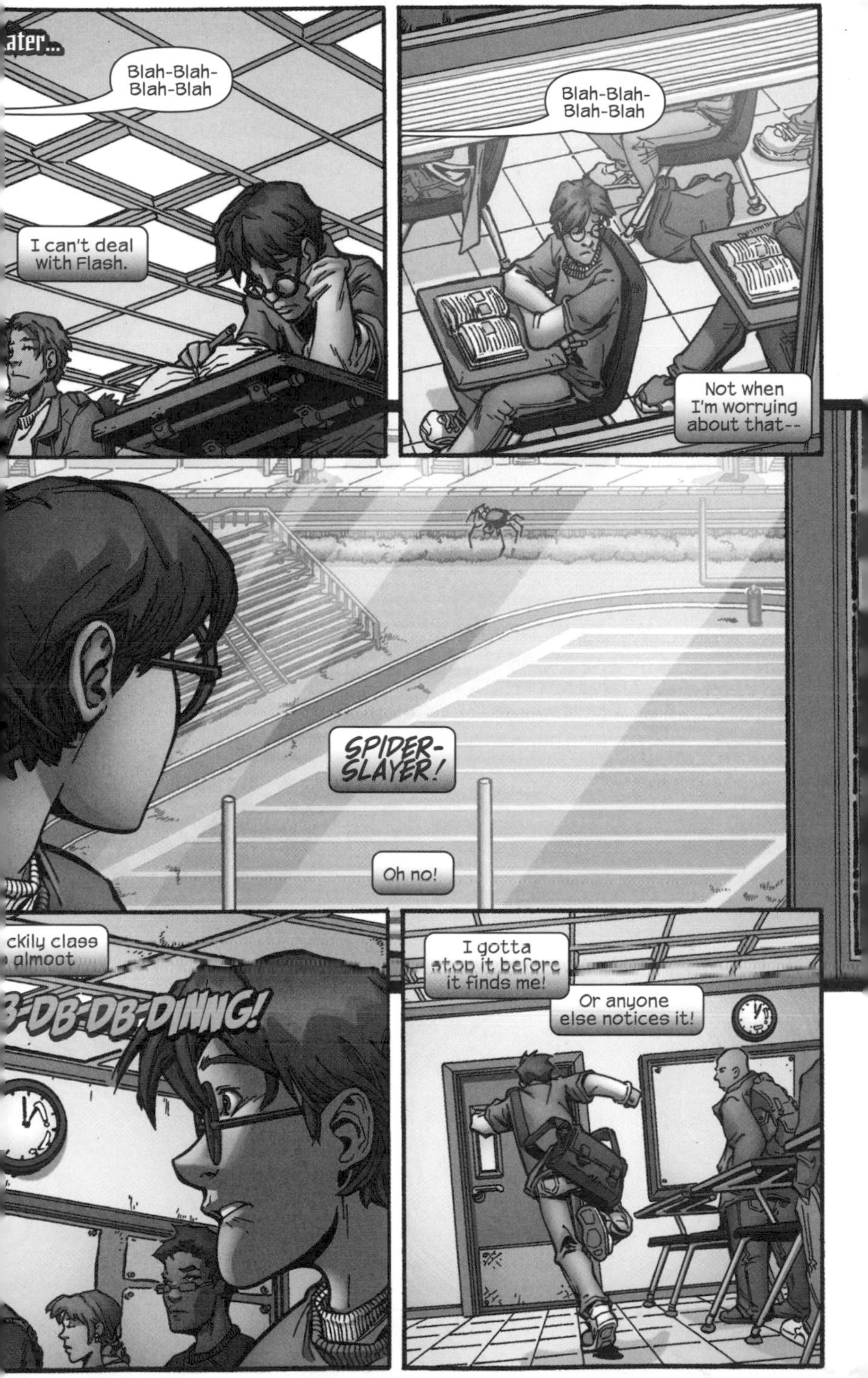
ater...
Blah-Blah-Blah-Blah
I can't deal with Flash.
Blah-Blah-Blah-Blah
Not when I'm worrying about that--
SPIDER-SLAYER!
Oh no!
ckily class
B-DB-DB-DINNG!
I gotta stop it before it finds me!
Or anyone else notices it!

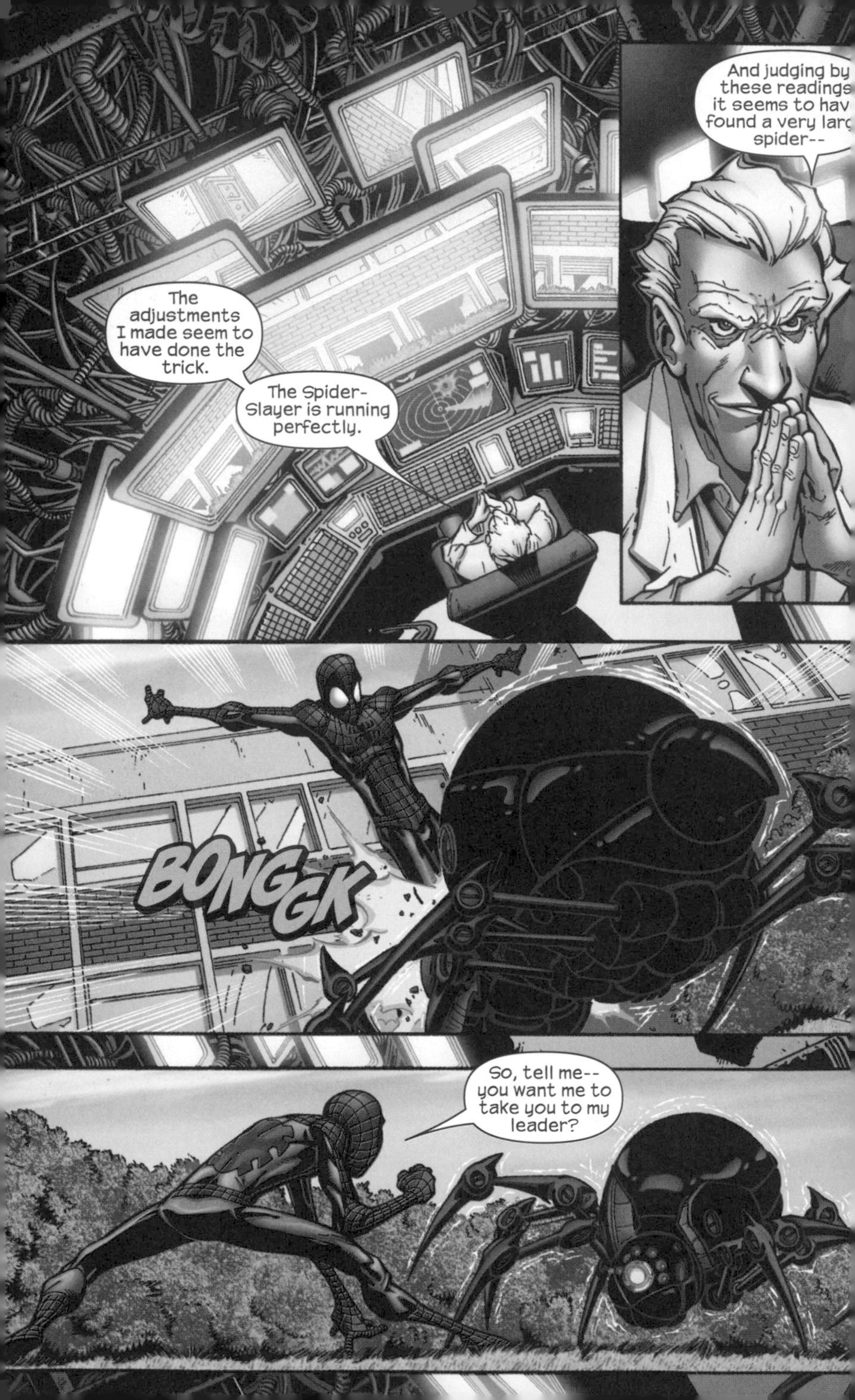
The adjustments I made seem to have done the trick.
The Spider-Slayer is running perfectly.
And judging by these readings it seems to hav found a very larc spider--
BONGGK
So, tell me-- you want me to take you to my leader?

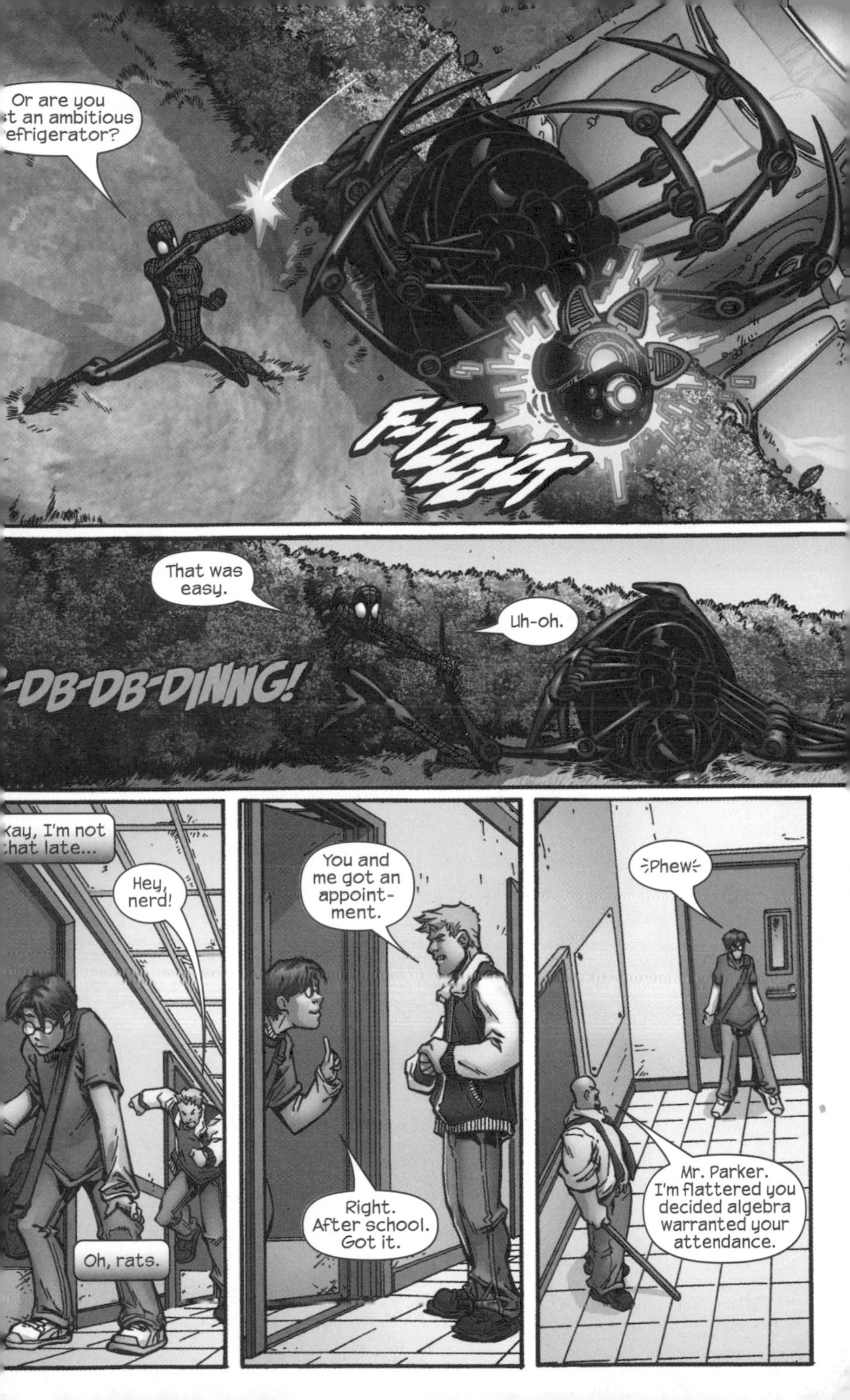

Or are you
t an ambitious
efrigerator?
F-TZZZT
That was
easy.
Uh-oh.
-DB-DB-DINNG!
Kay, I'm not
that late...
Hey,
nerd!
Oh, rats.
You and
me got an
appoint-
ment.
Right.
After school.
Got it.
Phew
Mr. Parker.
I'm flattered you
decided algebra
warranted your
attendance.

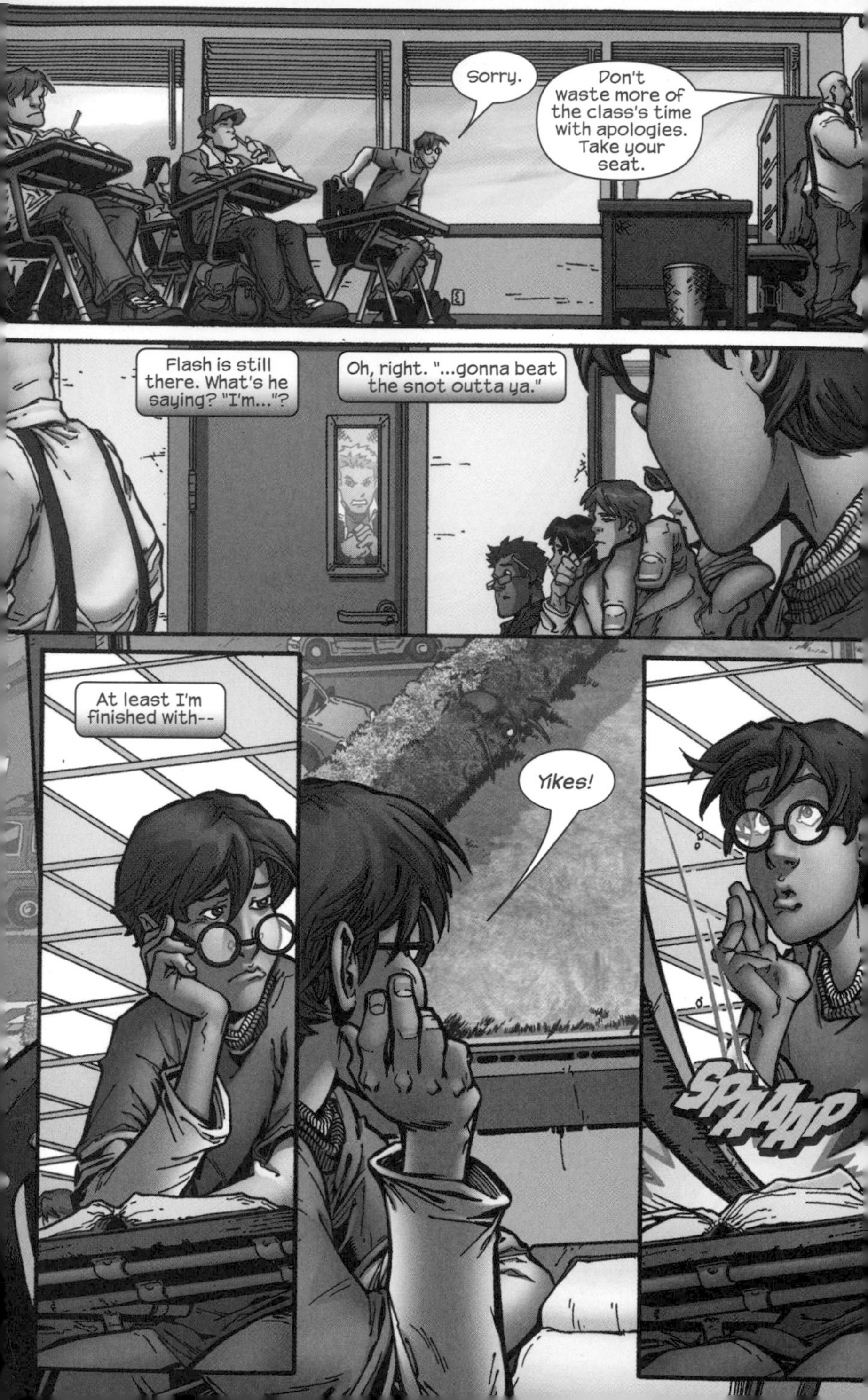
Sorry.
Don't waste more of the class's time with apologies. Take your seat.
Flash is still there. What's he saying? "I'm..."?
Oh, right. "...gonna beat the snot outta ya."
At least I'm finished with--
Yikes!
SPAAAAP

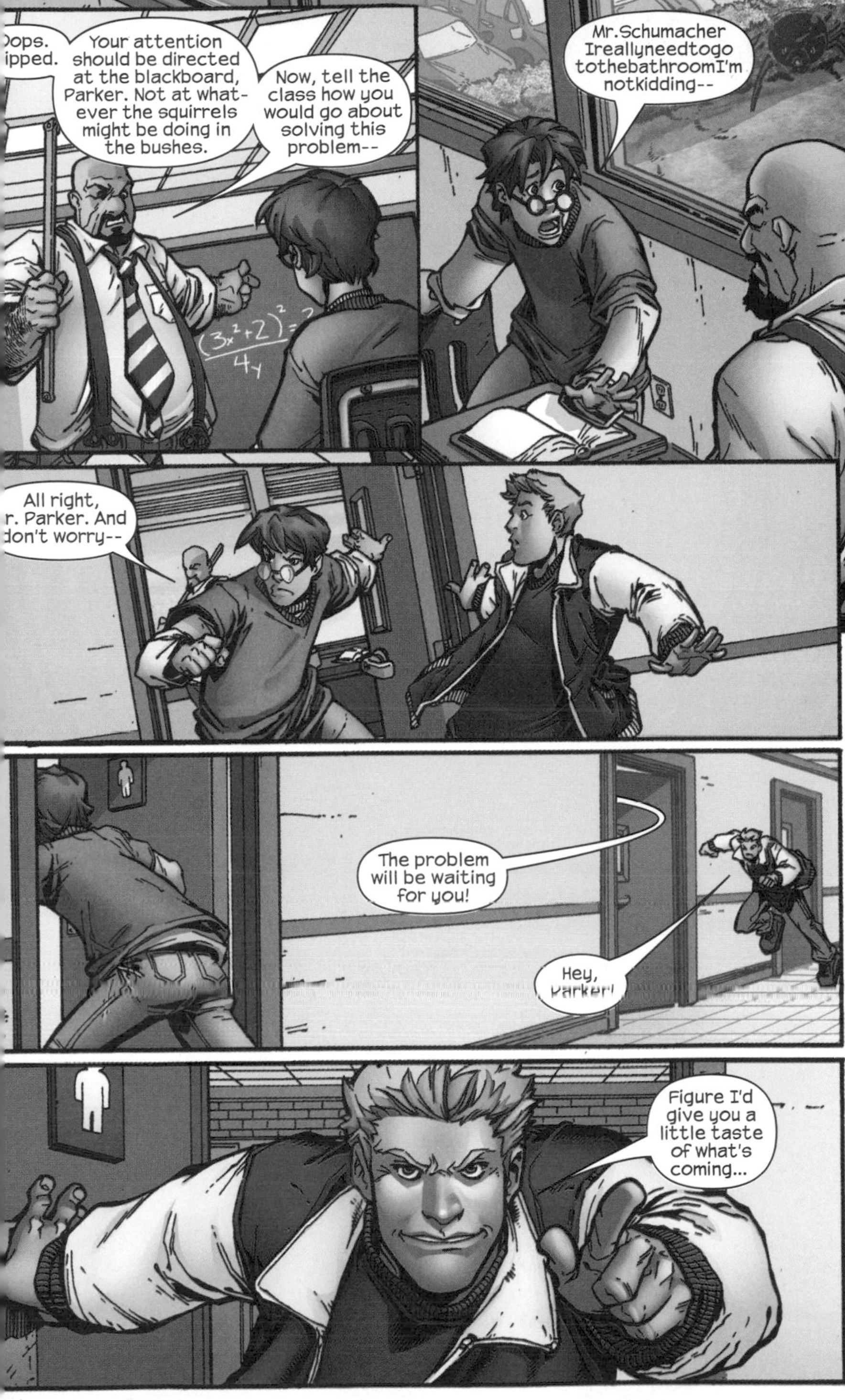
ops.
ipped.
Your attention should be directed at the blackboard, Parker. Not at whatever the squirrels might be doing in the bushes.
Now, tell the class how you would go about solving this problem--
$\frac{(3x^2+2)^2}{4y} = ?$
Mr.Schumacher IreallyneedtogotothebathroomI'm notkidding--
All right,
r. Parker. And
don't worry--
The problem will be waiting for you!
Hey, Parker!
Figure I'd give you a little taste of what's coming...

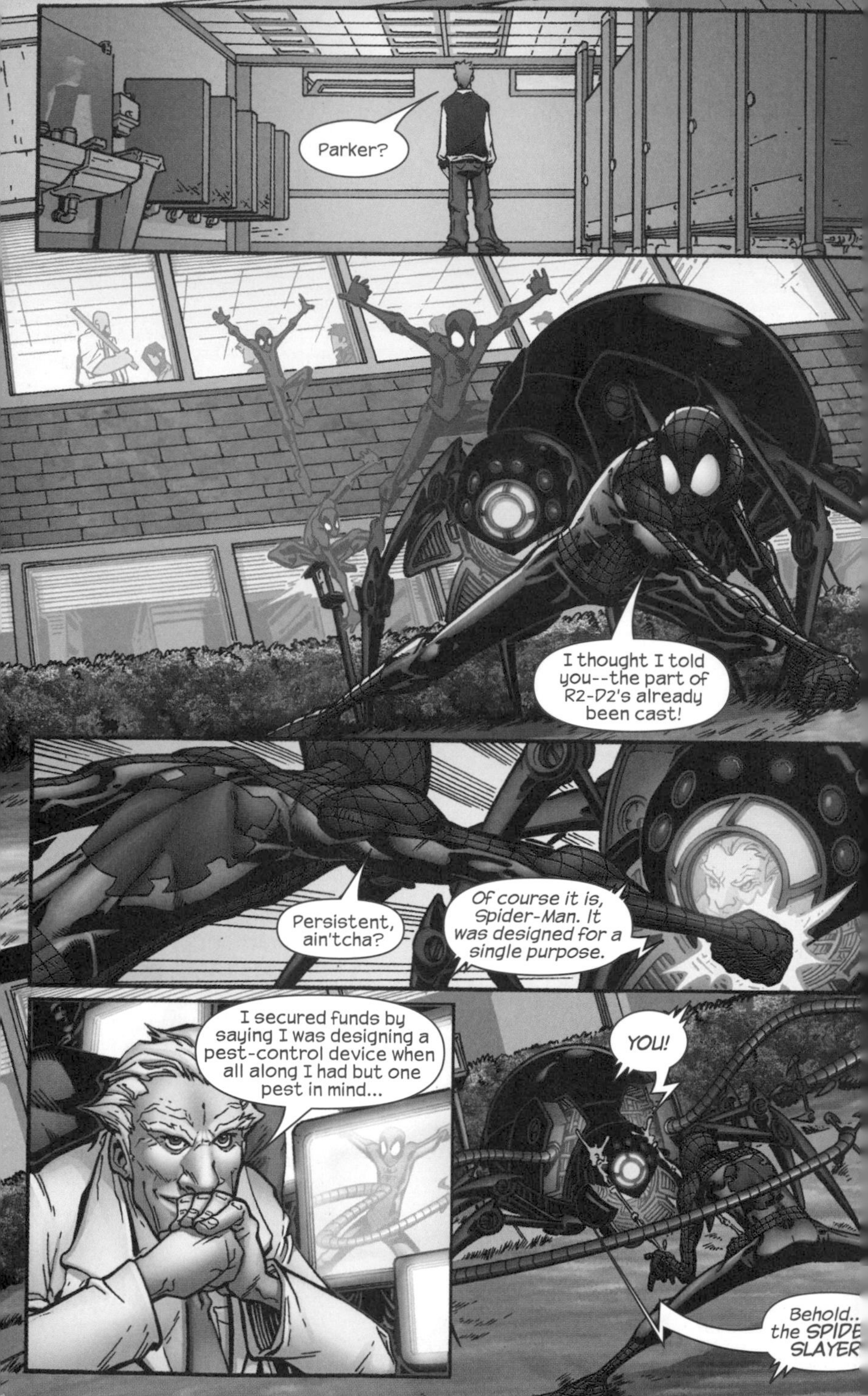
Parker?
I thought I told you--the part of R2-D2's already been cast!
Persistent, ain'tcha?
Of course it is, Spider-Man. It was designed for a single purpose.
I secured funds by saying I was designing a pest-control device when all along I had but one pest in mind...
YOU!
Behold.. the SPIDE SLAYER

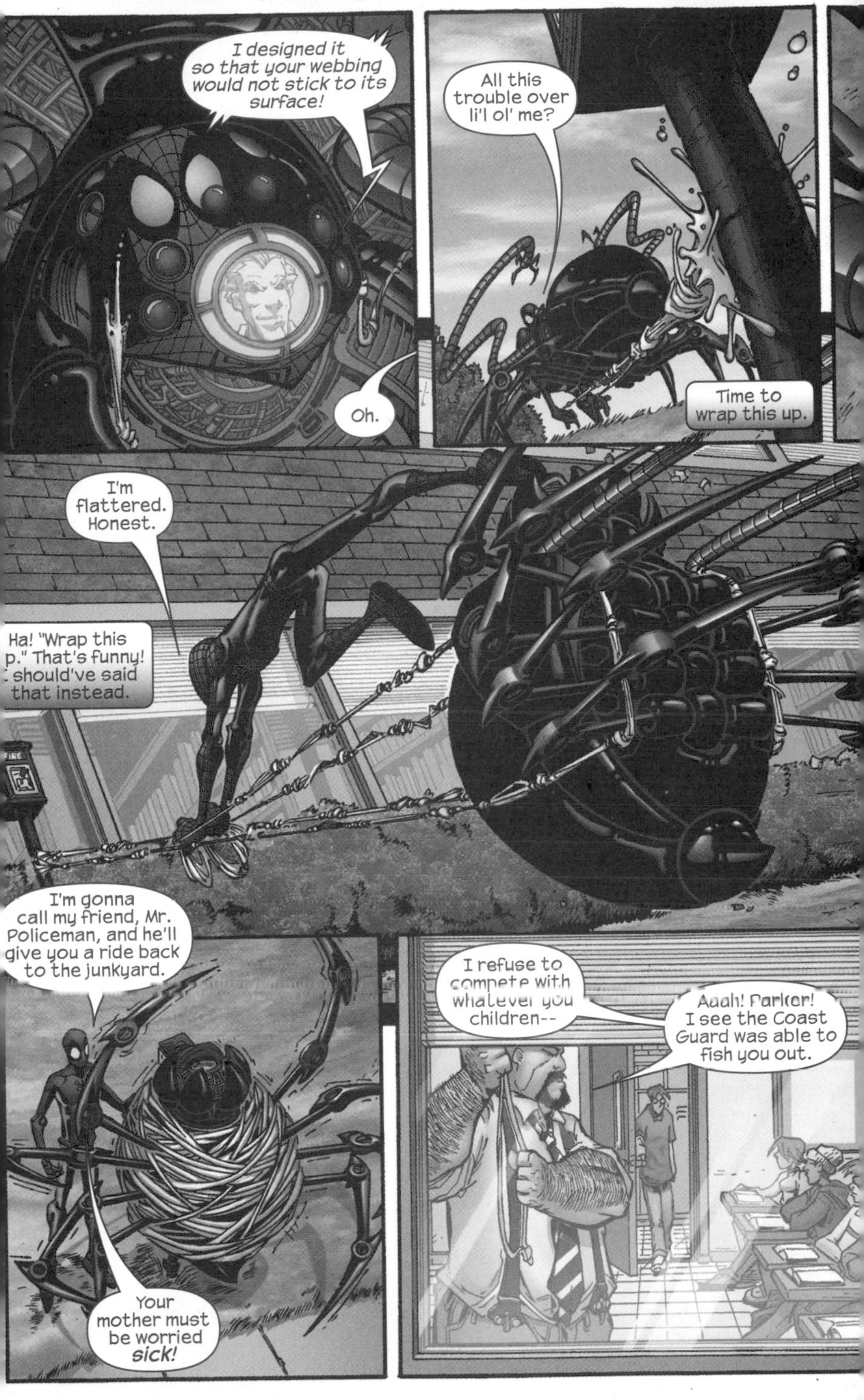

I designed it so that your webbing would not stick to its surface!
Oh.
All this trouble over li'l ol' me?
Time to wrap this up.
I'm flattered. Honest.
Ha! "Wrap this p." That's funny! should've said that instead.
I'm gonna call my friend, Mr. Policeman, and he'll give you a ride back to the junkyard.
Your mother must be worried *sick!*
I refuse to compete with whatever you children--
Aaah! Parker! I see the Coast Guard was able to fish you out.

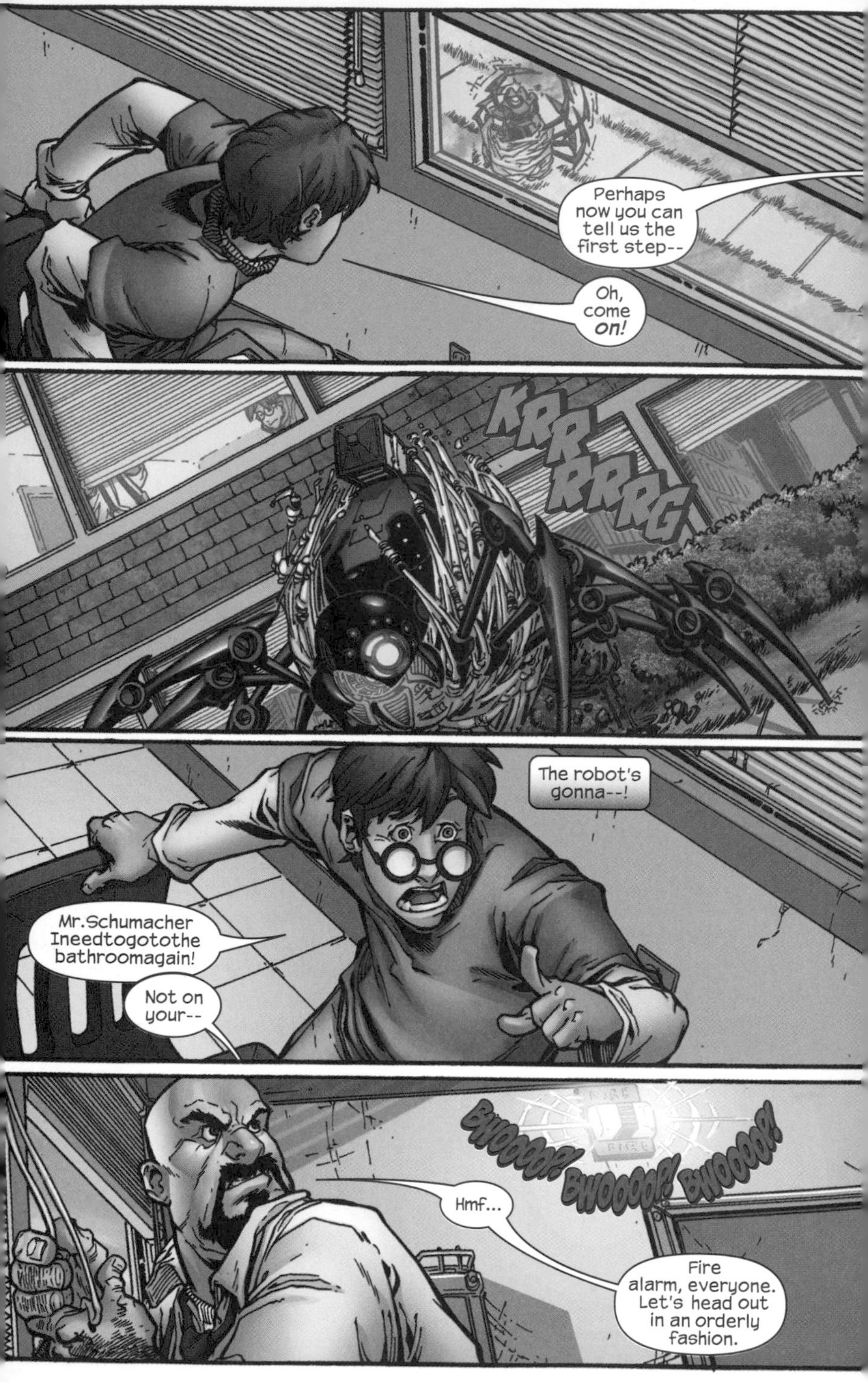
Perhaps now you can tell us the first step--
Oh, come on!
KRRRRRRG
The robot's gonna--!
Mr.Schumacher Ineedtogotothe bathroomagain!
Not on your--
BWOOOOP! BWOOOOP! BWOOOOP!
Hmf...
Fire alarm, everyone. Let's head out in an orderly fashion.

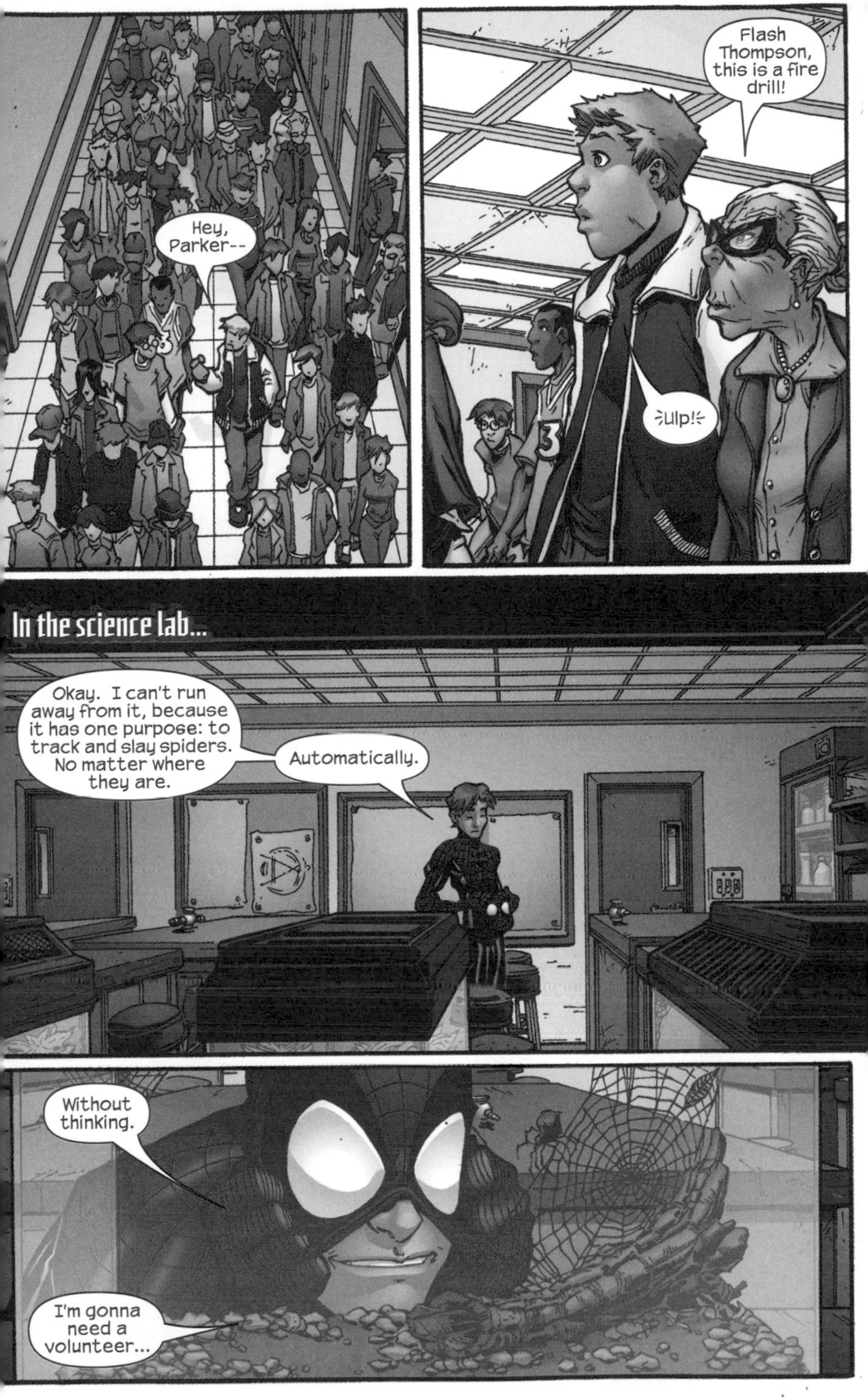
Hey, Parker--
Flash Thompson, this is a fire drill!
Ulp!
In the science lab...
Okay. I can't run away from it, because it has one purpose: to track and slay spiders. No matter where they are.
Automatically.
Without thinking.
I'm gonna need a volunteer...

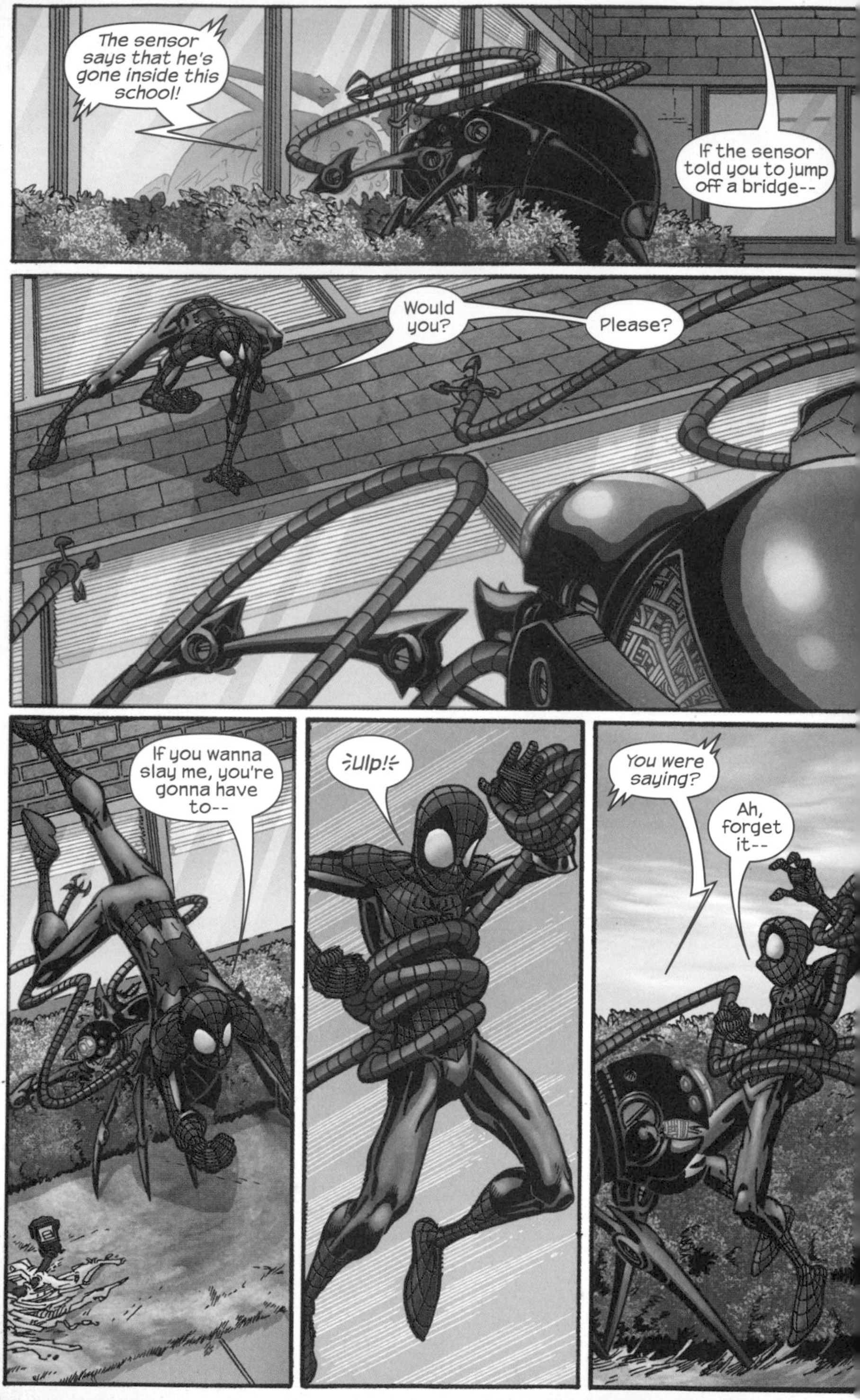
The sensor says that he's gone inside this school!
If the sensor told you to jump off a bridge--
Would you?
Please?
If you wanna slay me, you're gonna have to--
Ulp!
You were saying?
Ah, forget it--

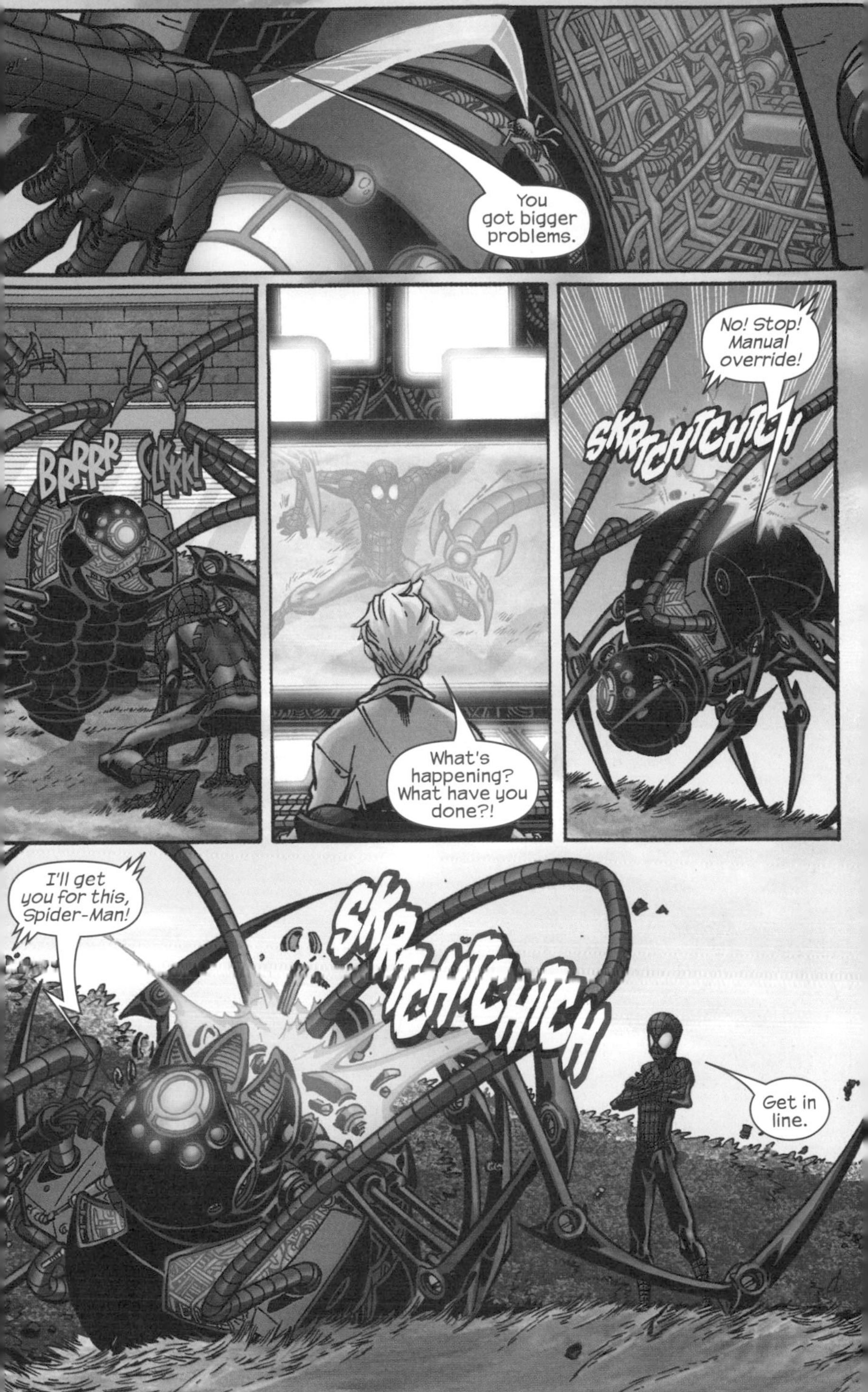
You got bigger problems.
BRRRR
CLIKKK!
What's happening? What have you done?!
No! Stop! Manual override!
SKRTCHTCHTCH
I'll get you for this, Spider-Man!
SKRTCHTCHTCH
Get in line.

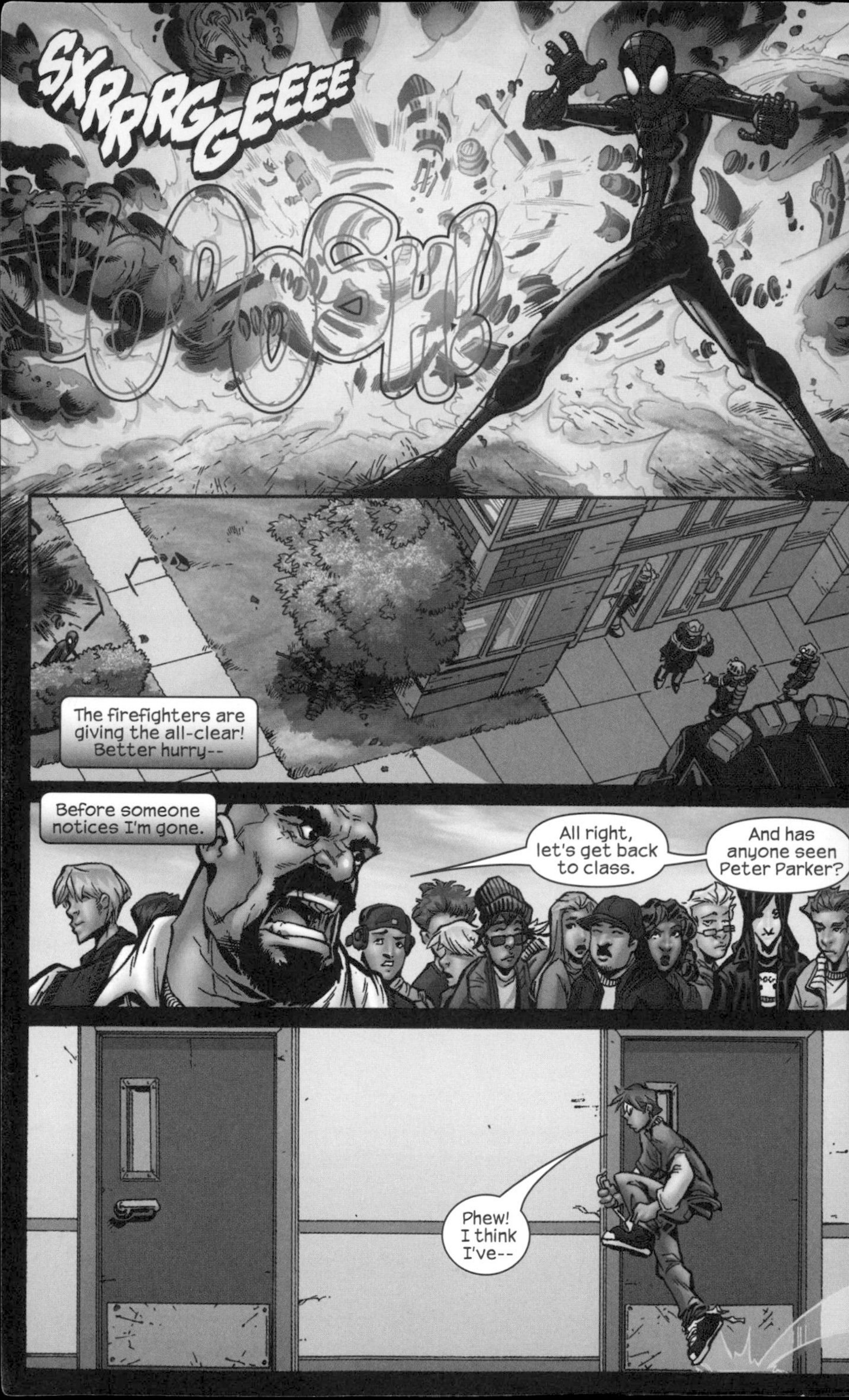
SXRRRGGEEEE
The firefighters are giving the all-clear! Better hurry--
Before someone notices I'm gone.
All right, let's get back to class.
And has anyone seen Peter Parker?
Phew! I think I've--

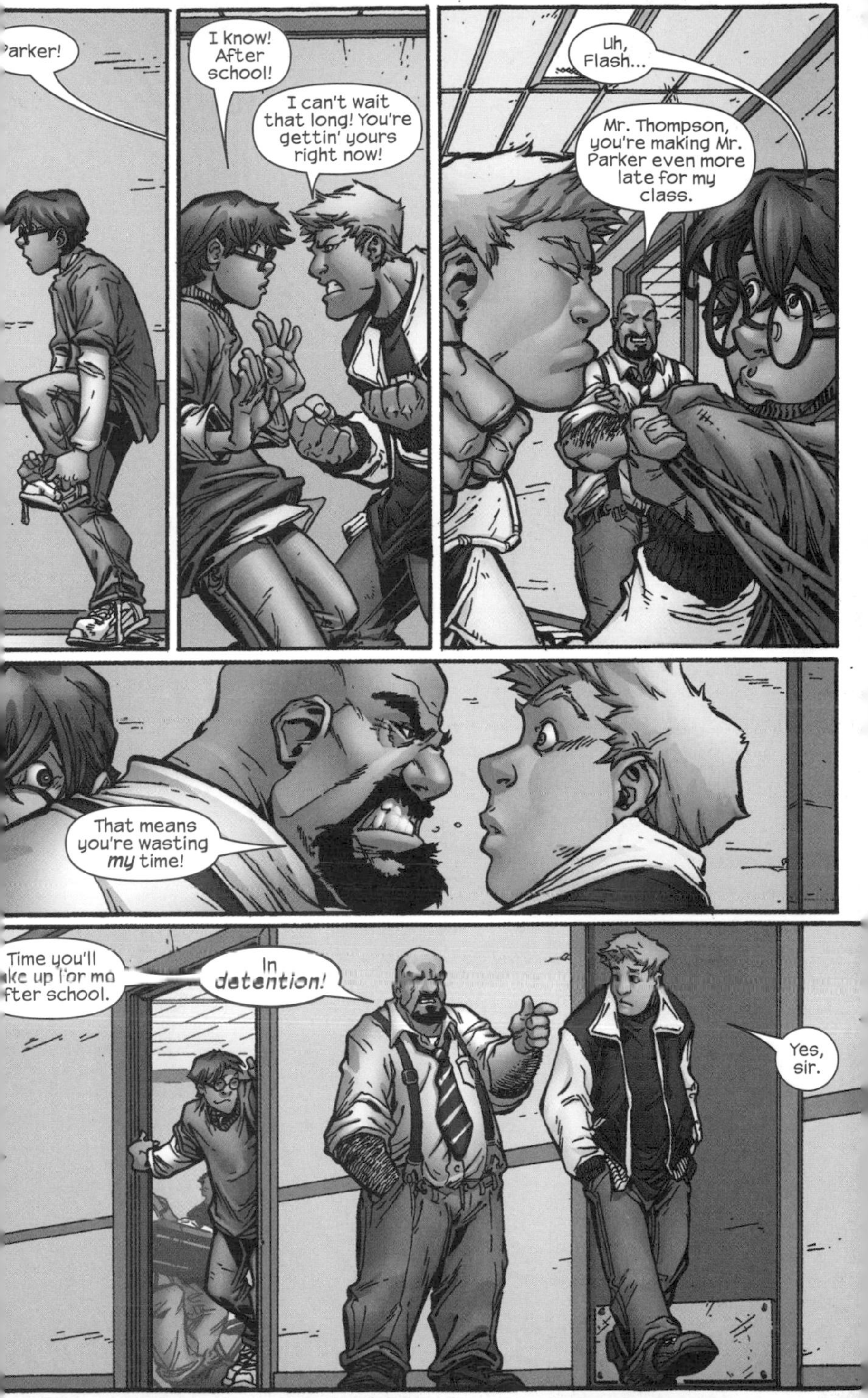
Parker!
I know! After school!
I can't wait that long! You're gettin' yours right now!
Uh, Flash...
Mr. Thompson, you're making Mr. Parker even more late for my class.
That means you're wasting *my* time!
Time you'll ke up for me fter school.
In *detention!*
Yes, sir.

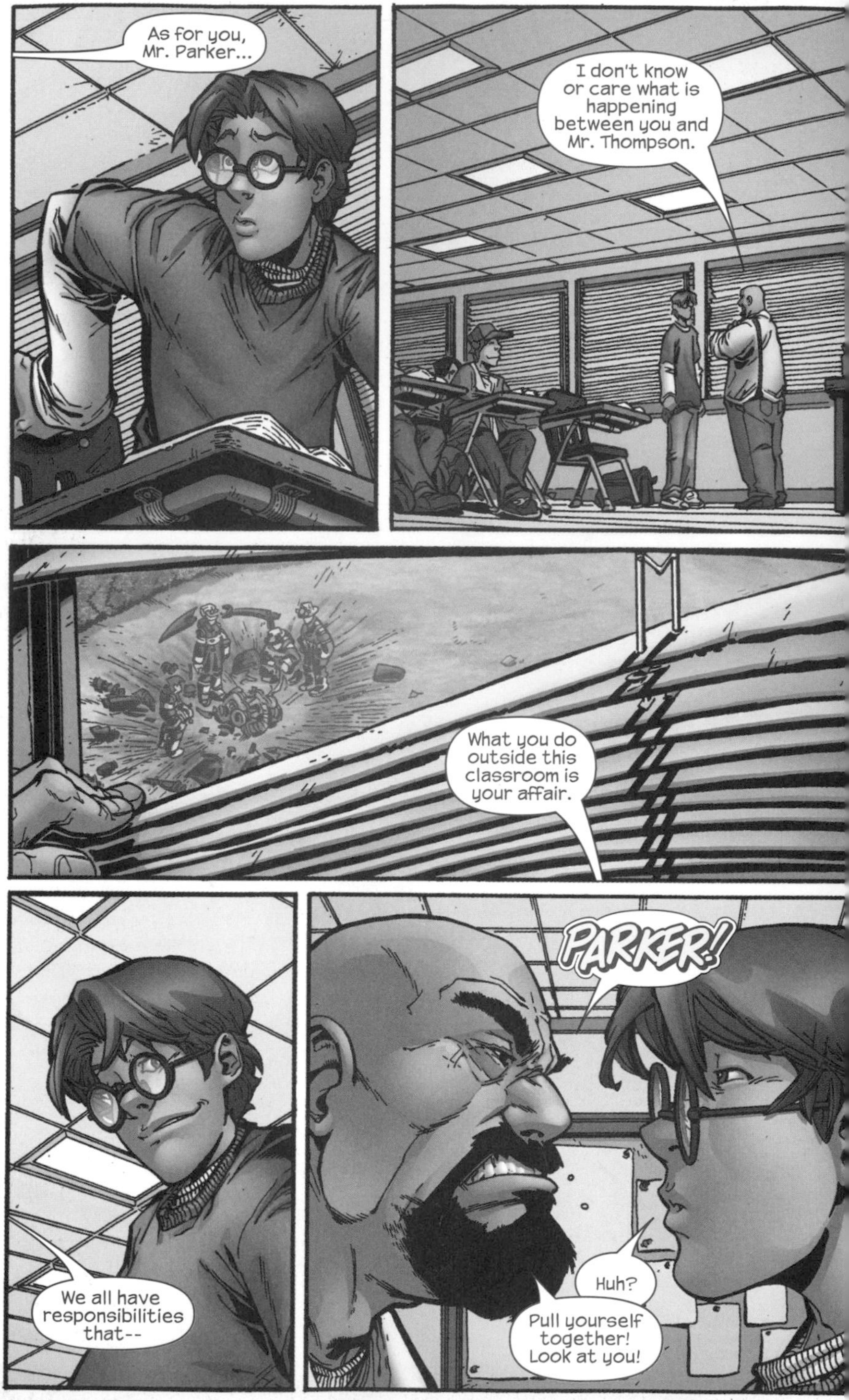
As for you, Mr. Parker...
I don't know or care what is happening between you and Mr. Thompson.
What you do outside this classroom is your affair.
We all have responsibilities that--
PARKER!
Huh?
Pull yourself together! Look at you!

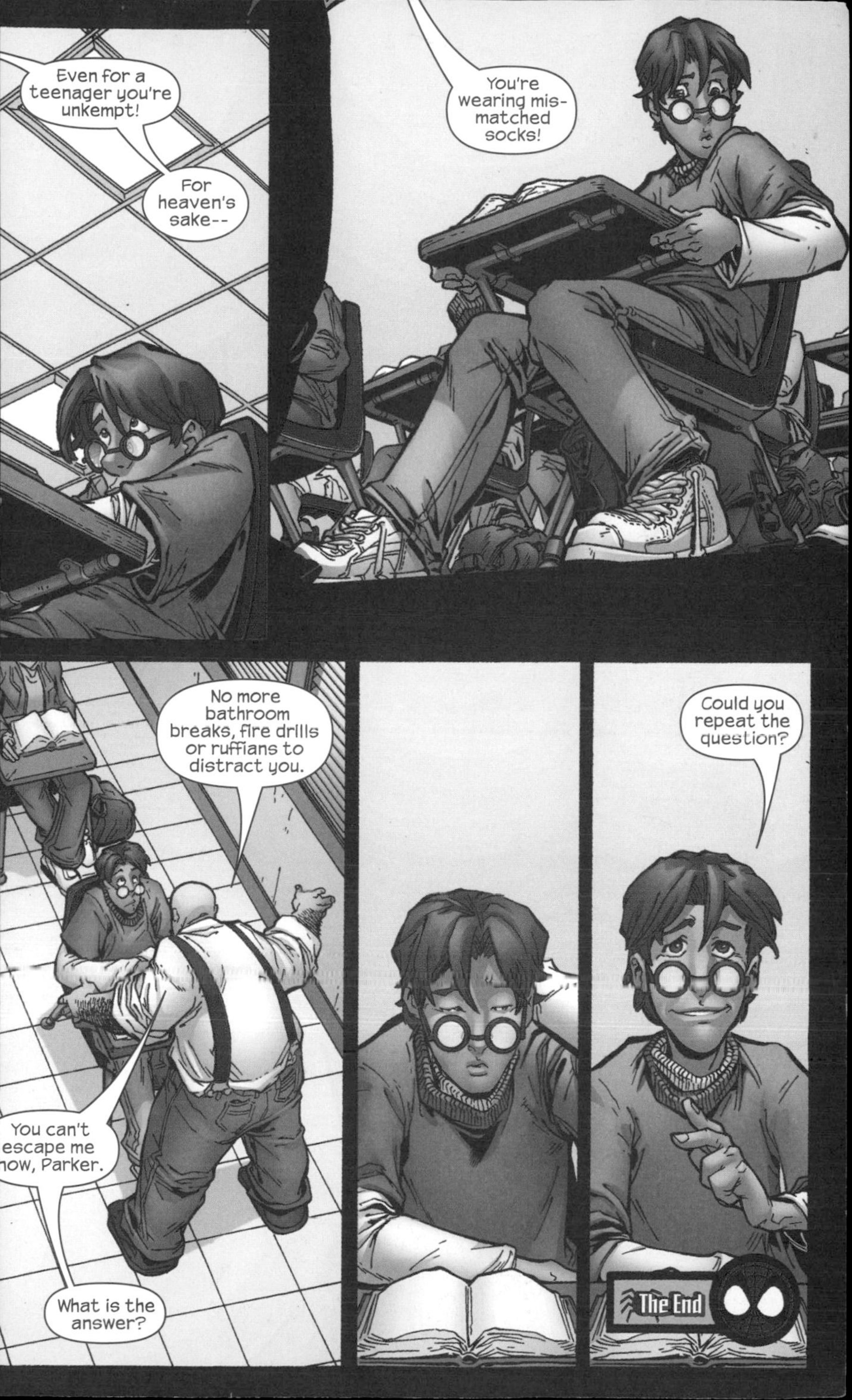

Even for a teenager you're unkempt!
For heaven's sake--
You're wearing mis-matched socks!
No more bathroom breaks, fire drills or ruffians to distract you.
You can't escape me now, Parker.
What is the answer?
Could you repeat the question?
The End

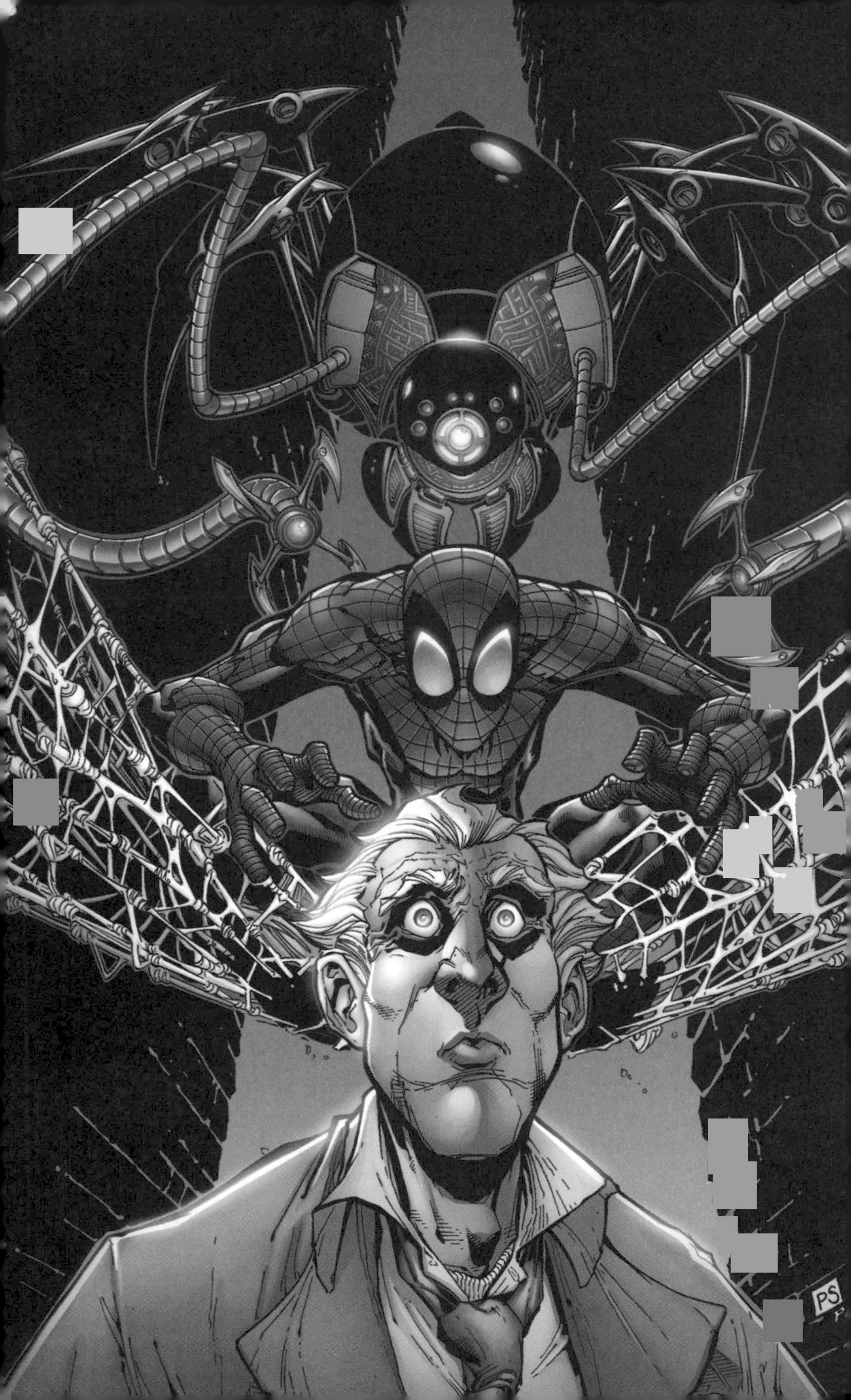

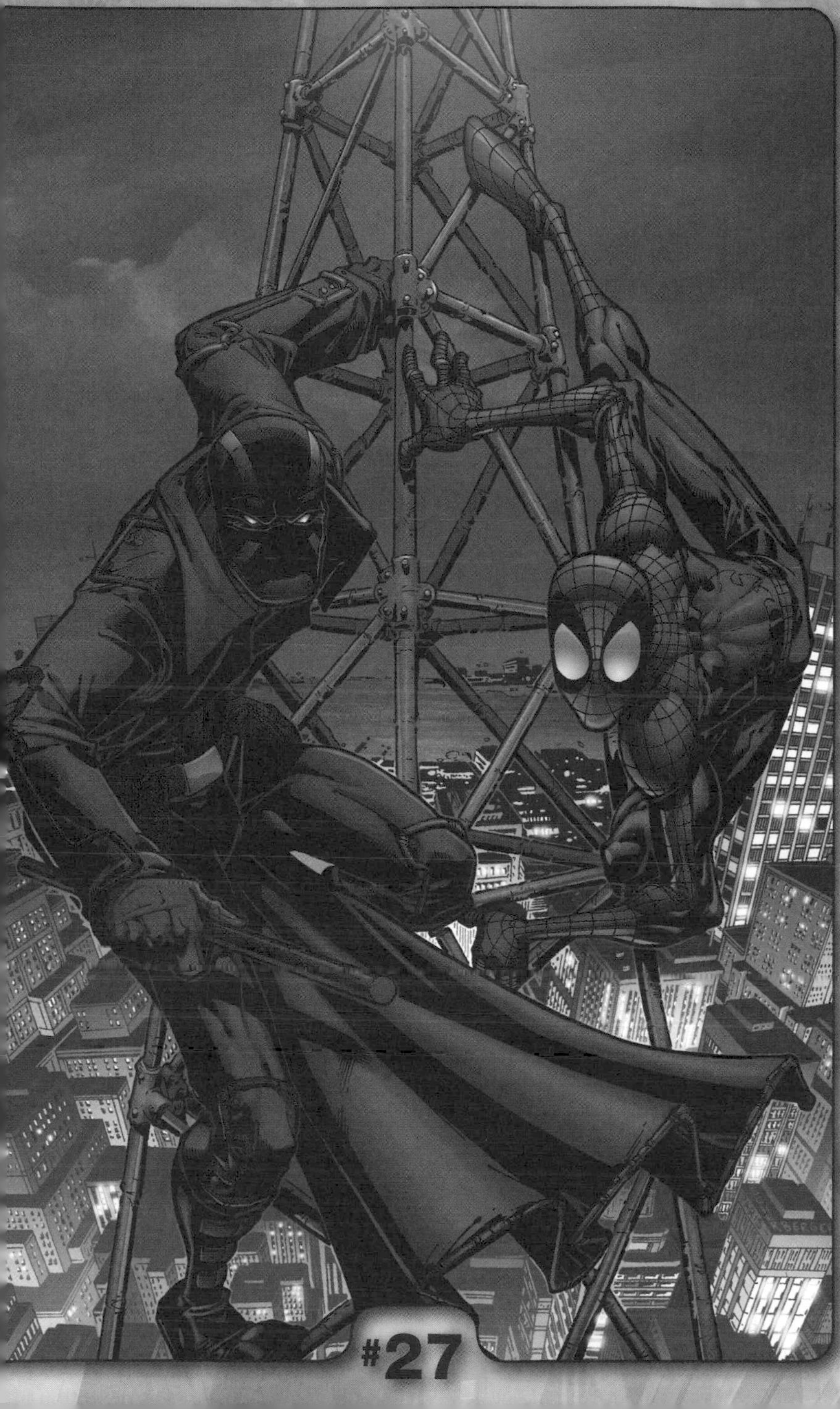
#27

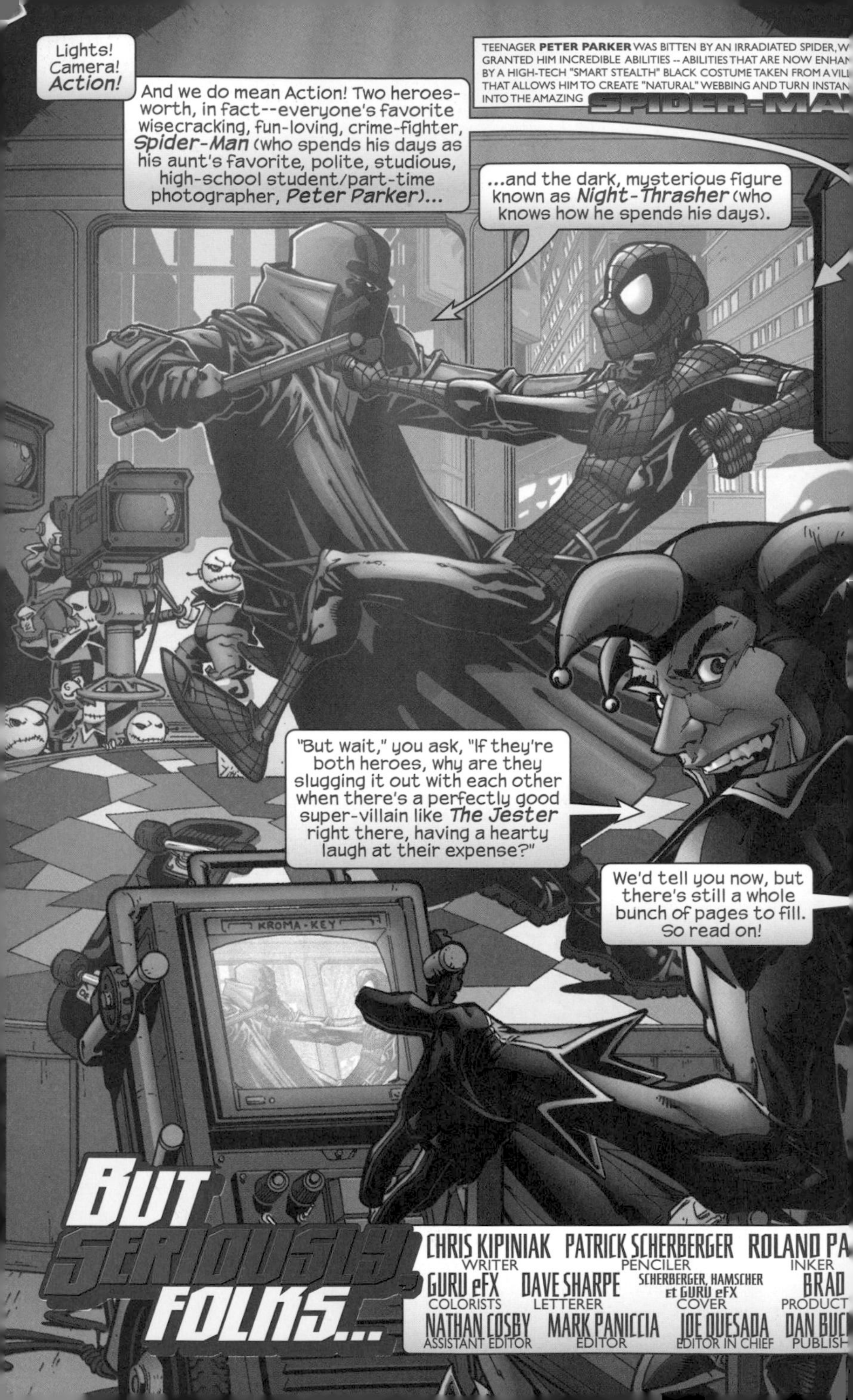

Lights! Camera! Action!
TEENAGER PETER PARKER WAS BITTEN BY AN IRRADIATED SPIDER, W GRANTED HIM INCREDIBLE ABILITIES -- ABILITIES THAT ARE NOW ENHAN BY A HIGH-TECH "SMART STEALTH" BLACK COSTUME TAKEN FROM A VILL THAT ALLOWS HIM TO CREATE "NATURAL" WEBBING AND TURN INSTAN INTO THE AMAZING SPIDER-MA
And we do mean Action! Two heroes-worth, in fact--everyone's favorite wisecracking, fun-loving, crime-fighter, Spider-Man (who spends his days as his aunt's favorite, polite, studious, high-school student/part-time photographer, Peter Parker)...
...and the dark, mysterious figure known as Night-Thrasher (who knows how he spends his days).
"But wait," you ask, "If they're both heroes, why are they slugging it out with each other when there's a perfectly good super-villain like The Jester right there, having a hearty laugh at their expense?"
We'd tell you now, but there's still a whole bunch of pages to fill. So read on!
KROMA-KEY
BUT SERIOUSLY, FOLKS...
CHRIS KIPINIAK WRITER
PATRICK SCHERBERGER PENCILER
ROLAND PA INKER
GURU eFX COLORISTS
DAVE SHARPE LETTERER
SCHERBERGER, HAMSCHER et GURU eFX COVER
BRAD PRODUCT
NATHAN COSBY ASSISTANT EDITOR
MARK PANICCIA EDITOR
JOE QUESADA EDITOR IN CHIEF
DAN BUC PUBLISH

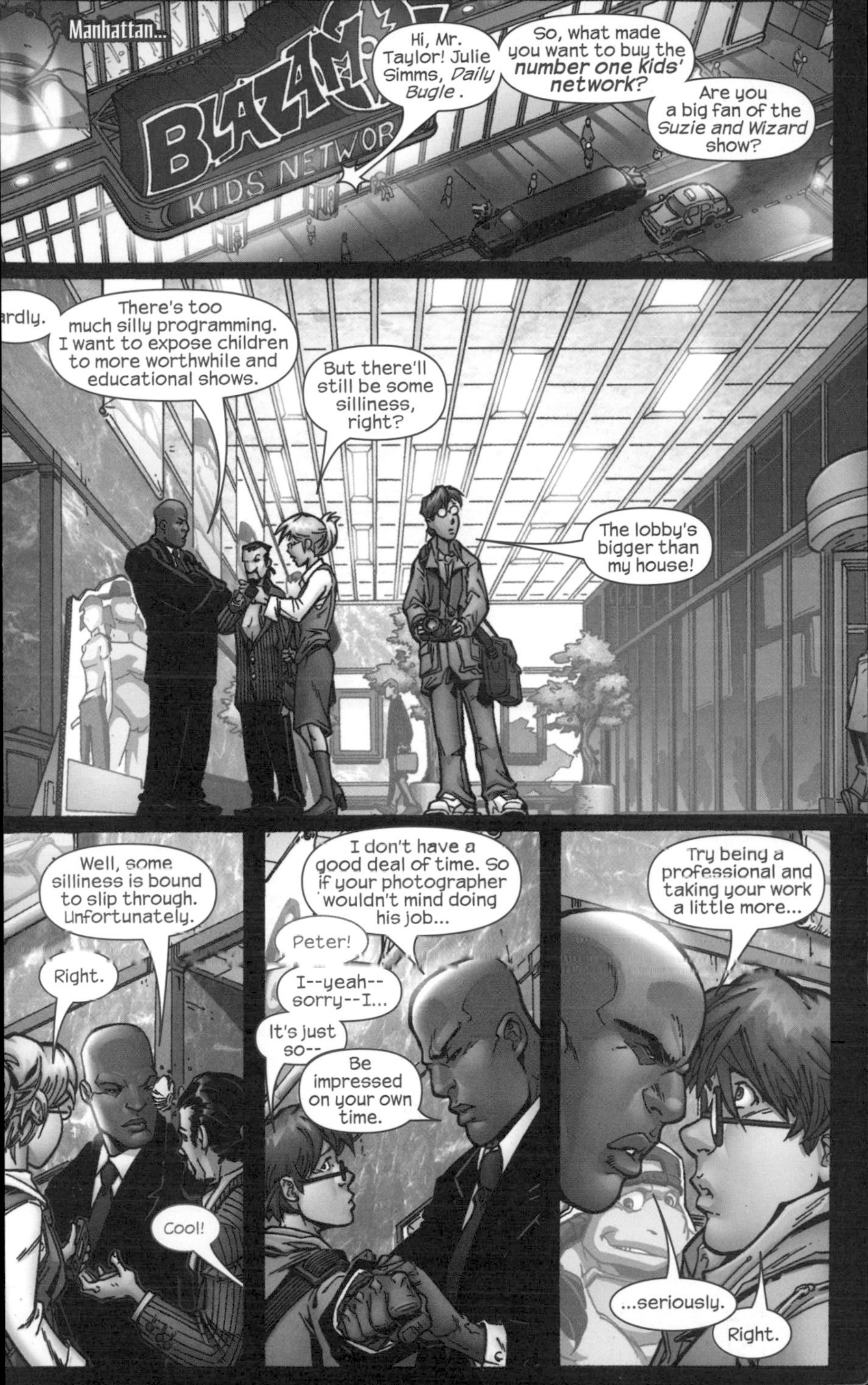
Manhattan...
BLAZAM
KIDS NETWOR
Hi, Mr. Taylor! Julie Simms, *Daily Bugle*.
So, what made you want to buy the **number one kids' network?**
Are you a big fan of the *Suzie and Wizard* show?
ardly.
There's too much silly programming. I want to expose children to more worthwhile and educational shows.
But there'll still be some silliness, right?
The lobby's bigger than my house!
Well, some silliness is bound to slip through. Unfortunately.
Right.
Cool!
I don't have a good deal of time. So if your photographer wouldn't mind doing his job...
Peter!
I--yeah--sorry--I...
It's just so--
Be impressed on your own time.
Try being a professional and taking your work a little more...
...seriously.
Right.

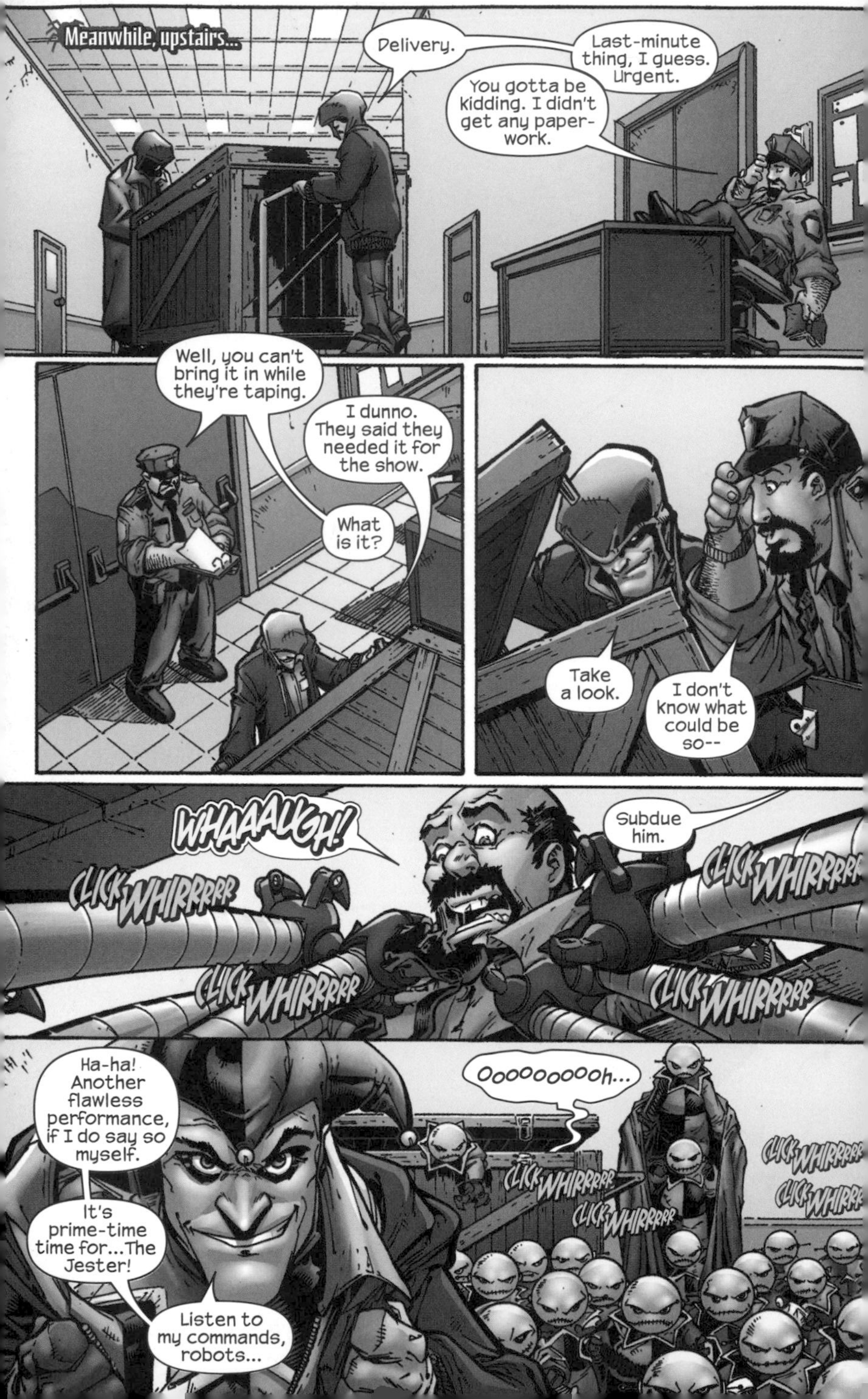

Meanwhile, upstairs...
Delivery.
Last-minute thing, I guess. Urgent.
You gotta be kidding. I didn't get any paper-work.
Well, you can't bring it in while they're taping.
I dunno. They said they needed it for the show.
What is it?
Take a look.
I don't know what could be so--
WHAAAUGH!
Subdue him.
CLICK WHIRRRRR
CLICK WHIRRRRR
CLICK WHIRRRRR
CLICK WHIRRRRR
Ha-ha! Another flawless performance, if I do say so myself.
It's prime-time time for...The Jester!
Listen to my commands, robots...
Oooooooooh...
CLICK WHIRRRRR
CLICK WHIRRRRR

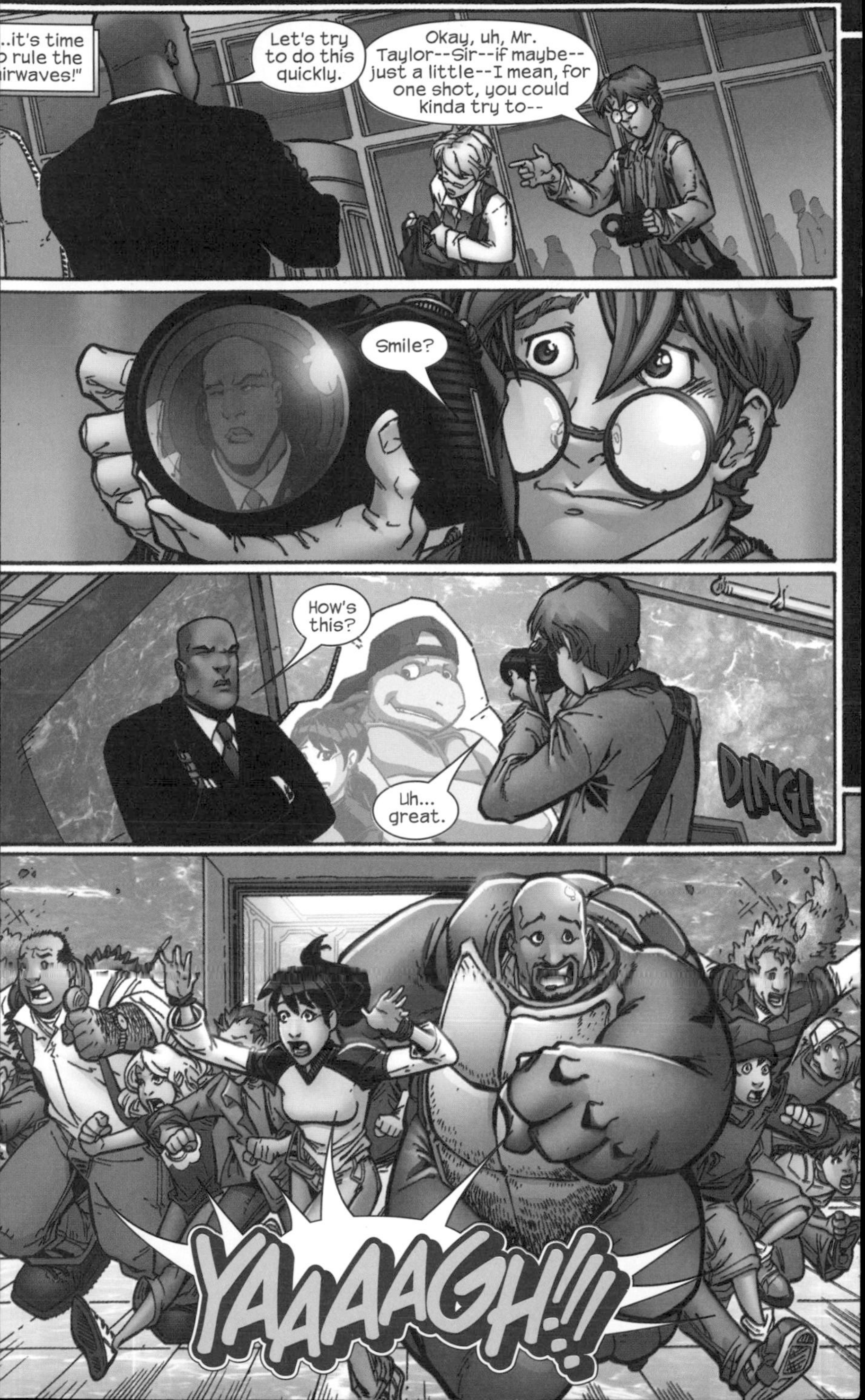
...it's time
o rule the
irwaves!"
Let's try to do this quickly.
Okay, uh, Mr. Taylor--Sir--if maybe--just a little--I mean, for one shot, you could kinda try to--
Smile?
How's this?
Uh... great.
DING!
YAAAAGH!!!

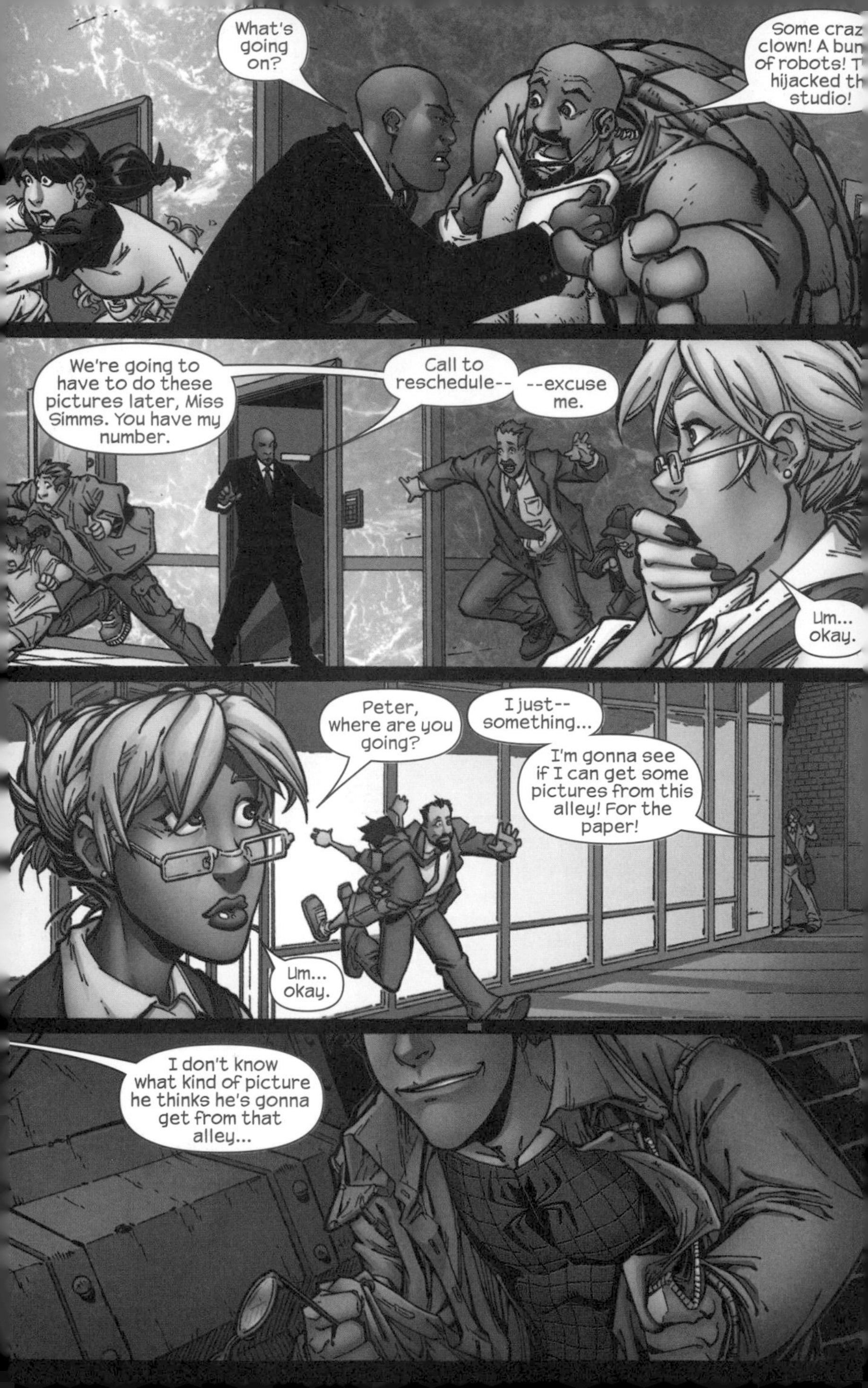

What's going on?
Some craz clown! A bun of robots! T hijacked th studio!
We're going to have to do these pictures later, Miss Simms. You have my number.
Call to reschedule--
--excuse me.
Um... okay.
Peter, where are you going?
I just-- something...
I'm gonna see if I can get some pictures from this alley! For the paper!
Um... okay.
I don't know what kind of picture he thinks he's gonna get from that alley...

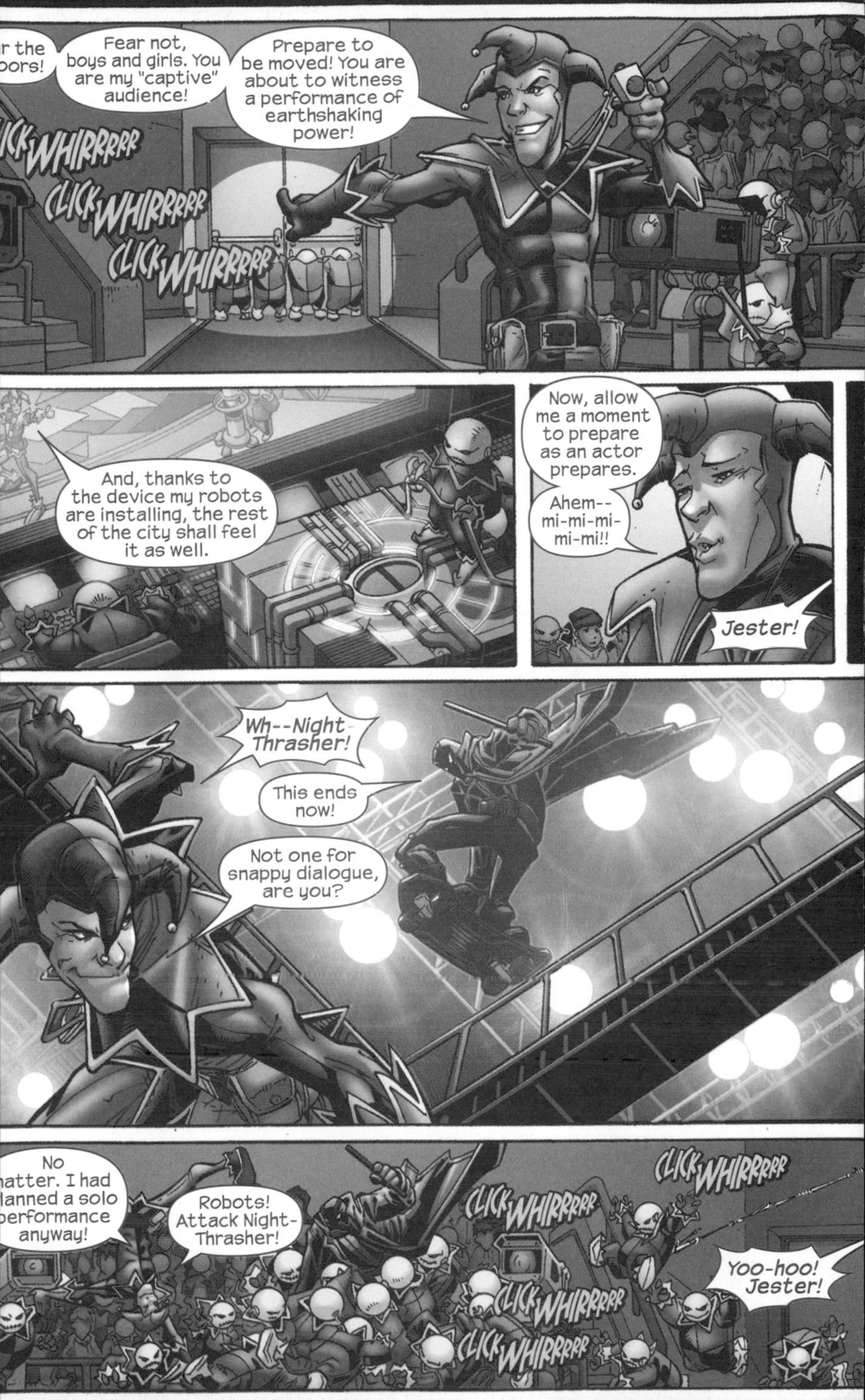
r the
oors!
Fear not, boys and girls. You are my "captive" audience!
Prepare to be moved! You are about to witness a performance of earthshaking power!
ICK WHIRRRRR
CLICK WHIRRRRR
CLICK WHIRRRRR
And, thanks to the device my robots are installing, the rest of the city shall feel it as well.
Now, allow me a moment to prepare as an actor prepares.
Ahem-- mi-mi-mi- mi-mi!!
Jester!
Wh--Night-Thrasher!
This ends now!
Not one for snappy dialogue, are you?
No
atter. I had
lanned a solo
erformance
anyway!
Robots! Attack Night-Thrasher!
CLICK WHIRRRRR
CLICK WHIRRRRR
CLICK WHIRRRRR
CLICK WHIRRRRR
Yoo-hoo! Jester!

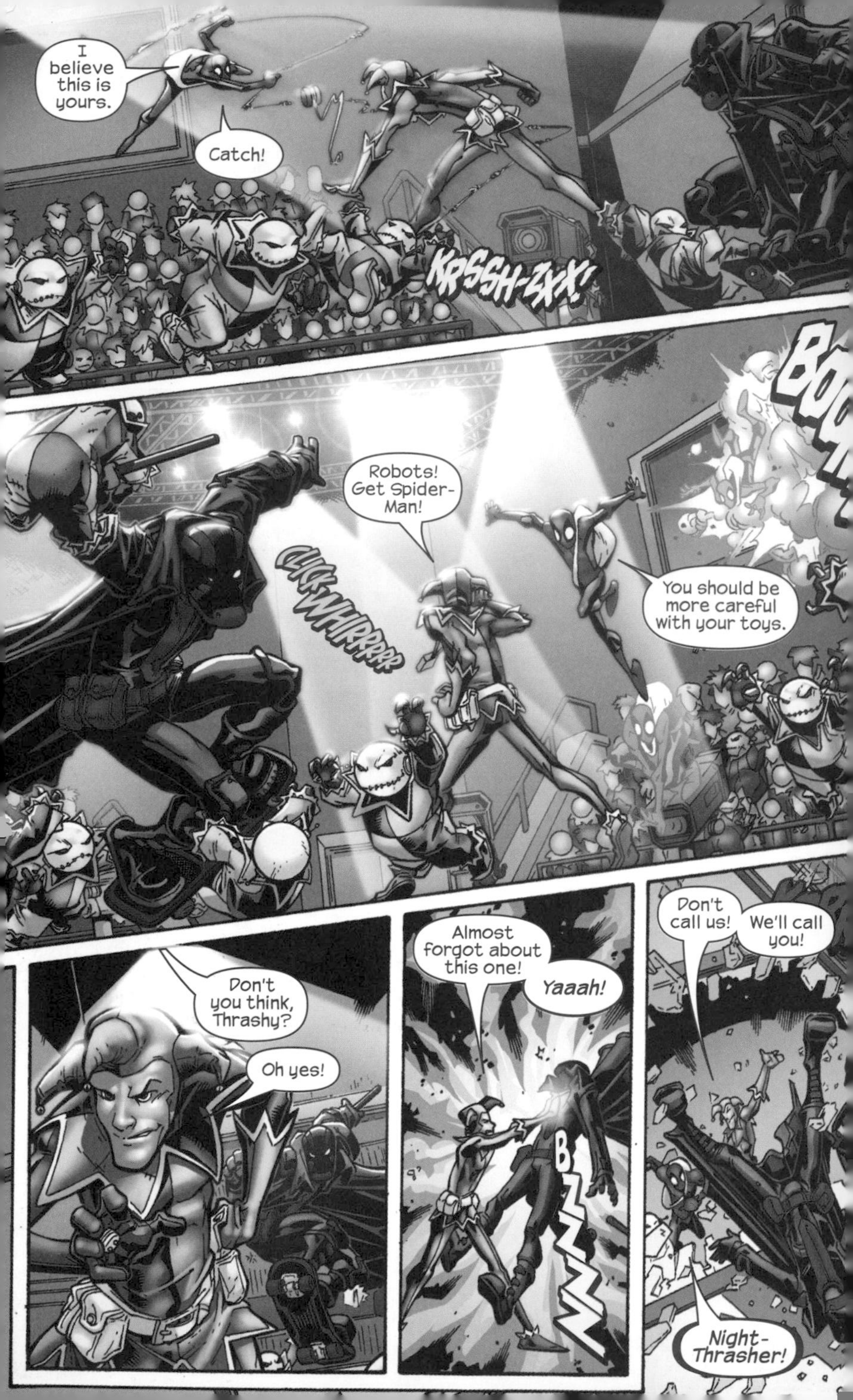

I believe this is yours.
Catch!
KRSSH-ZXX!
BOOM
Robots! Get Spider-Man!
CLICK WHIRRRR
You should be more careful with your toys.
Don't you think, Thrashy?
Oh yes!
Almost forgot about this one!
Yaaah!
BZZZM
Don't call us!
We'll call you!
Night-Thrasher!

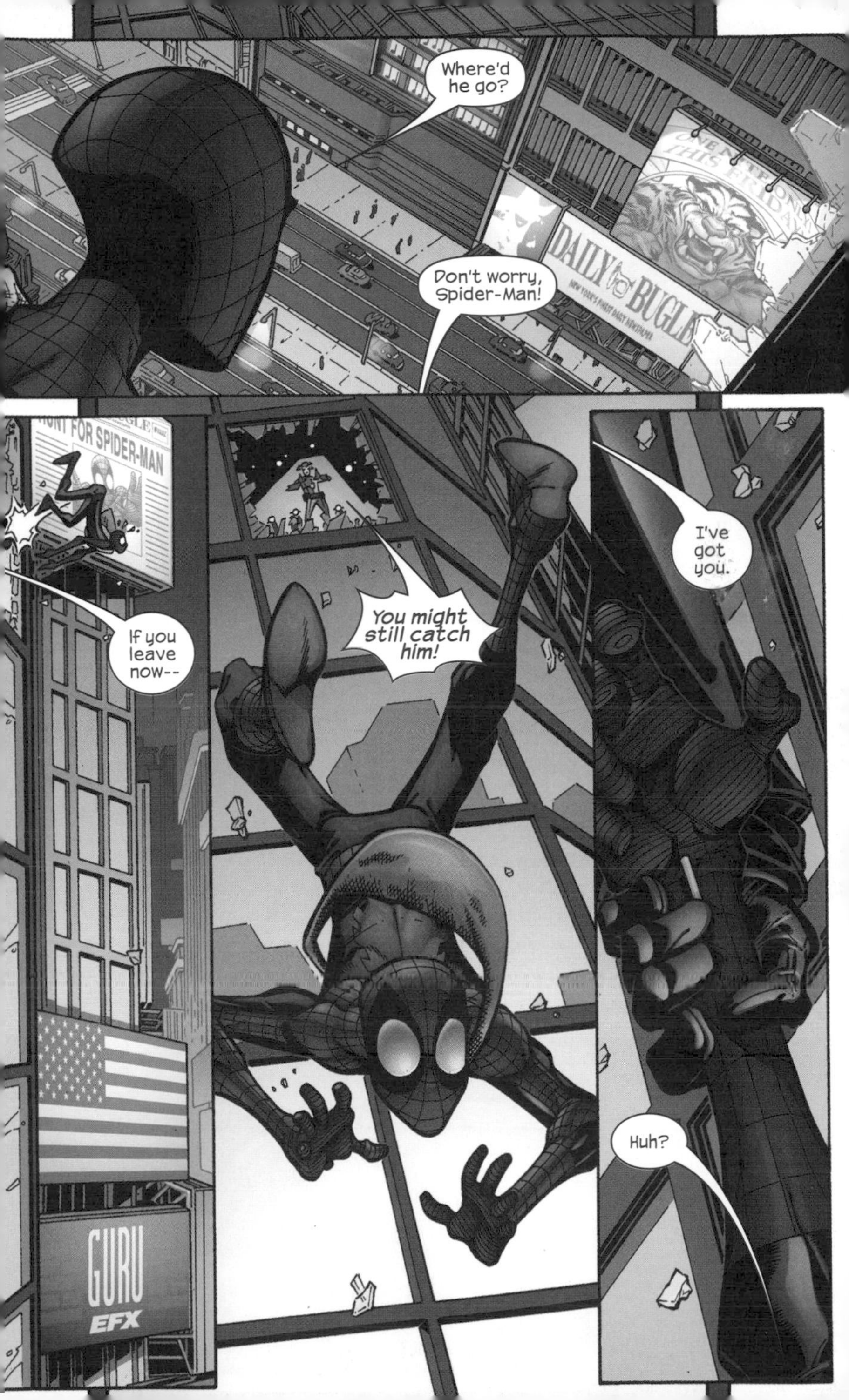
Where'd he go?
THIS FRIDAY
DAILY BUGLE
Don't worry, Spider-Man!
FOR SPIDER-MAN
If you leave now--
You might still catch him!
I've got you.
Huh?
GURU
EFX

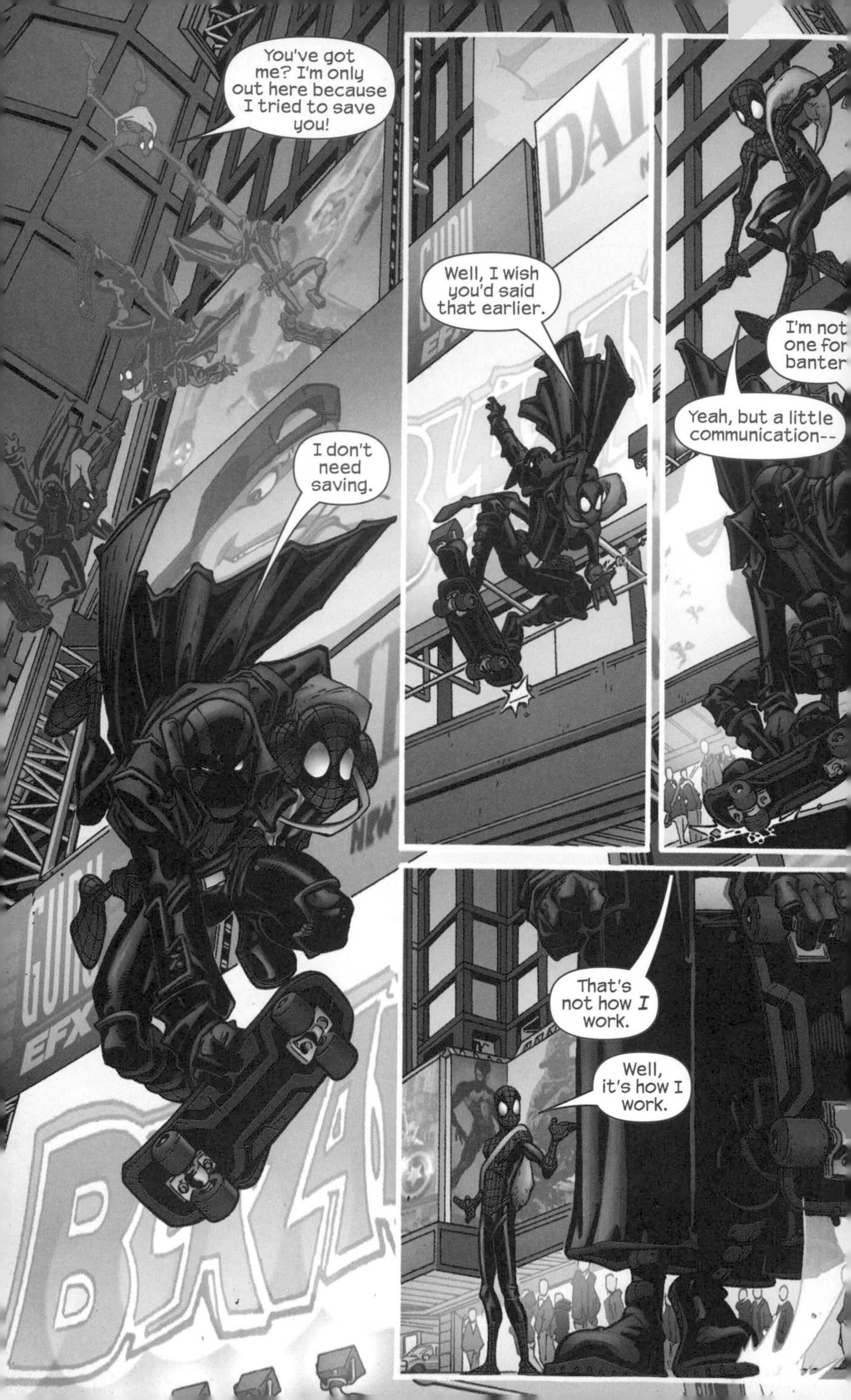
You've got me? I'm only out here because I tried to save you!
I don't need saving.
Well, I wish you'd said that earlier.
I'm not one for banter
Yeah, but a little communication--
That's not how *I* work.
Well, it's how I work.

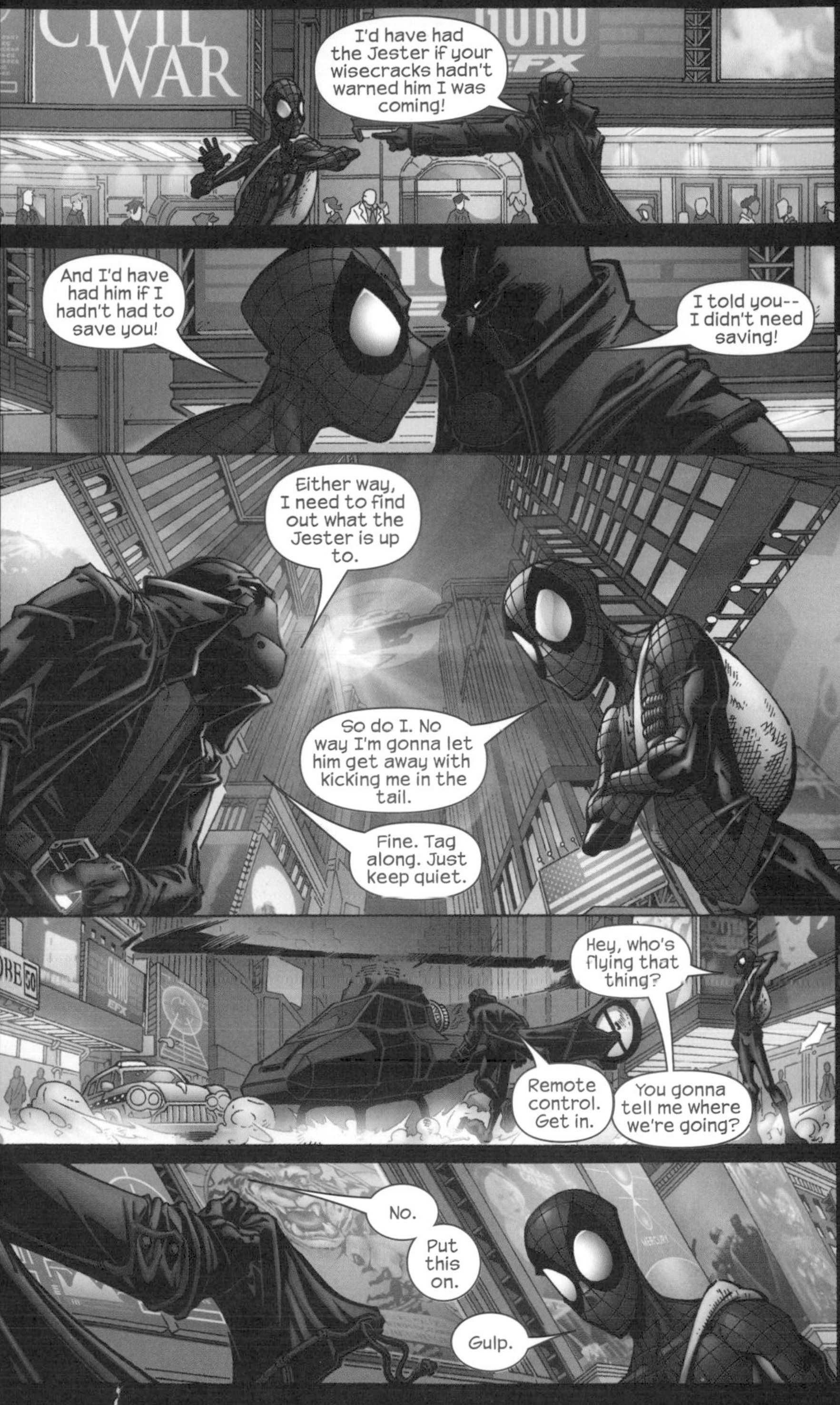
CIVIL WAR
I'd have had the Jester if your wisecracks hadn't warned him I was coming!
And I'd have had him if I hadn't had to save you!
I told you-- I didn't need saving!
Either way, I need to find out what the Jester is up to.
So do I. No way I'm gonna let him get away with kicking me in the tail.
Fine. Tag along. Just keep quiet.
Hey, who's flying that thing?
Remote control. Get in.
You gonna tell me where we're going?
No.
Put this on.
Gulp.

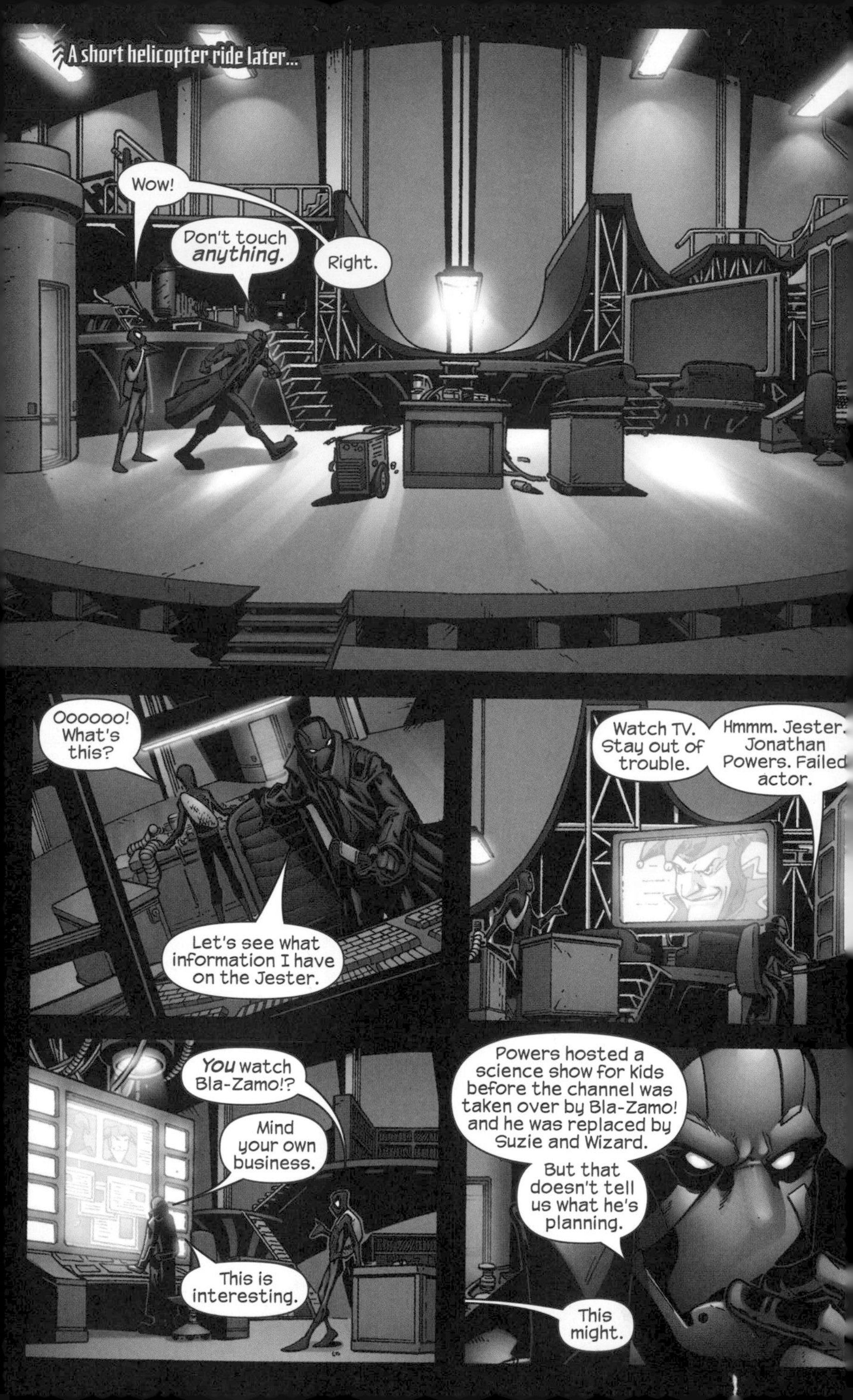
A short helicopter ride later...
Wow!
Don't touch *anything.*
Right.
Oooooo! What's this?
Let's see what information I have on the Jester.
Watch TV. Stay out of trouble.
Hmmm. Jester. Jonathan Powers. Failed actor.
You watch Bla-Zamo!?
Mind your own business.
This is interesting.
Powers hosted a science show for kids before the channel was taken over by Bla-Zamo! and he was replaced by Suzie and Wizard.
But that doesn't tell us what he's planning.
This might.

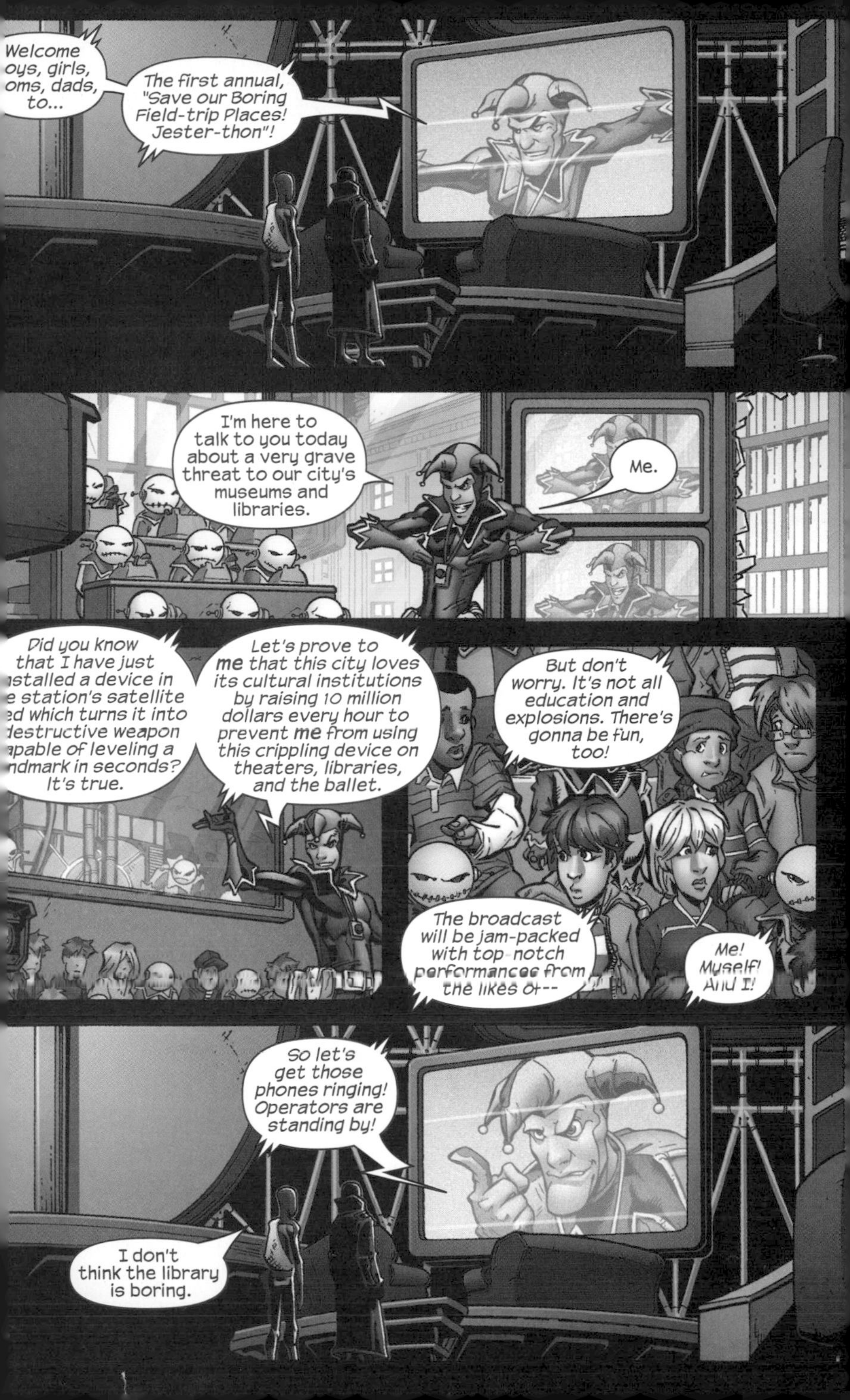
Welcome
oys, girls,
oms, dads,
to...
The first annual, "Save our Boring Field-trip Places! Jester-thon"!
I'm here to talk to you today about a very grave threat to our city's museums and libraries.
Me.
Did you know that I have just
1stalled a device in
e station's satellite
ed which turns it into
destructive weapon
apable of leveling a
ndmark in seconds?
It's true.
Let's prove to me that this city loves its cultural institutions by raising 10 million dollars every hour to prevent me from using this crippling device on theaters, libraries, and the ballet.
But don't worry. It's not all education and explosions. There's gonna be fun, too!
The broadcast will be jam-packed with top-notch performances from the likes of--
Me! Myself! And I!
So let's get those phones ringing! Operators are standing by!
I don't think the library is boring.

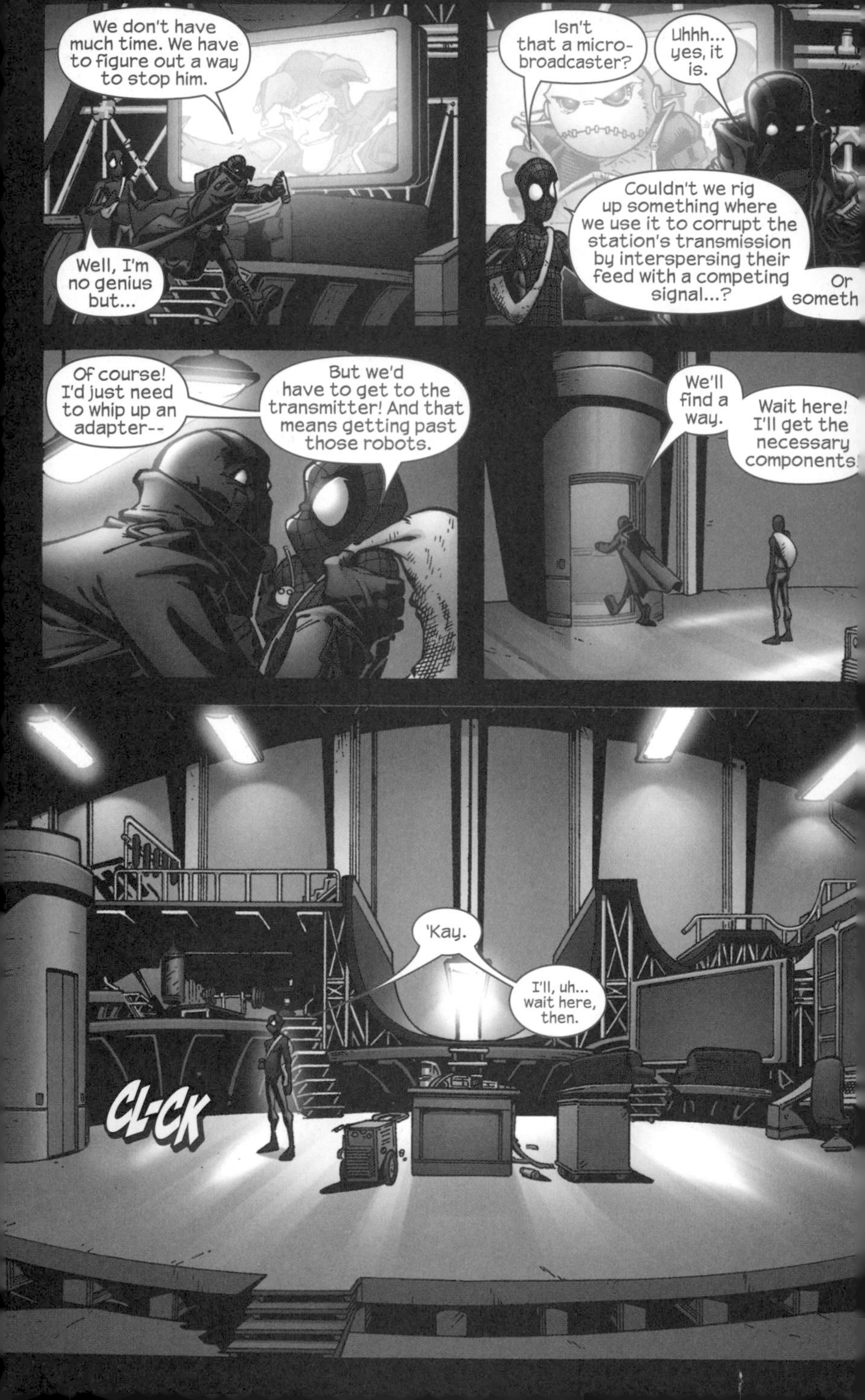
We don't have much time. We have to figure out a way to stop him.
Well, I'm no genius but...
Isn't that a micro-broadcaster?
Uhhh... yes, it is.
Couldn't we rig up something where we use it to corrupt the station's transmission by interspersing their feed with a competing signal...?
Or someth
Of course! I'd just need to whip up an adapter--
But we'd have to get to the transmitter! And that means getting past those robots.
We'll find a way.
Wait here! I'll get the necessary components
'Kay.
I'll, uh... wait here, then.
CL-CK

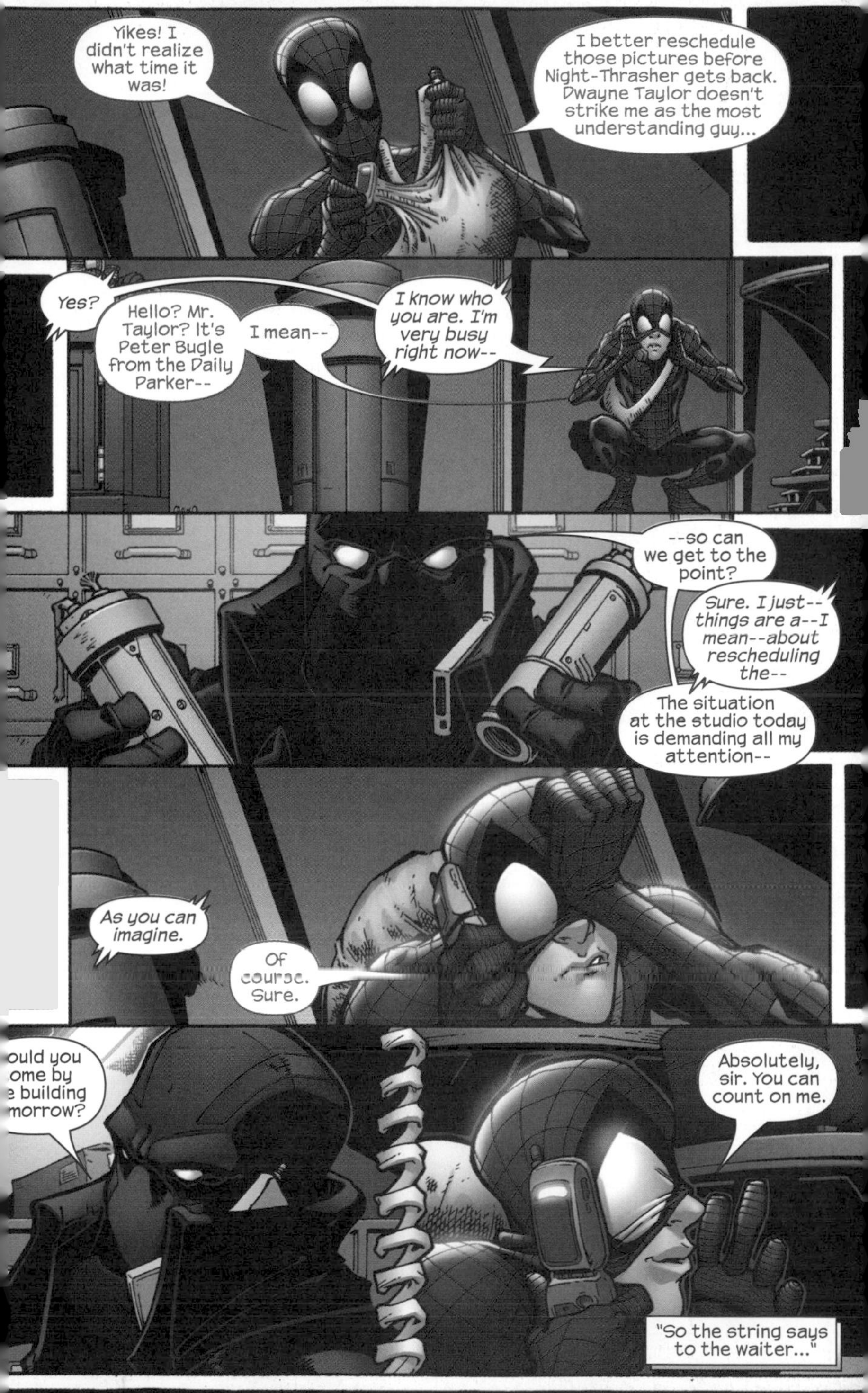
Yikes! I didn't realize what time it was!
I better reschedule those pictures before Night-Thrasher gets back. Dwayne Taylor doesn't strike me as the most understanding guy...
Yes?
Hello? Mr. Taylor? It's Peter Bugle from the Daily Parker--
I mean--
I know who you are. I'm very busy right now--
--so can we get to the point?
Sure. I just--things are a--I mean--about rescheduling the--
The situation at the studio today is demanding all my attention--
As you can imagine.
Of course. Sure.
ould you ome by e building morrow?
Absolutely, sir. You can count on me.
"So the string says to the waiter..."

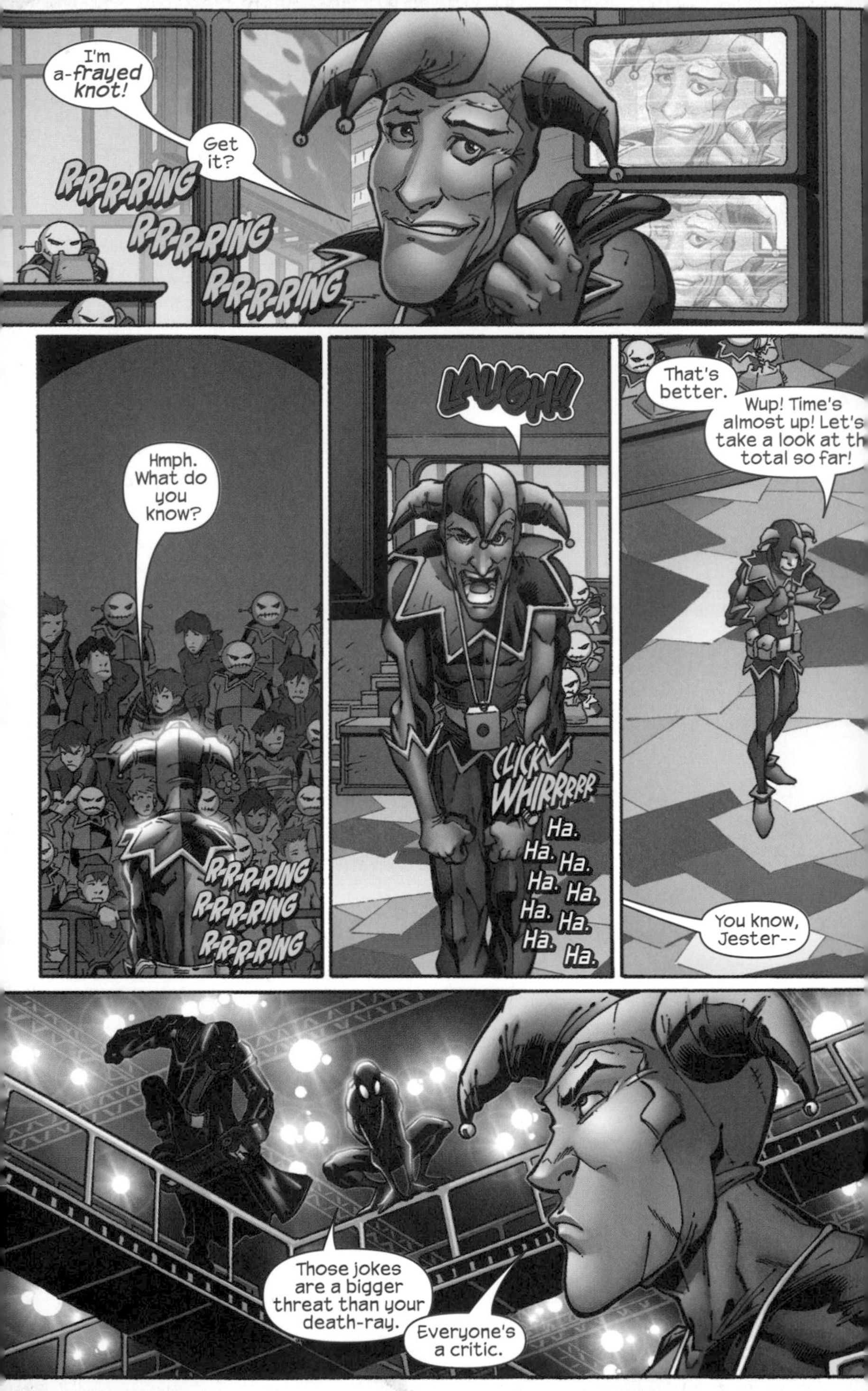
I'm a-frayed knot!
Get it?
R-R-R-RING
R-R-R-RING
R-R-R-RING
Hmph. What do you know?
R-R-R-RING
R-R-R-RING
R-R-R-RING
LAUGH!!
CLICK
WHIRRRRR
Ha. Ha. Ha. Ha. Ha. Ha. Ha. Ha. Ha.
That's better.
Wup! Time's almost up! Let's take a look at th total so far!
You know, Jester--
Those jokes are a bigger threat than your death-ray.
Everyone's a critic.

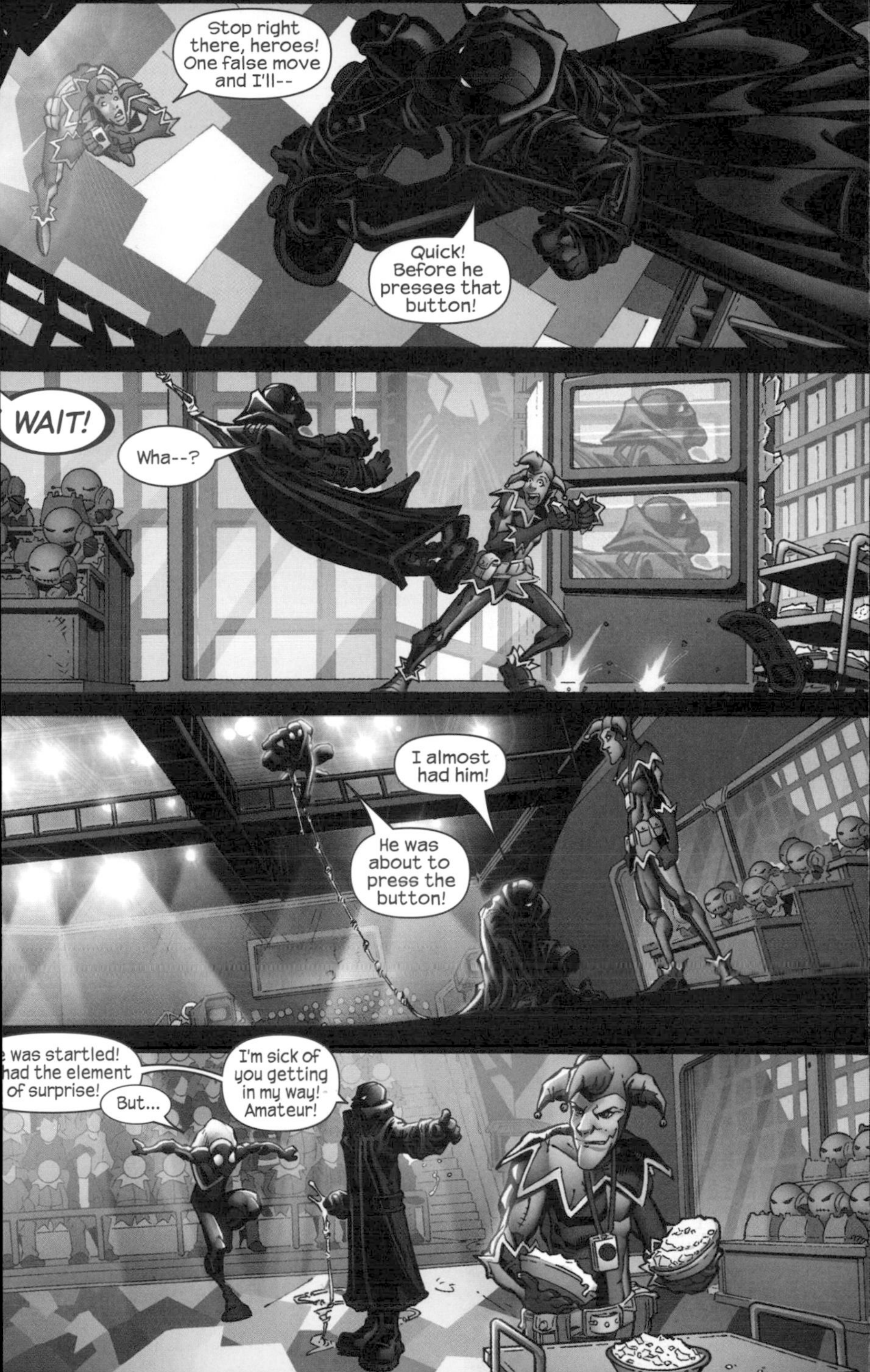
Stop right there, heroes! One false move and I'll--
Quick! Before he presses that button!
WAIT!
Wha--?
I almost had him!
He was about to press the button!
was startled! had the element of surprise!
But...
I'm sick of you getting in my way! Amateur!

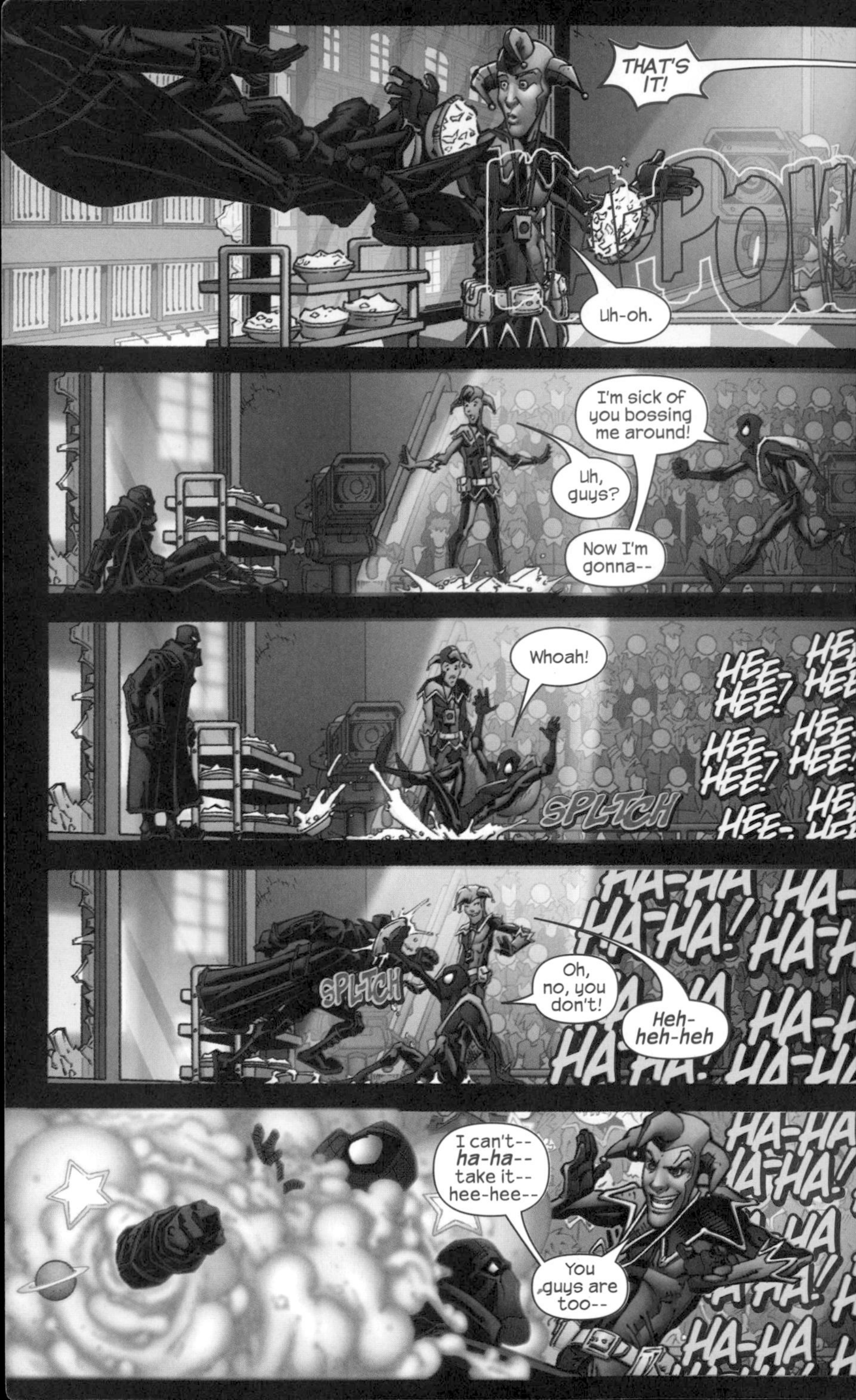

THAT'S IT!
POW
Uh-oh.
I'm sick of you bossing me around!
Uh, guys?
Now I'm gonna--
Whoah!
HEE-HEE!
SPL-TCH
HA-HA HA-HA!
SPL-TCH
Oh, no, you don't!
Heh-heh-heh
I can't-- ha-ha-- take it-- hee-hee--
You guys are too--
HA-HA HA-HA!

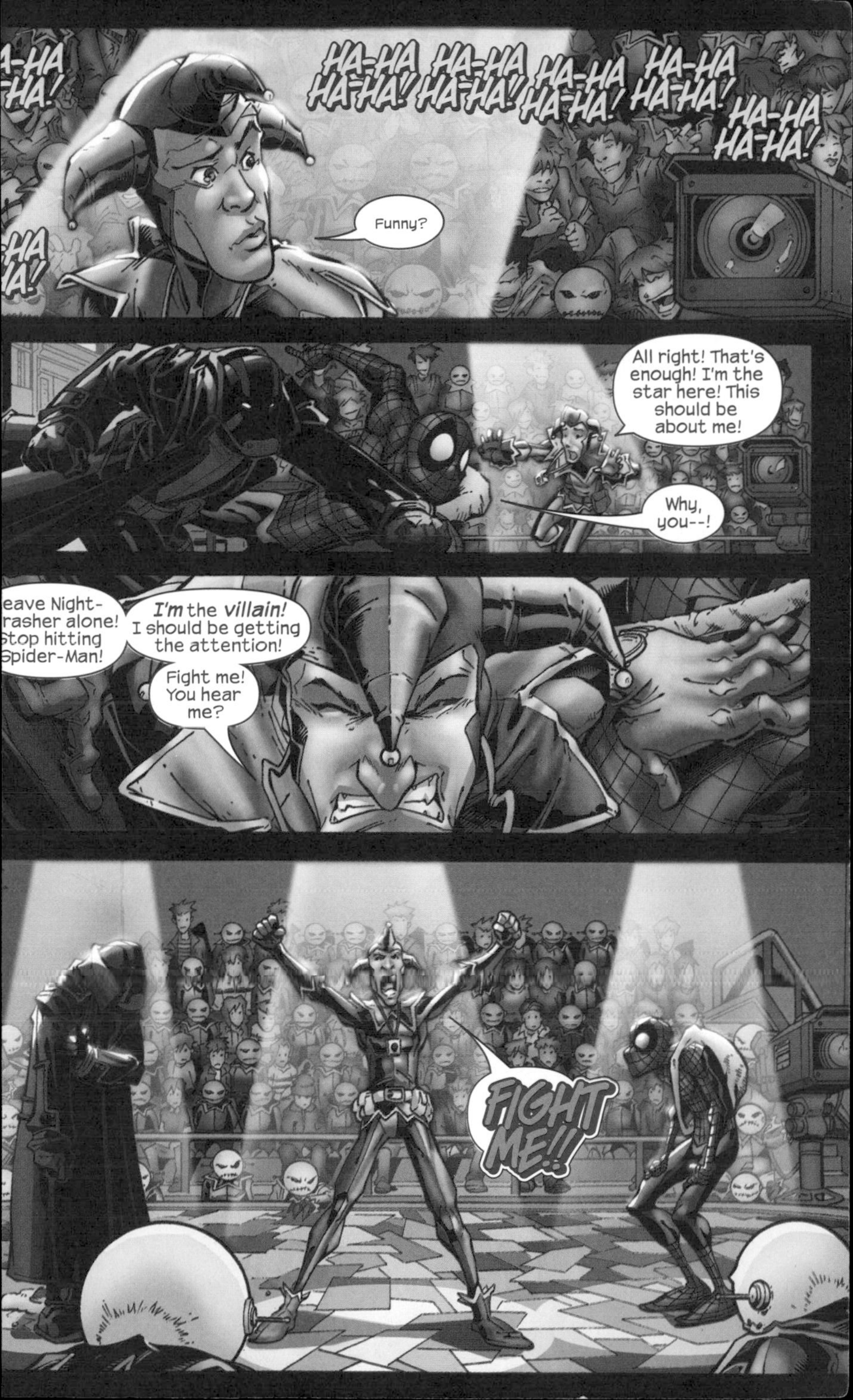

HA-HA HA-HA HA-HA HA-HA HA-HA!
HA-HA HA-HA! HA-HA! HA-HA! HA-HA!
HA-HA HA-HA!
Funny?
All right! That's enough! I'm the star here! This should be about me!
Why, you--!
I'm the villain! I should be getting the attention!
Fight me! You hear me?
FIGHT ME!!

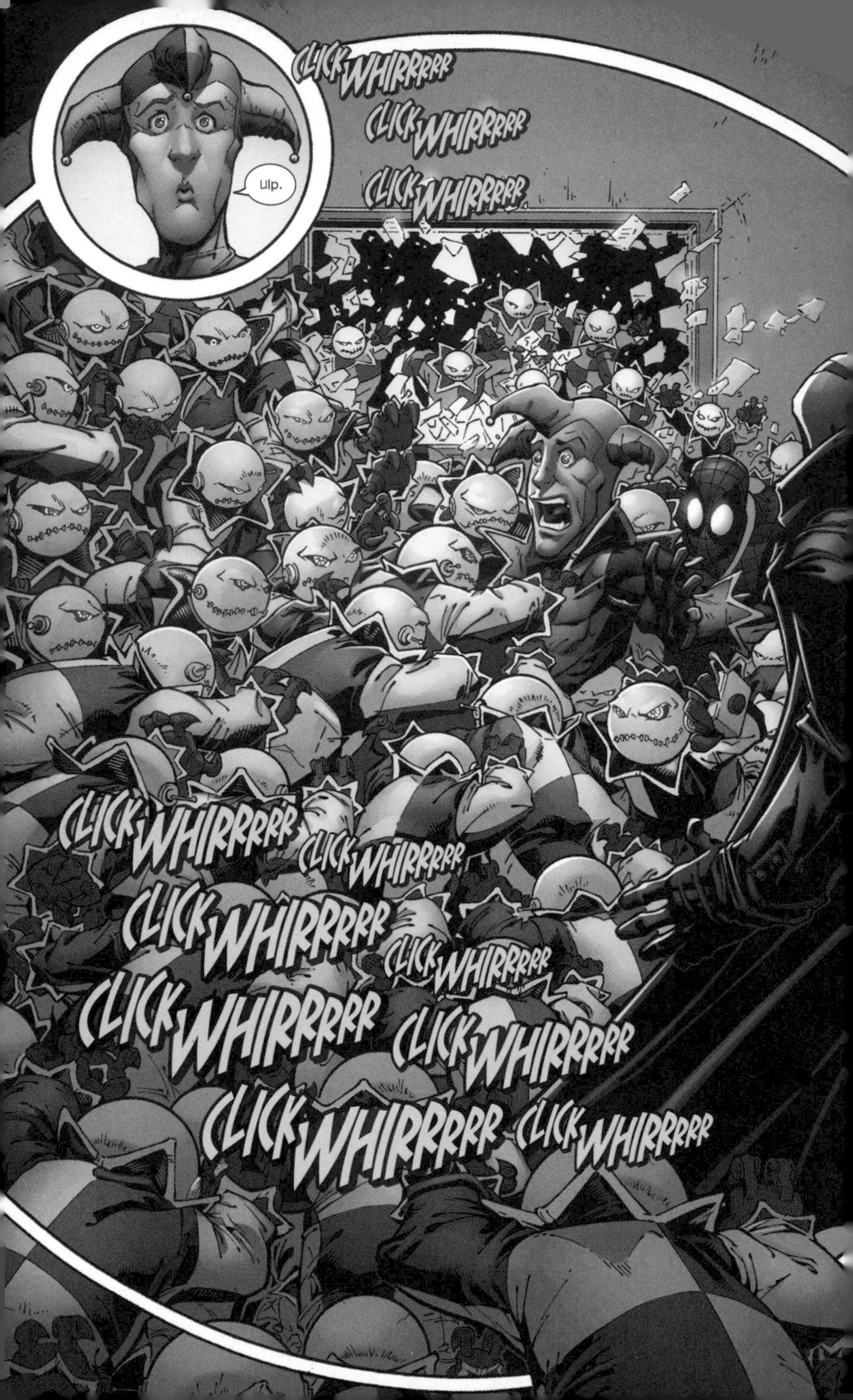
CLICK WHIRRRRR
CLICK WHIRRRRR
CLICK WHIRRRRR.
ulp.
CLICK WHIRRRRR
CLICK WHIRRRRR
CLICK WHIRRRRR
CLICK WHIRRRRR
CLICK WHIRRRRR
CLICK WHIRRRRR
CLICK WHIRRRRR
CLICK WHIRRRRR

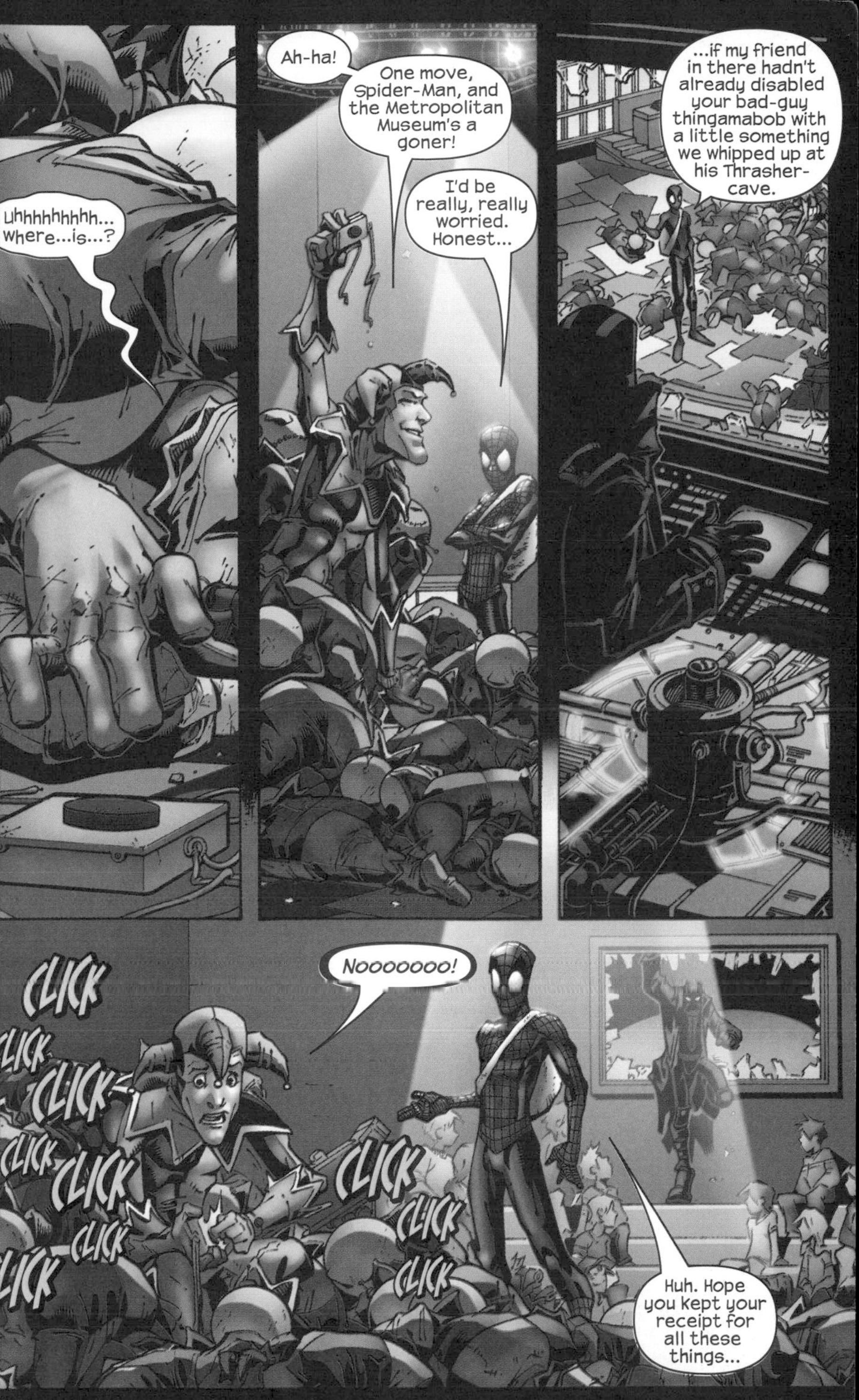
Uhhhhhhhh... where...is...?
Ah-ha!
One move, Spider-Man, and the Metropolitan Museum's a goner!
I'd be really, really worried. Honest...
...if my friend in there hadn't already disabled your bad-guy thingamabob with a little something we whipped up at his Thrasher-cave.
CLICK
CLICK
CLICK
CLICK
CLICK
CLICK
CLICK
Noooooooo!
CLICK
CLICK
CLICK
Huh. Hope you kept your receipt for all these things...

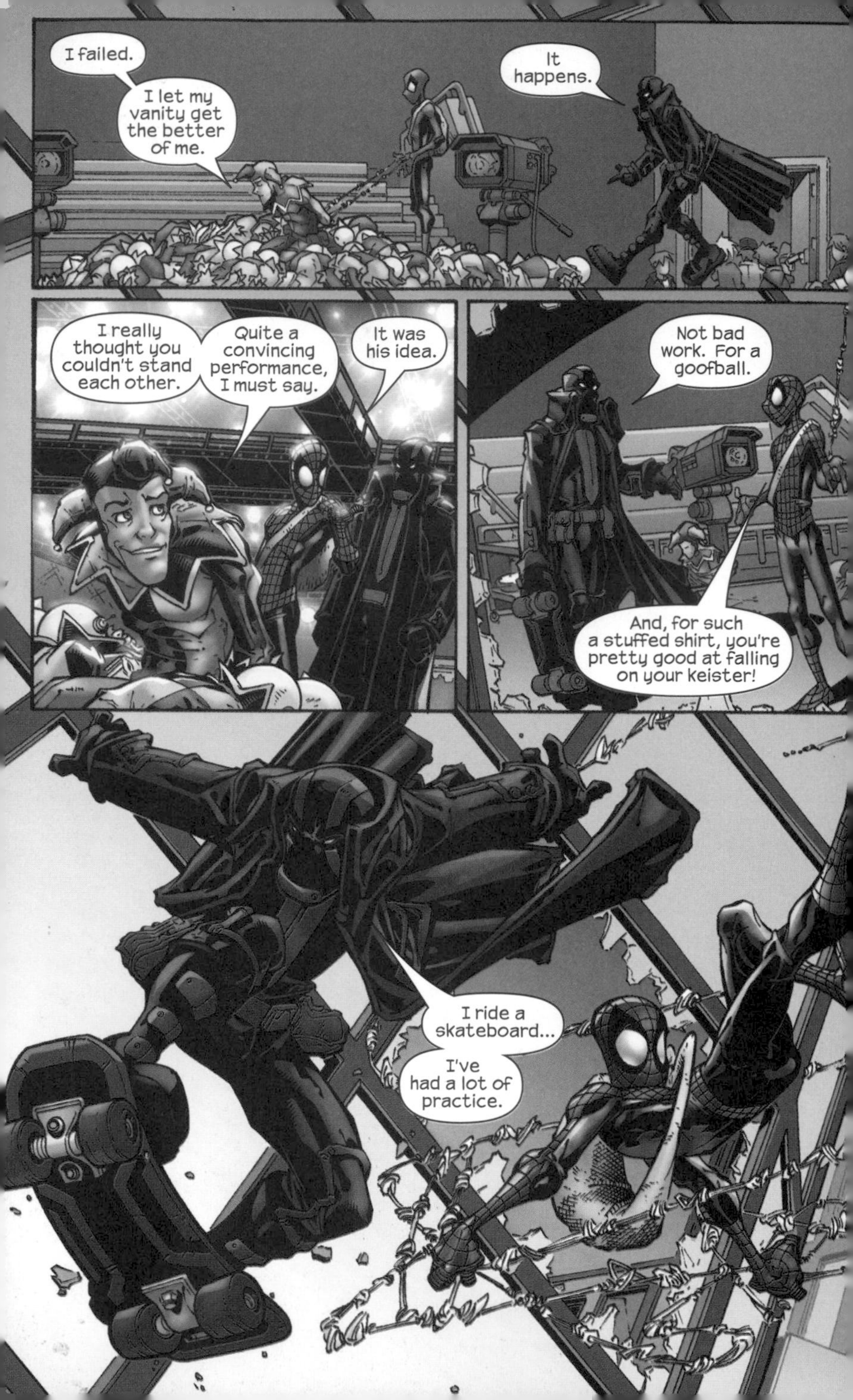
I failed.
I let my vanity get the better of me.
It happens.
I really thought you couldn't stand each other.
Quite a convincing performance, I must say.
It was his idea.
Not bad work. For a goofball.
And, for such a stuffed shirt, you're pretty good at falling on your keister!
I ride a skateboard...
I've had a lot of practice.

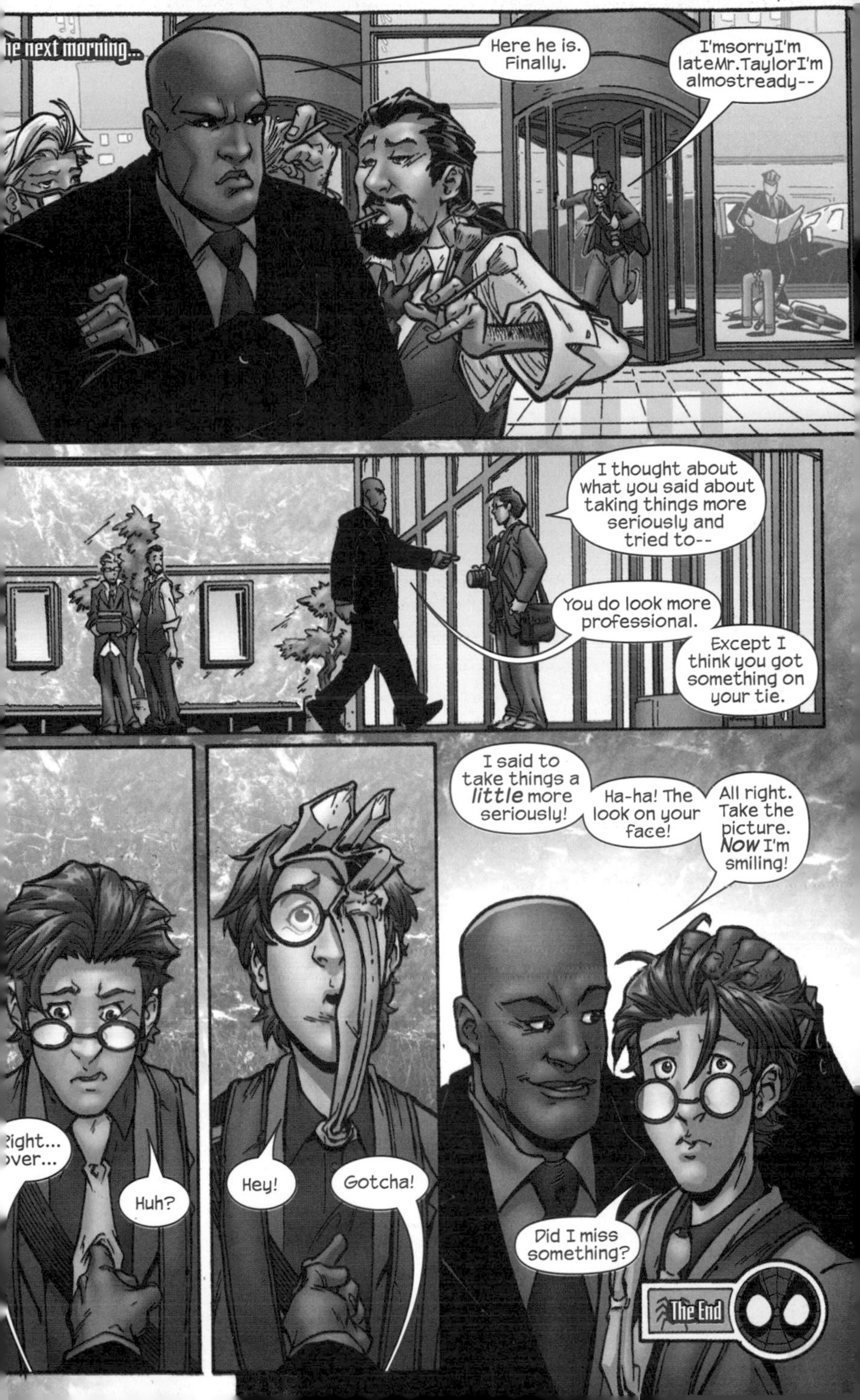
he next morning...
Here he is. Finally.
I'msorryI'm lateMr.TaylorI'm almostready--
I thought about what you said about taking things more seriously and tried to--
You do look more professional.
Except I think you got something on your tie.
Right... over...
Huh?
Hey!
Gotcha!
I said to take things a *little* more seriously!
Ha-ha! The look on your face!
All right. Take the picture. *NOW* I'm smiling!
Did I miss something?
The End

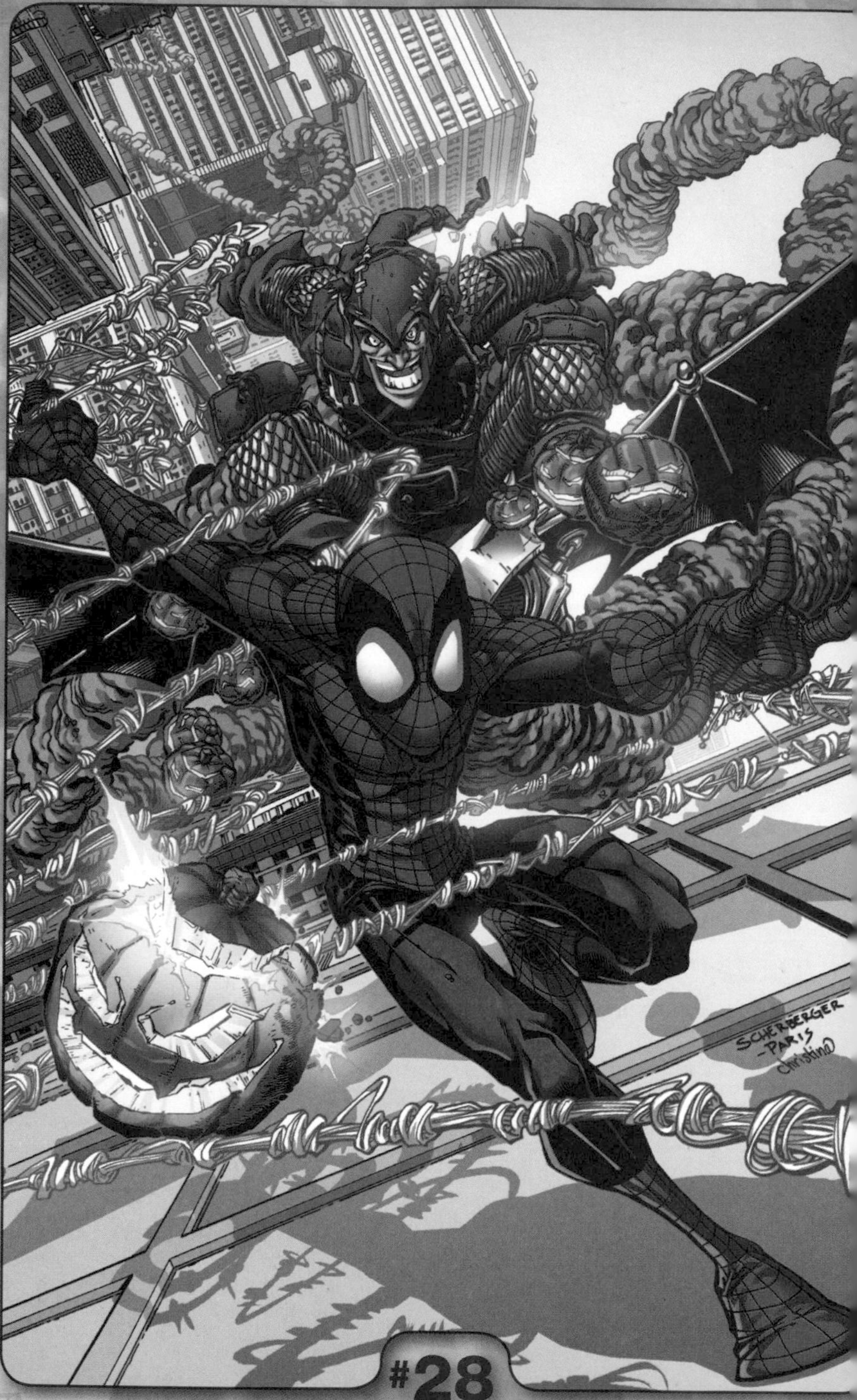
SCHERBERGER
-PARIS
christina

#28

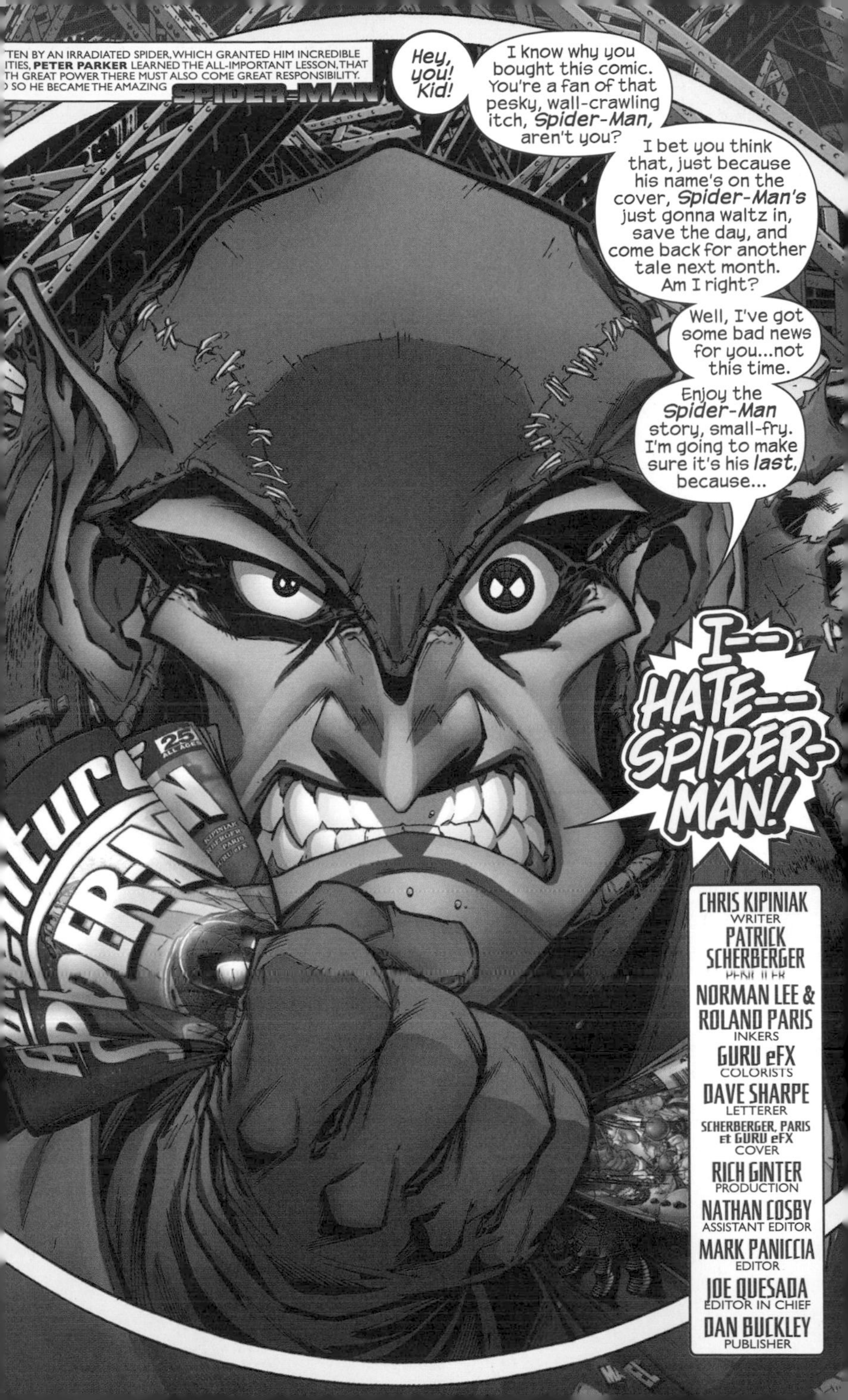
TEN BY AN IRRADIATED SPIDER, WHICH GRANTED HIM INCREDIBLE
ITIES, PETER PARKER LEARNED THE ALL-IMPORTANT LESSON, THAT
TH GREAT POWER THERE MUST ALSO COME GREAT RESPONSIBILITY.
SO HE BECAME THE AMAZING SPIDER-MAN
Hey, you! Kid!
I know why you bought this comic. You're a fan of that pesky, wall-crawling itch, Spider-Man, aren't you?
I bet you think that, just because his name's on the cover, Spider-Man's just gonna waltz in, save the day, and come back for another tale next month. Am I right?
Well, I've got some bad news for you...not this time.
Enjoy the Spider-Man story, small-fry. I'm going to make sure it's his last, because...
I-- HATE-- SPIDER-MAN!
CHRIS KIPINIAK
WRITER
PATRICK SCHERBERGER
PENCILER
NORMAN LEE & ROLAND PARIS
INKERS
GURU eFX
COLORISTS
DAVE SHARPE
LETTERER
SCHERBERGER, PARIS et GURU eFX
COVER
RICH GINTER
PRODUCTION
NATHAN COSBY
ASSISTANT EDITOR
MARK PANICCIA
EDITOR
JOE QUESADA
EDITOR IN CHIEF
DAN BUCKLEY
PUBLISHER

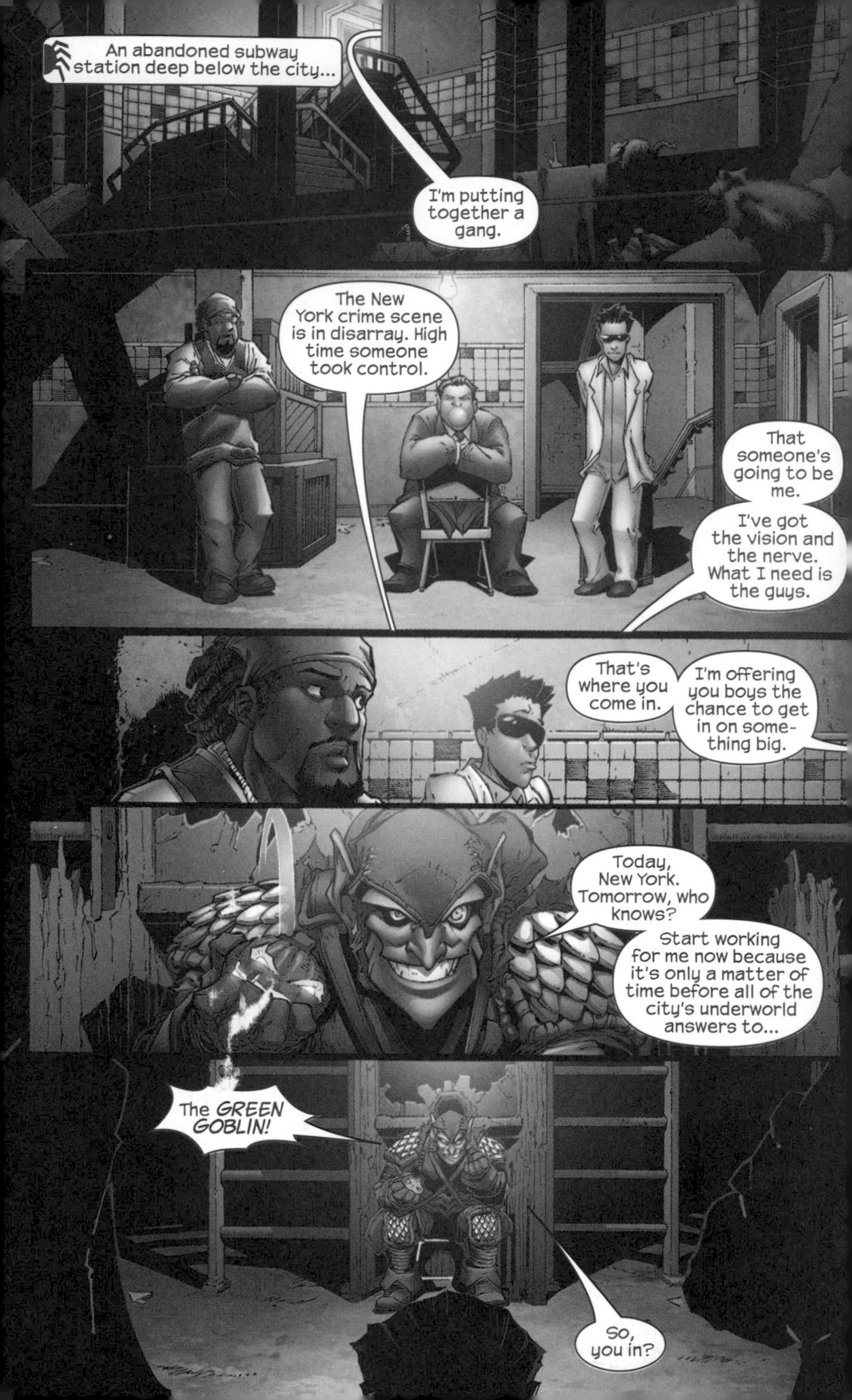
An abandoned subway station deep below the city...
I'm putting together a gang.
The New York crime scene is in disarray. High time someone took control.
That someone's going to be me.
I've got the vision and the nerve. What I need is the guys.
That's where you come in.
I'm offering you boys the chance to get in on something big.
Today, New York. Tomorrow, who knows?
Start working for me now because it's only a matter of time before all of the city's underworld answers to...
The GREEN GOBLIN!
So, you in?

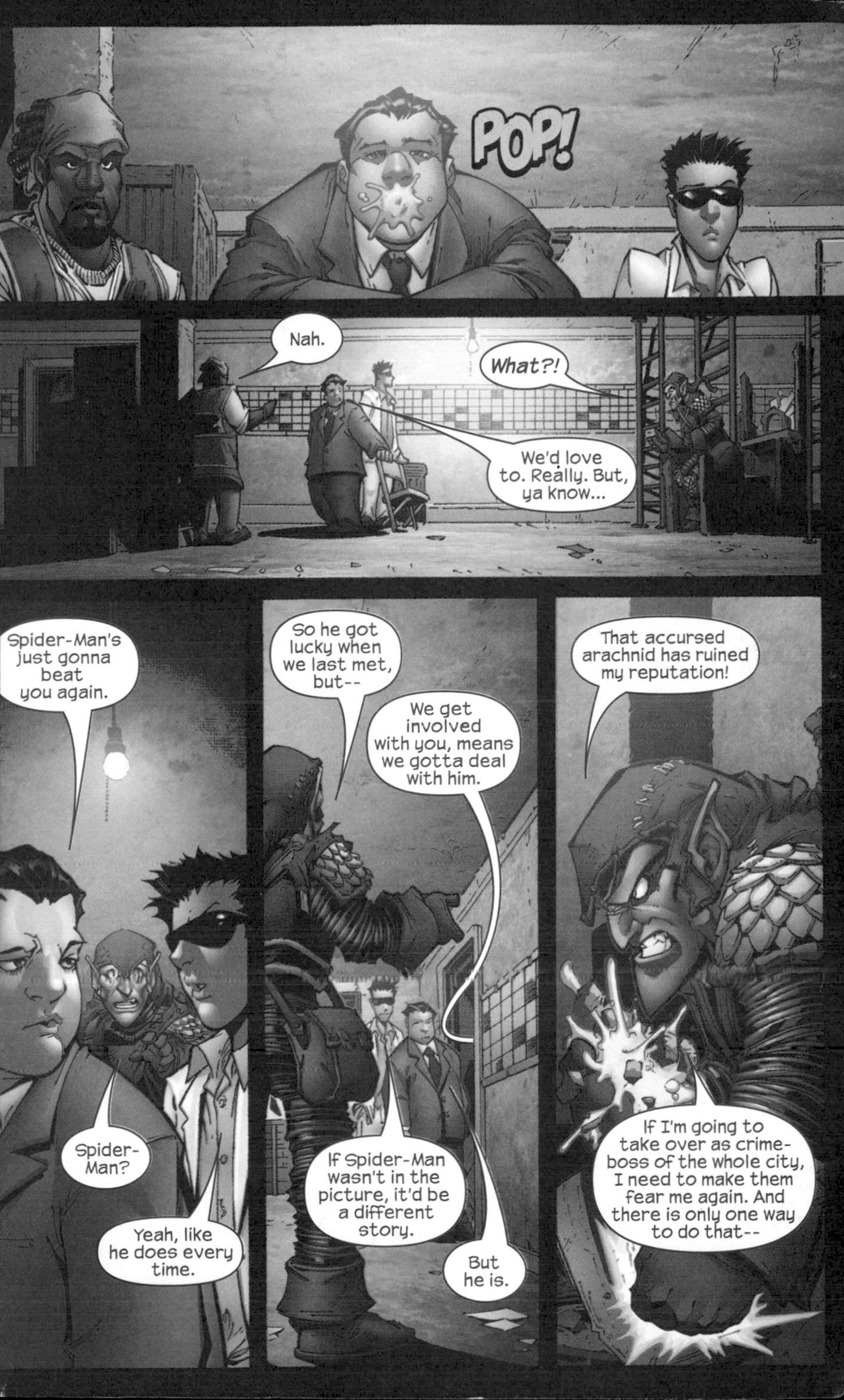
POP!
Nah.
What?!
We'd love to. Really. But, ya know...
Spider-Man's just gonna beat you again.
Spider-Man?
Yeah, like he does every time.
So he got lucky when we last met, but--
We get involved with you, means we gotta deal with him.
If Spider-Man wasn't in the picture, it'd be a different story.
But he is.
That accursed arachnid has ruined my reputation!
If I'm going to take over as crime-boss of the whole city, I need to make them fear me again. And there is only one way to do that--

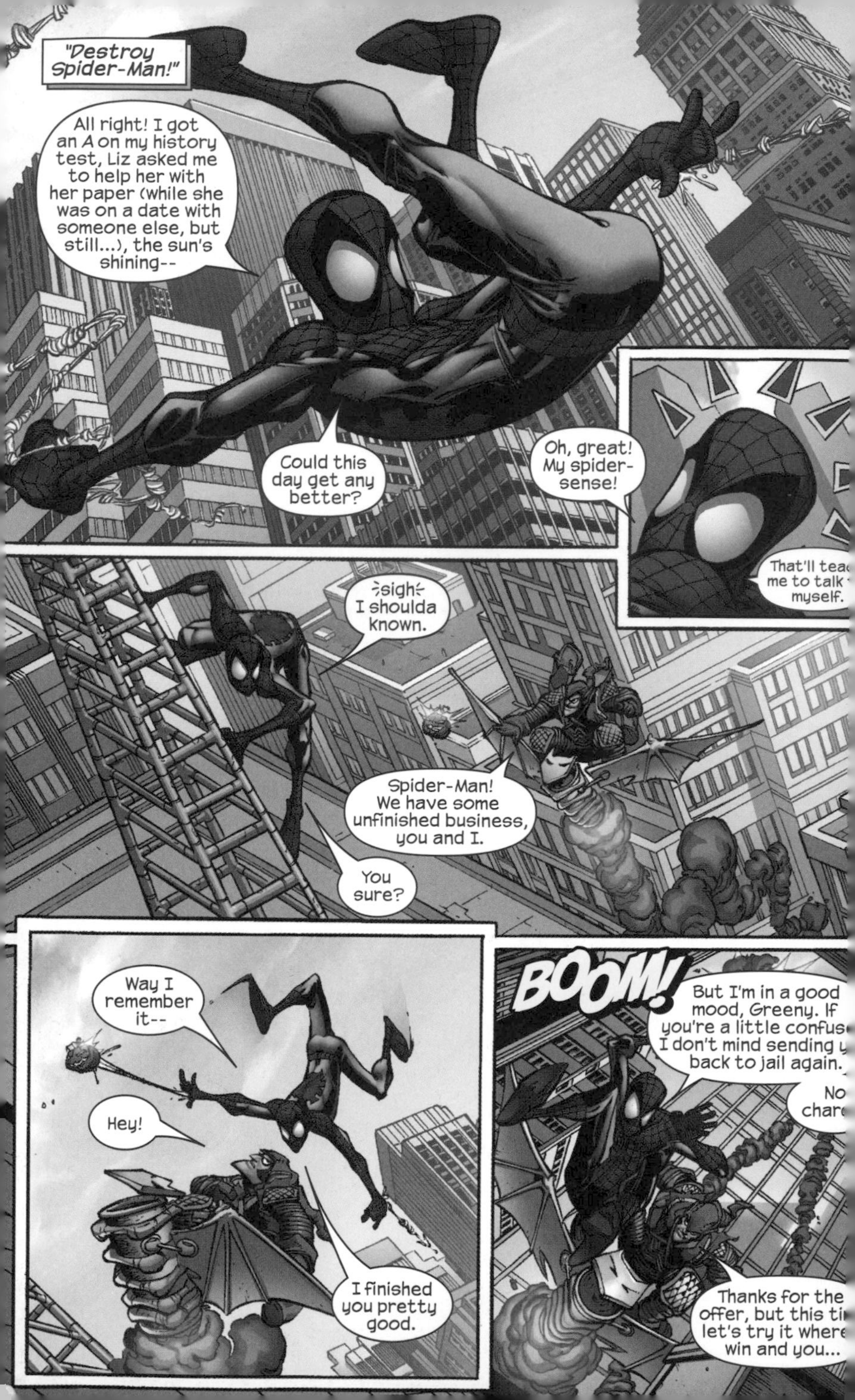
"Destroy Spider-Man!"
All right! I got an A on my history test, Liz asked me to help her with her paper (while she was on a date with someone else, but still...), the sun's shining--
Could this day get any better?
Oh, great! My spider-sense!
That'll tea me to talk myself.
sigh I shoulda known.
Spider-Man! We have some unfinished business, you and I.
You sure?
Way I remember it--
Hey!
I finished you pretty good.
BOOM!
But I'm in a good mood, Greeny. If you're a little confus I don't mind sending y back to jail again.
No char
Thanks for the offer, but this ti let's try it where win and you...

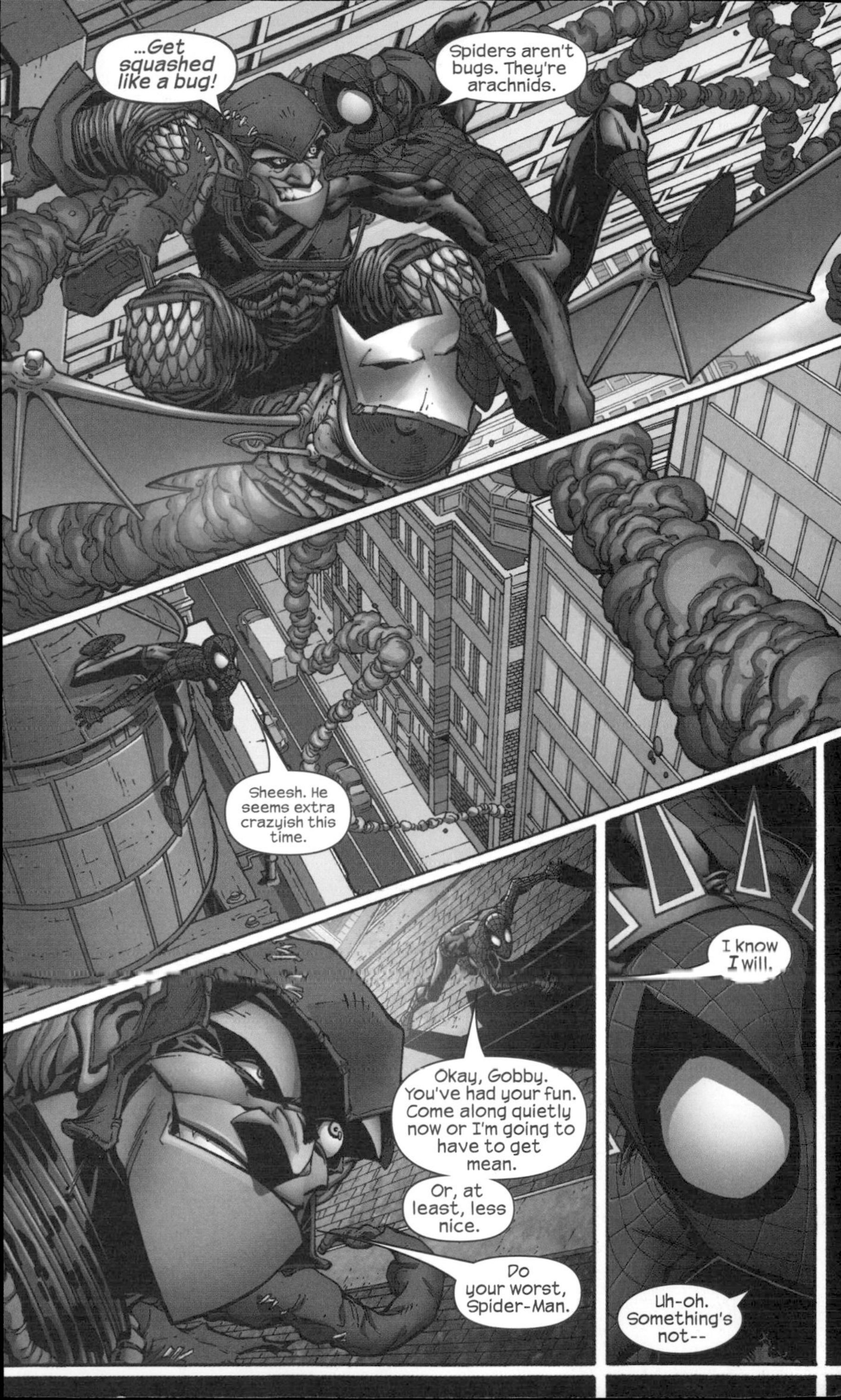
...Get squashed like a bug!
Spiders aren't bugs. They're arachnids.
Sheesh. He seems extra crazyish this time.
Okay, Gobby. You've had your fun. Come along quietly now or I'm going to have to get mean.
Or, at least, less nice.
Do your worst, Spider-Man.
I know I will.
Uh-oh. Something's not--

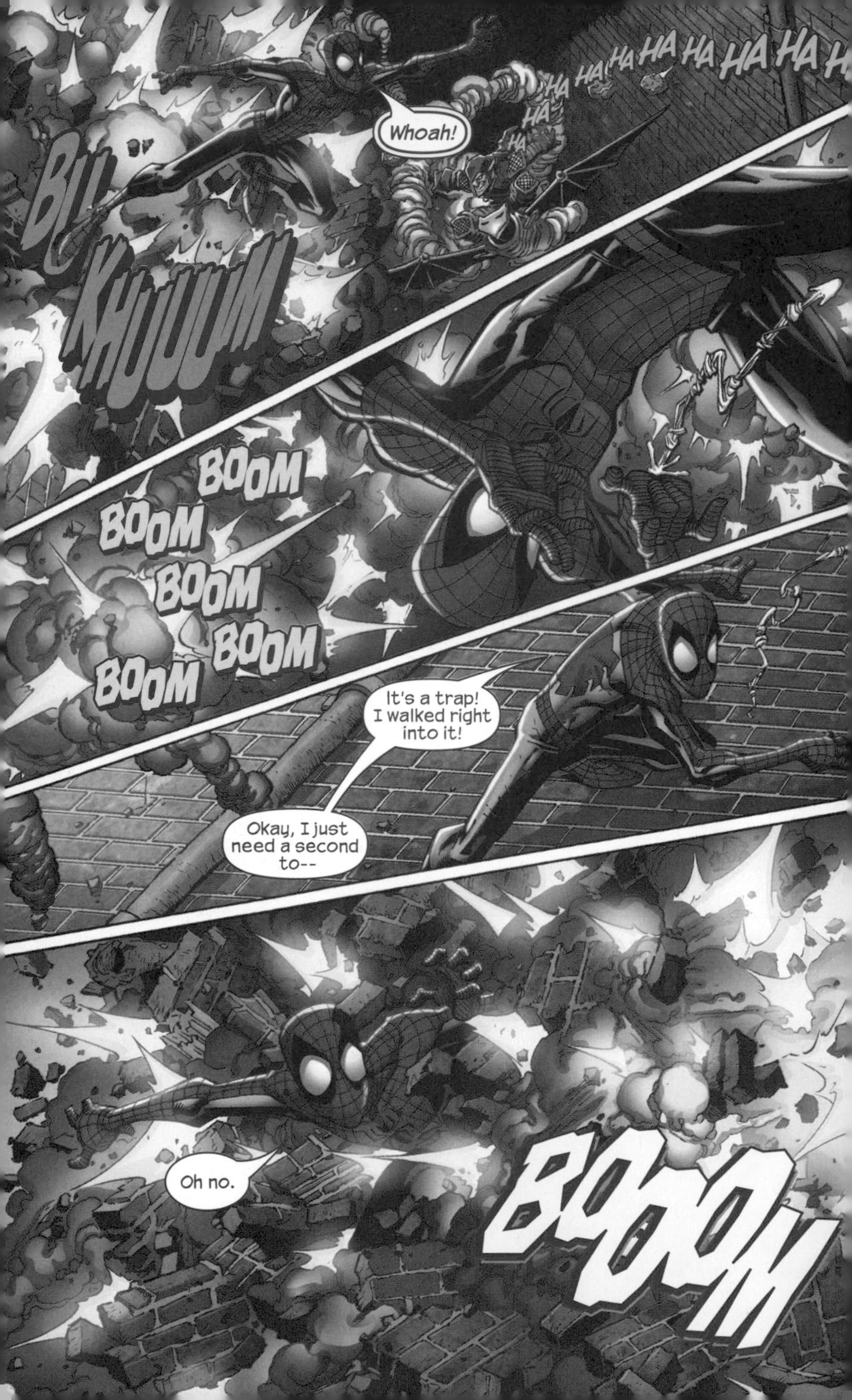

HA HA HA HA HA HA HA HA HA
Whoah!
BLI KHUUUUM!
BOOM
BOOM
BOOM
BOOM
BOOM
It's a trap! I walked right into it!
Okay, I just need a second to--
Oh no.
BOOOM

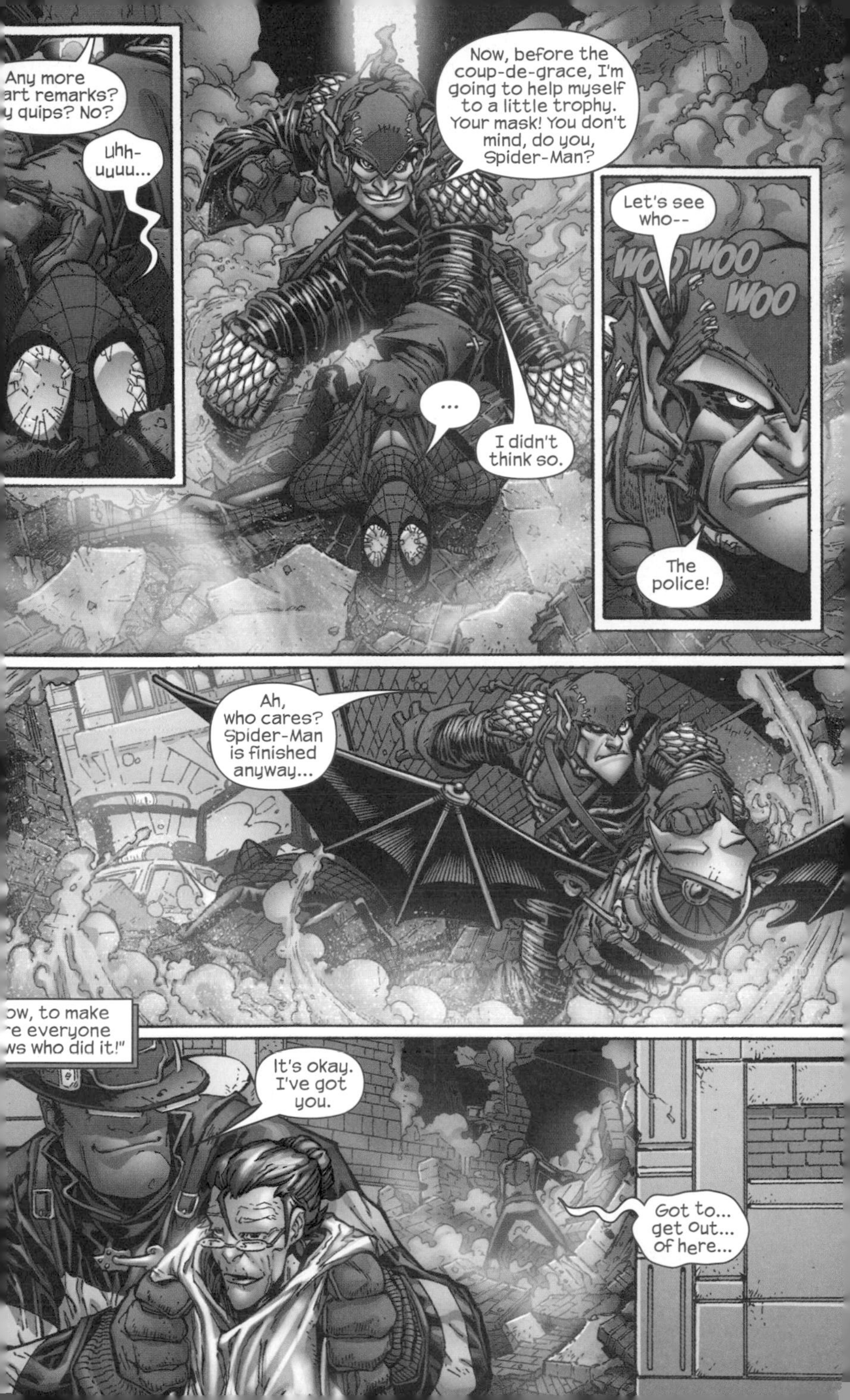

Any more
art remarks?
y quips? No?
Uhh-
uuuu...
Now, before the coup-de-grace, I'm going to help myself to a little trophy. Your mask! You don't mind, do you, Spider-Man?
...
I didn't think so.
Let's see who--
WOO WOO WOO
The police!
Ah, who cares? Spider-Man is finished anyway...
ow, to make
e everyone
ws who did it!"
It's okay. I've got you.
Got to... get out... of here...

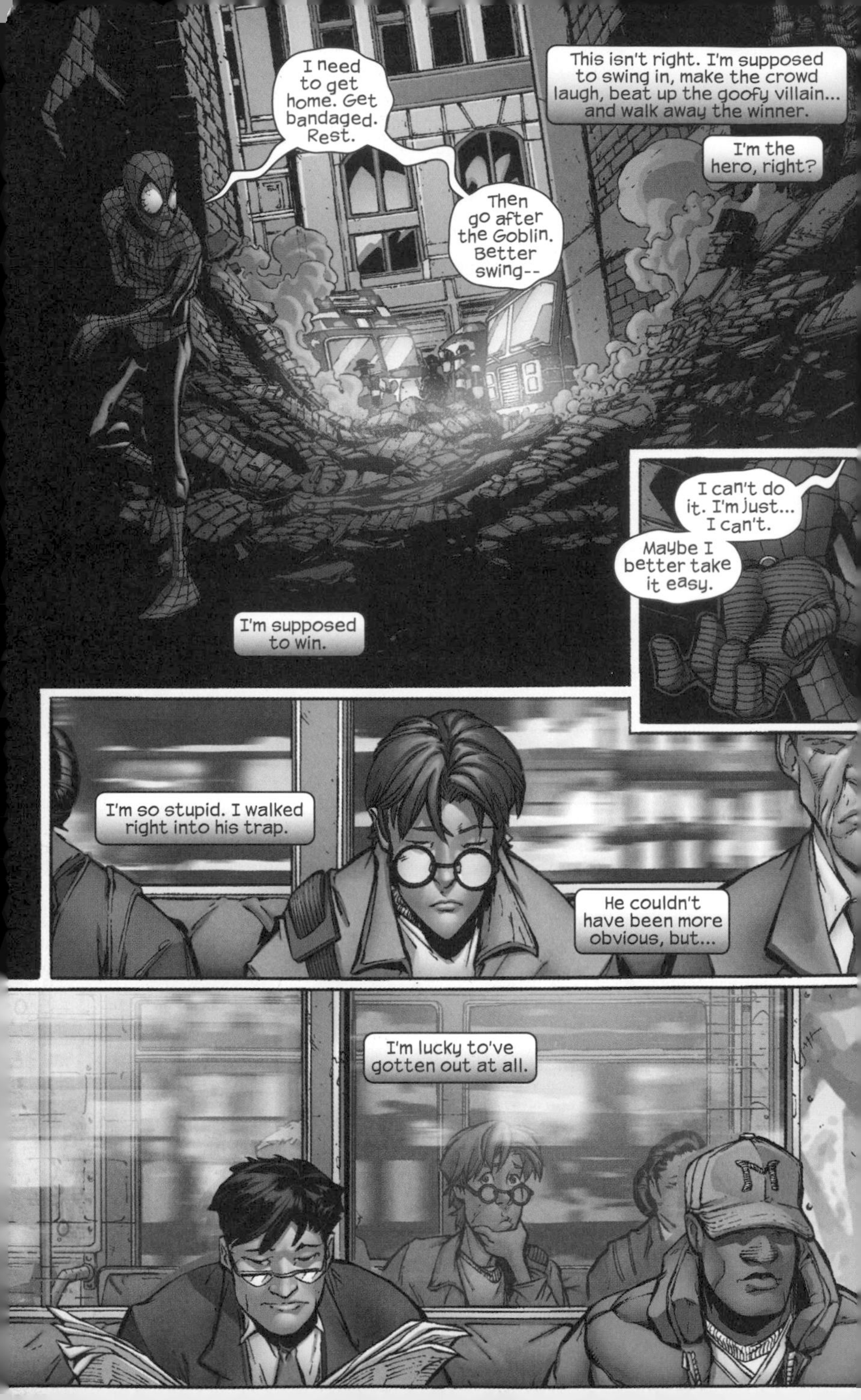
I need to get home. Get bandaged. Rest.
Then go after the Goblin. Better swing--
This isn't right. I'm supposed to swing in, make the crowd laugh, beat up the goofy villain... and walk away the winner.
I'm the hero, right?
I'm supposed to win.
I can't do it. I'm just... I can't.
Maybe I better take it easy.
I'm so stupid. I walked right into his trap.
He couldn't have been more obvious, but...
I'm lucky to've gotten out at all.

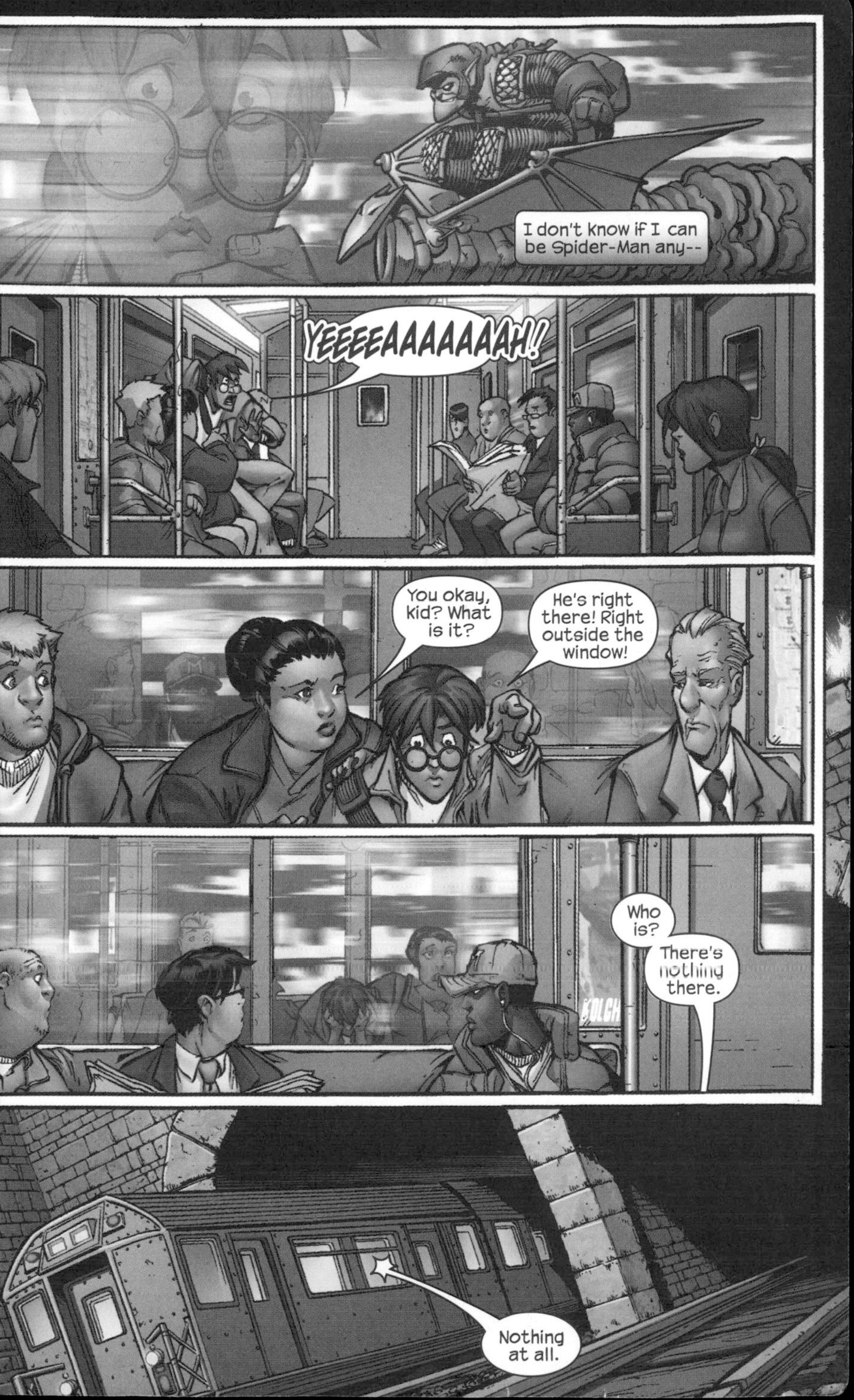
I don't know if I can be Spider-Man any--
YEEEEAAAAAAAH!
You okay, kid? What is it?
He's right there! Right outside the window!
Who is?
There's nothing there.
Nothing at all.

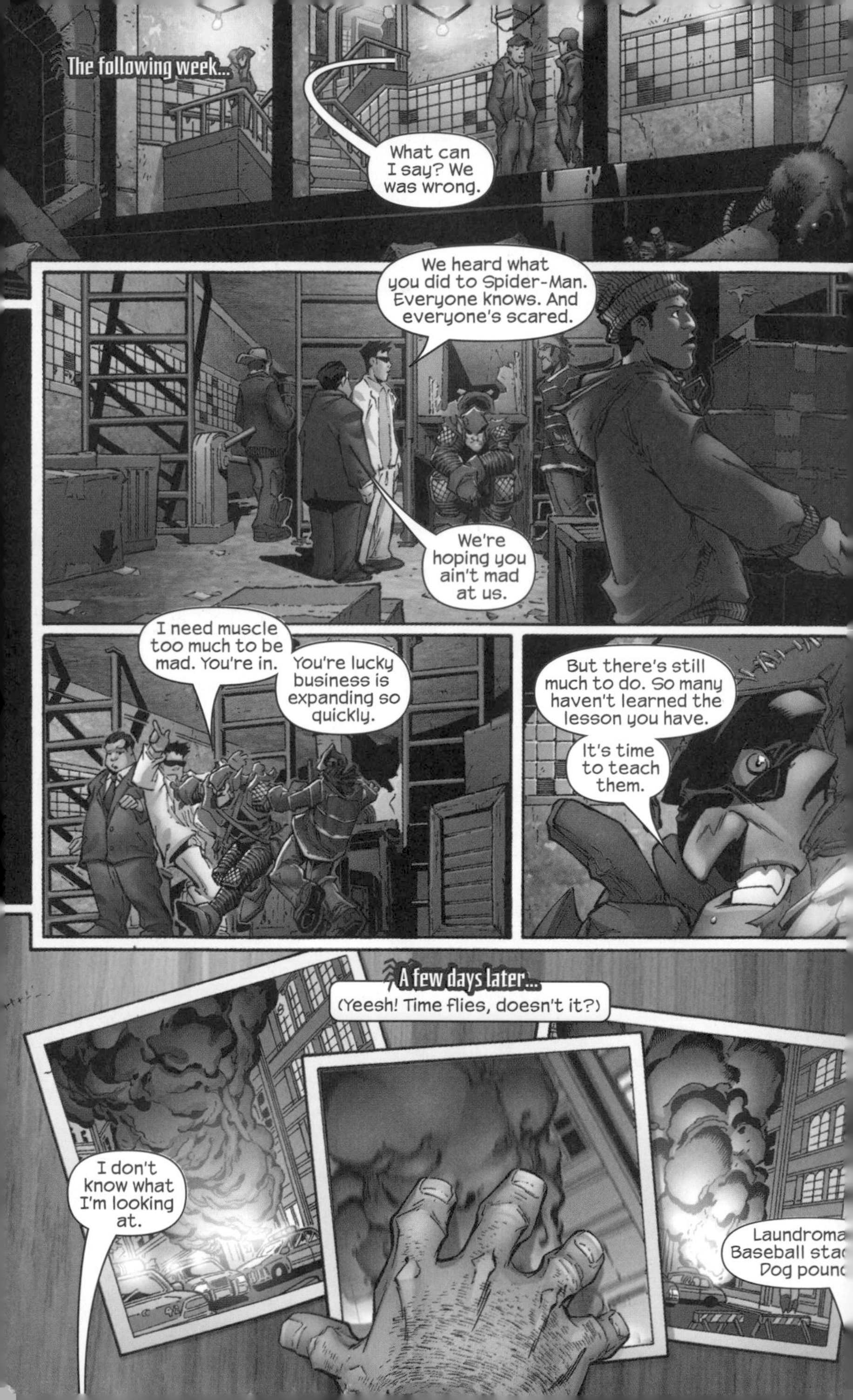

The following week...
What can I say? We was wrong.
We heard what you did to Spider-Man. Everyone knows. And everyone's scared.
We're hoping you ain't mad at us.
I need muscle too much to be mad. You're in.
You're lucky business is expanding so quickly.
But there's still much to do. So many haven't learned the lesson you have.
It's time to teach them.
A few days later...
(Yeesh! Time flies, doesn't it?)
I don't know what I'm looking at.
Laundroma
Baseball sta
Dog poun

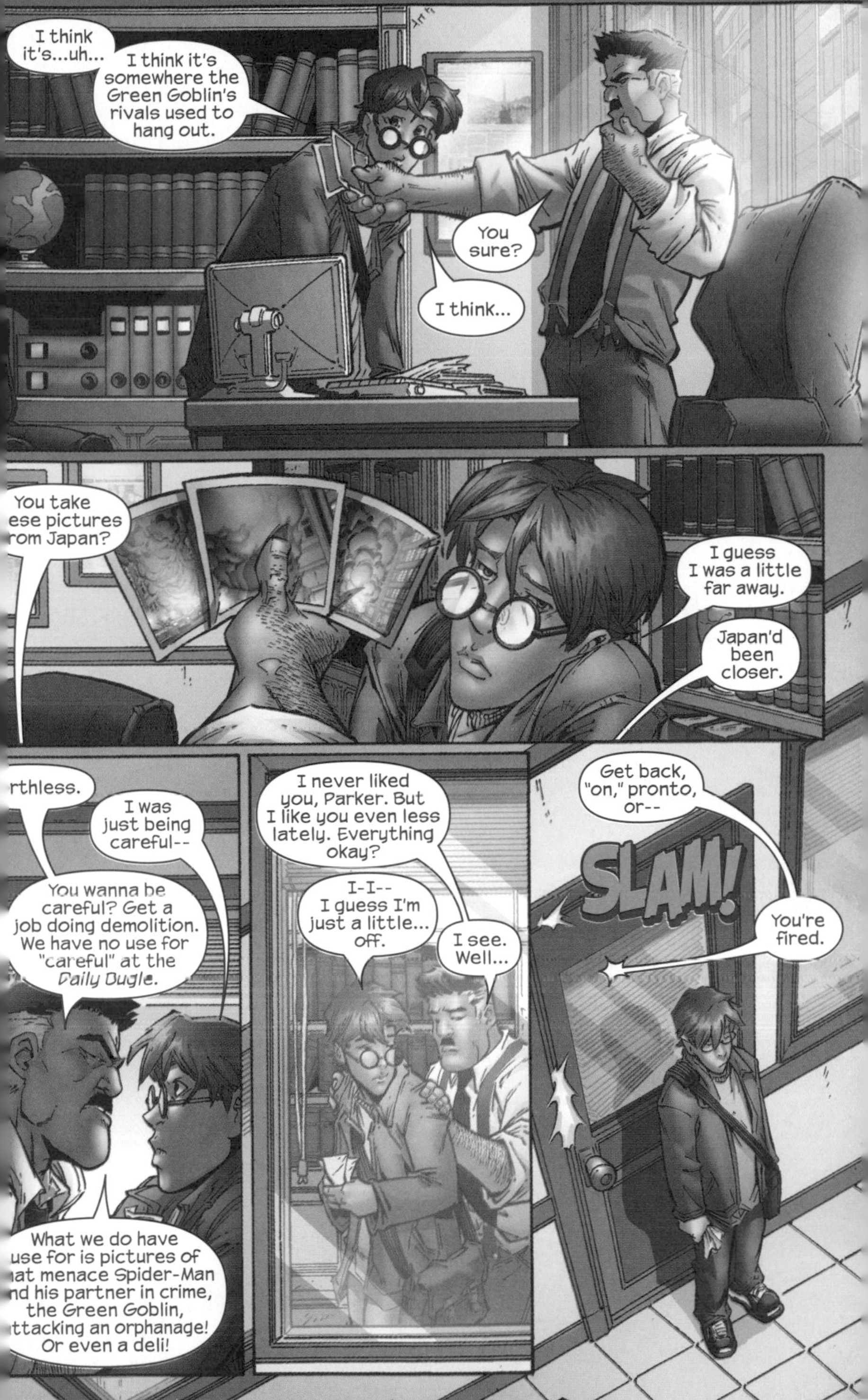
I think it's...uh...
I think it's somewhere the Green Goblin's rivals used to hang out.
You sure?
I think...
You take ese pictures rom Japan?
I guess I was a little far away.
Japan'd been closer.
rthless.
I was just being careful--
You wanna be careful? Get a job doing demolition. We have no use for "careful" at the Daily Bugle.
What we do have use for is pictures of hat menace Spider-Man nd his partner in crime, the Green Goblin, ttacking an orphanage! Or even a deli!
I never liked you, Parker. But I like you even less lately. Everything okay?
I-I-- I guess I'm just a little... off.
I see. Well...
Get back, "on," pronto, or--
SLAM!
You're fired.

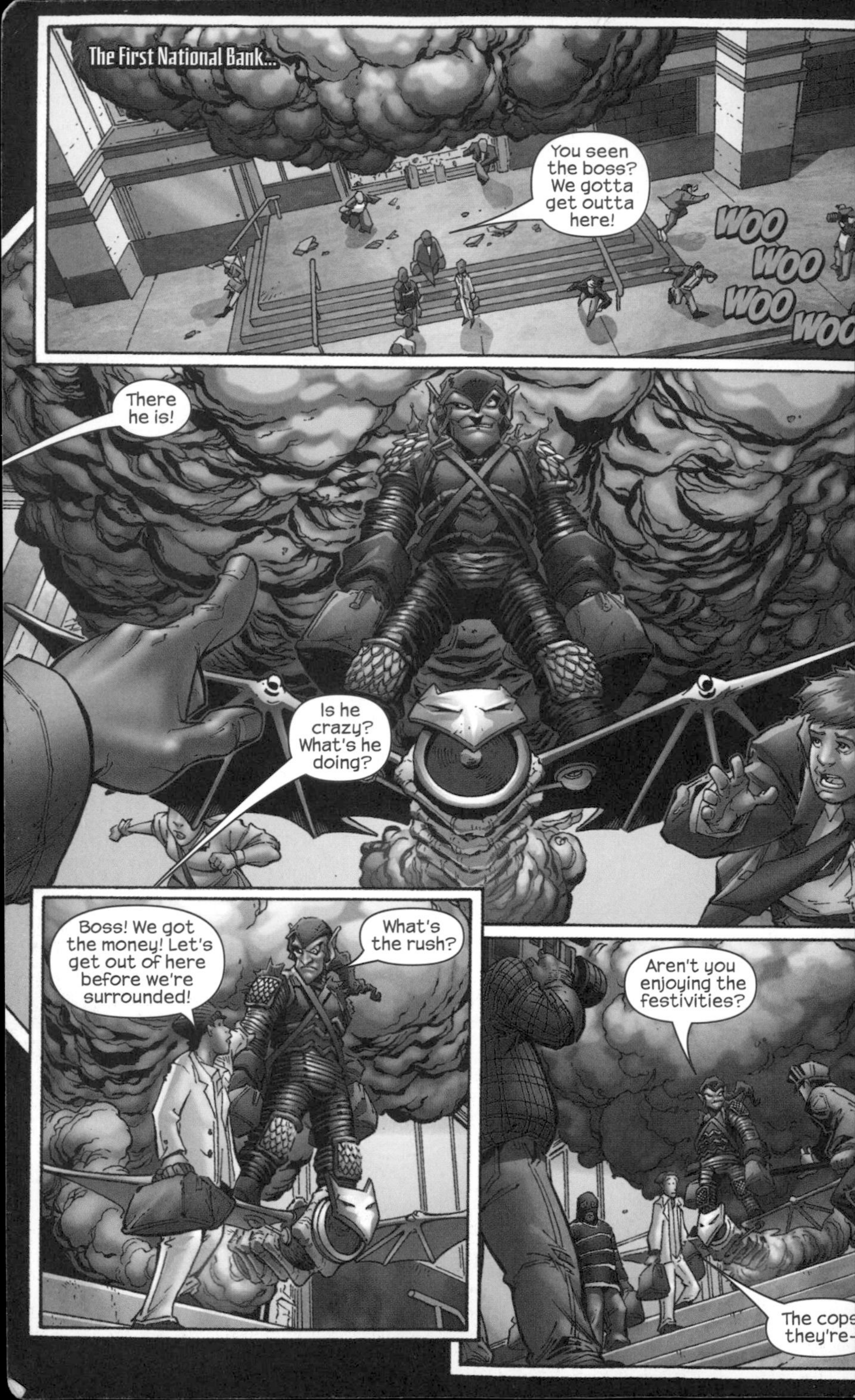
The First National Bank...
You seen the boss? We gotta get outta here!
WOO WOO WOO WOO
There he is!
Is he crazy? What's he doing?
Boss! We got the money! Let's get out of here before we're surrounded!
What's the rush?
Aren't you enjoying the festivities?
The cops they're-

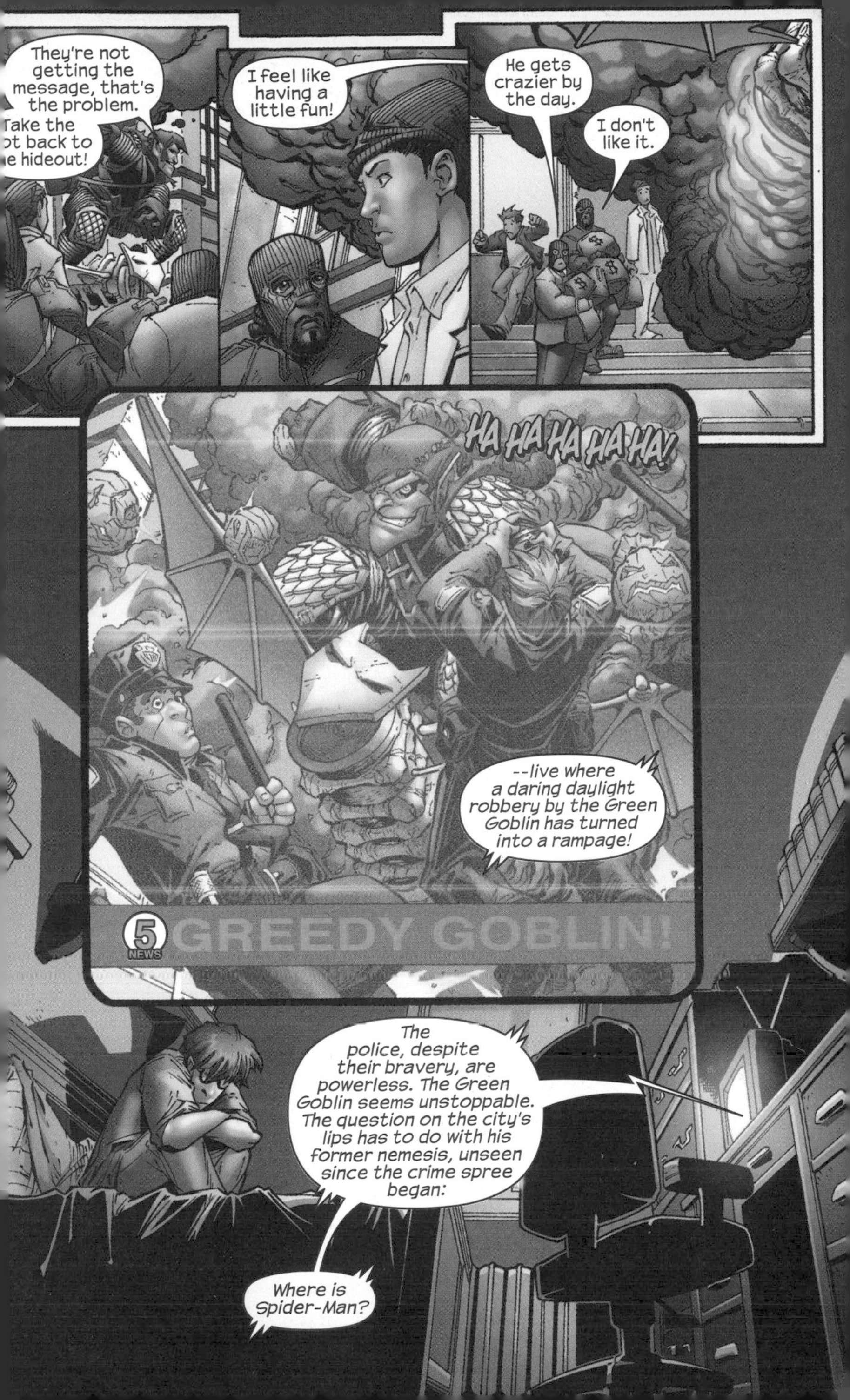
They're not getting the message, that's the problem.
Take the ot back to e hideout!
I feel like having a little fun!
He gets crazier by the day.
I don't like it.
HA HA HA HA HA!
--live where a daring daylight robbery by the Green Goblin has turned into a rampage!
5 NEWS
GREEDY GOBLIN!
The police, despite their bravery, are powerless. The Green Goblin seems unstoppable. The question on the city's lips has to do with his former nemesis, unseen since the crime spree began:
Where is Spider-Man?

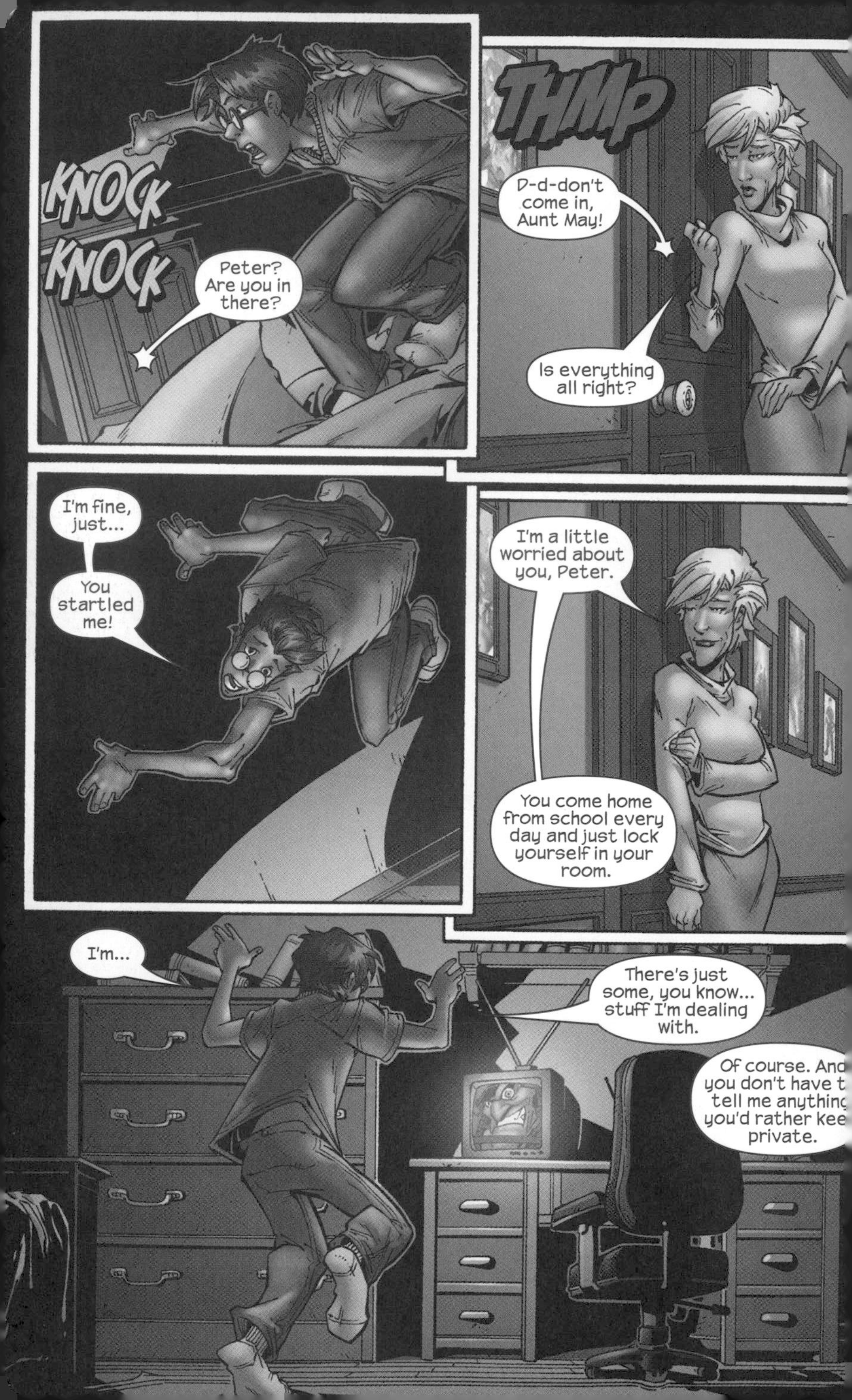
KNOCK KNOCK
Peter? Are you in there?
THMP
D-d-don't come in, Aunt May!
Is everything all right?
I'm fine, just...
You startled me!
I'm a little worried about you, Peter.
You come home from school every day and just lock yourself in your room.
I'm...
There's just some, you know... stuff I'm dealing with.
Of course. And you don't have to tell me anything you'd rather keep private.

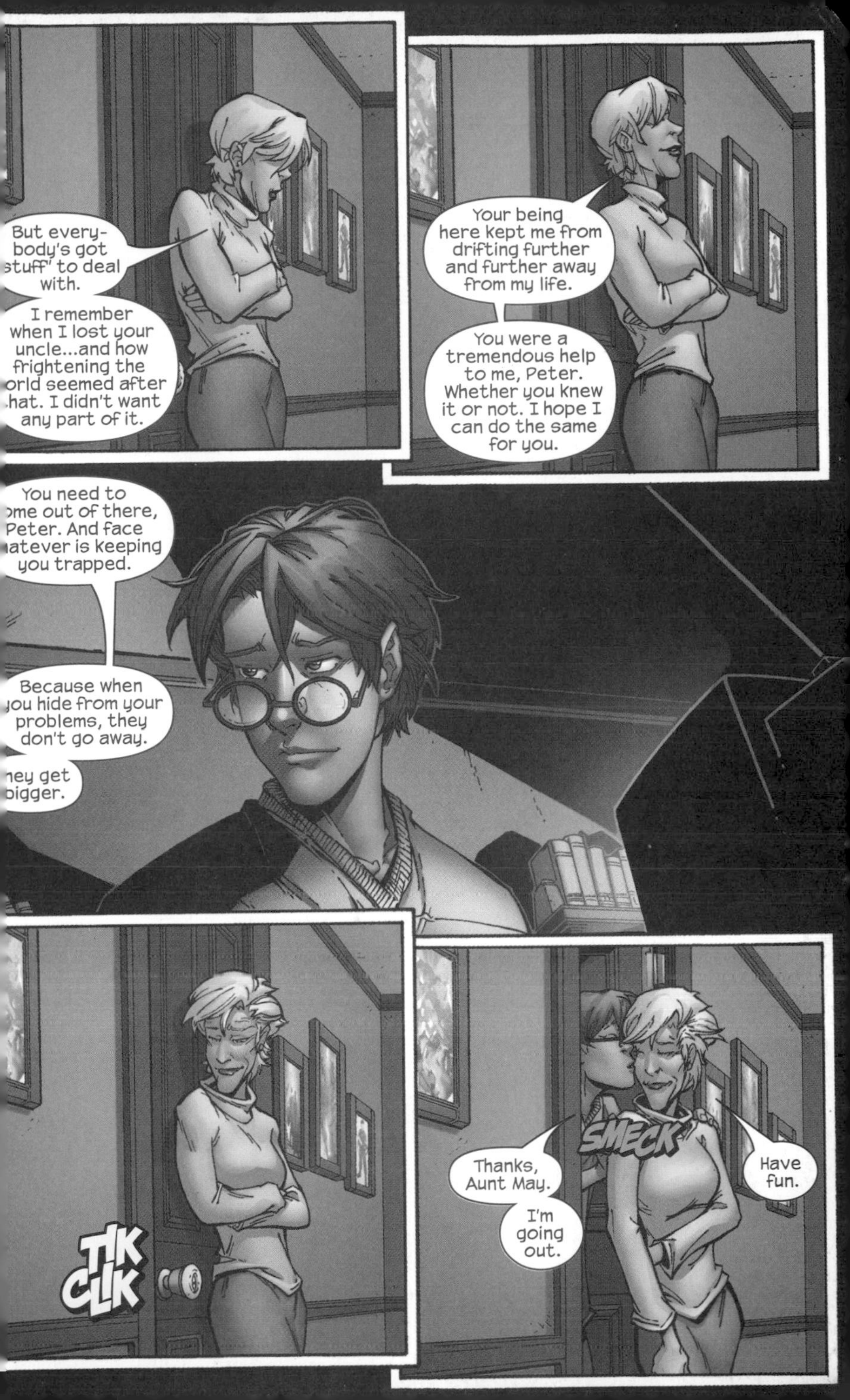
But every-body's got stuff to deal with.
I remember when I lost your uncle...and how frightening the orld seemed after hat. I didn't want any part of it.
Your being here kept me from drifting further and further away from my life.
You were a tremendous help to me, Peter. Whether you knew it or not. I hope I can do the same for you.
You need to ome out of there, Peter. And face atever is keeping you trapped.
Because when ou hide from your problems, they don't go away.
ney get oigger.
TIK CLIK
SMECK
Thanks, Aunt May.
I'm going out.
Have fun.

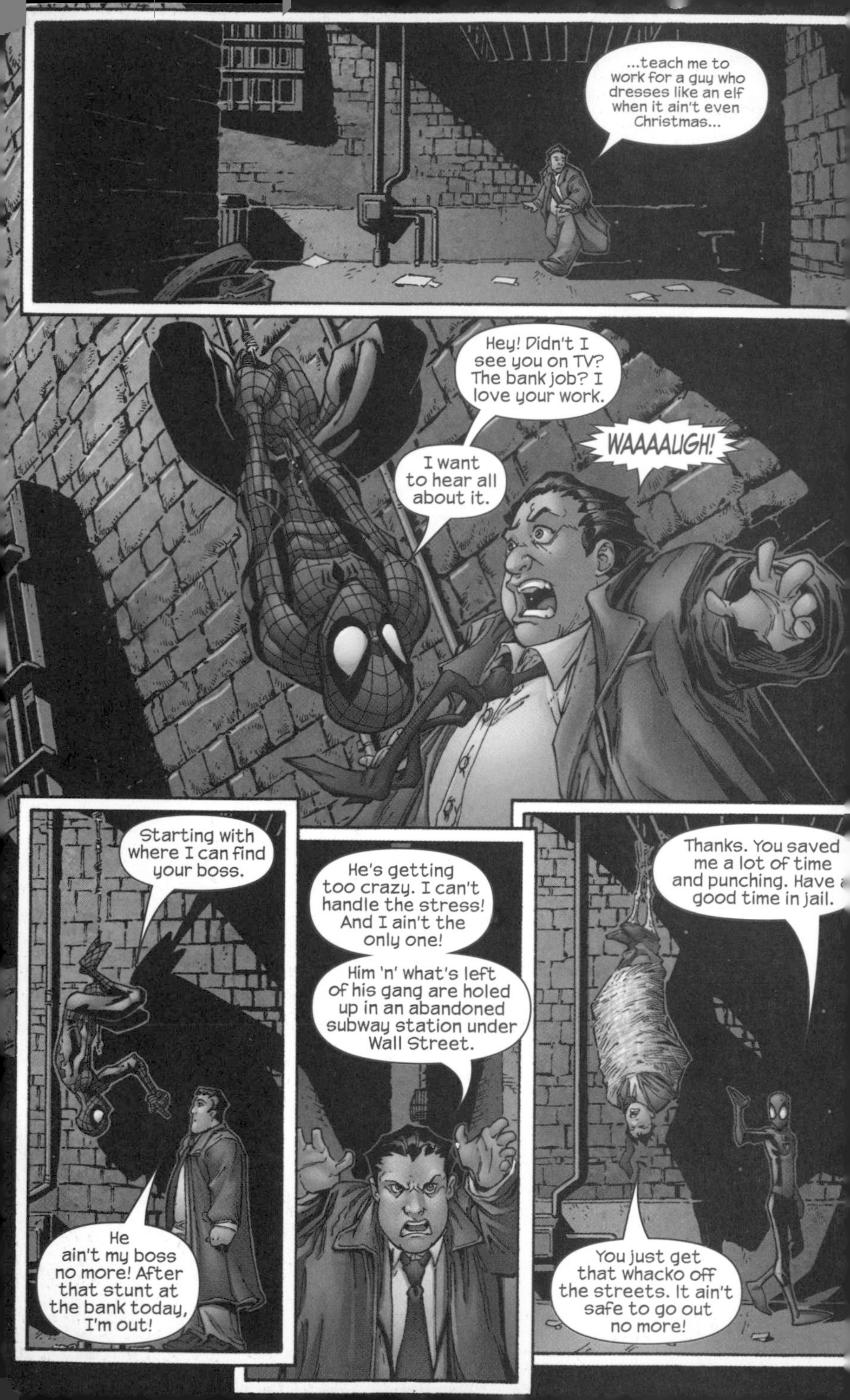
...teach me to work for a guy who dresses like an elf when it ain't even Christmas...
Hey! Didn't I see you on TV? The bank job? I love your work.
I want to hear all about it.
WAAAAUGH!
Starting with where I can find your boss.
He ain't my boss no more! After that stunt at the bank today, I'm out!
He's getting too crazy. I can't handle the stress! And I ain't the only one!
Him 'n' what's left of his gang are holed up in an abandoned subway station under Wall Street.
Thanks. You saved me a lot of time and punching. Have a good time in jail.
You just get that whacko off the streets. It ain't safe to go out no more!

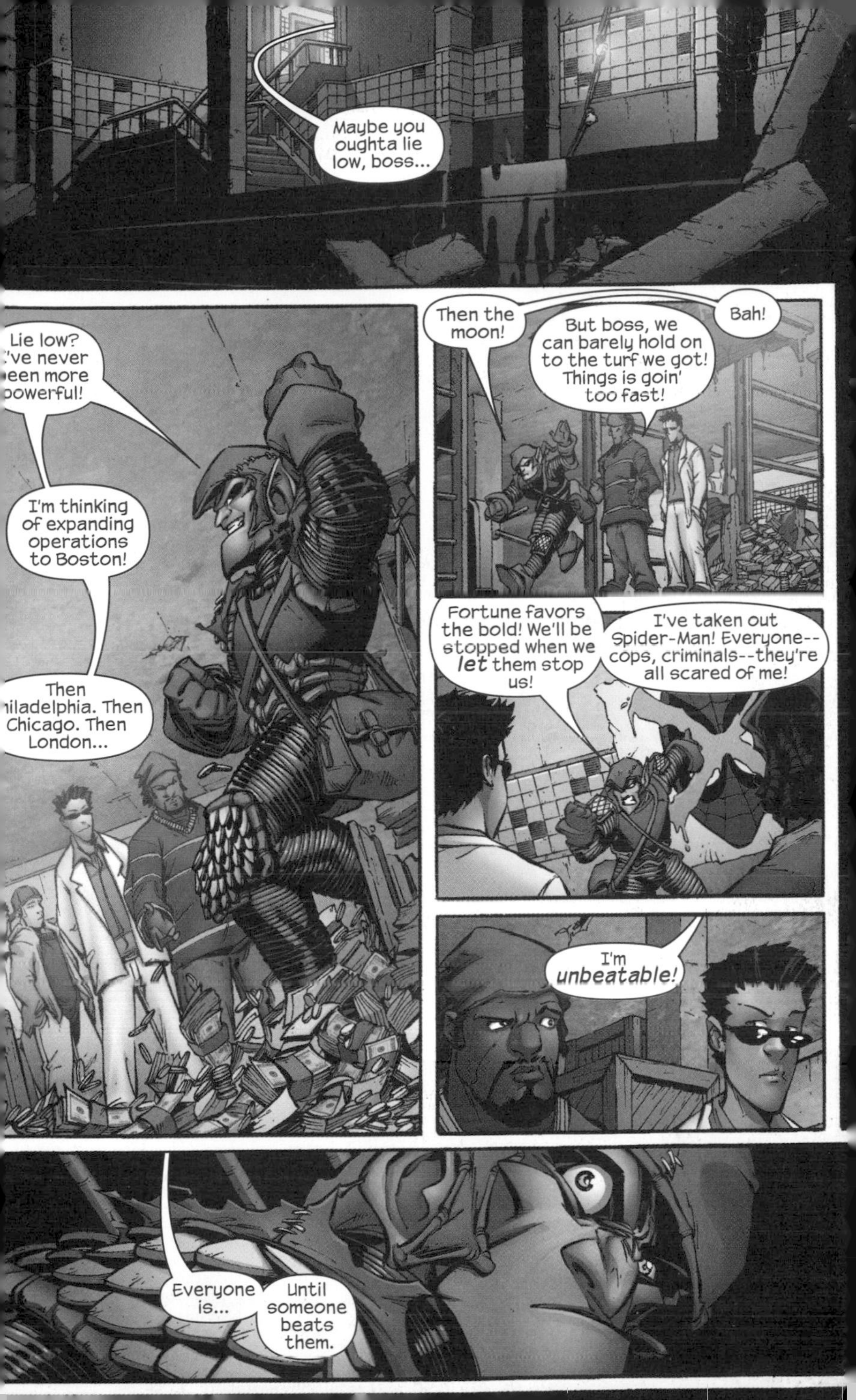
Maybe you oughta lie low, boss...
Lie low? 've never een more powerful!
I'm thinking of expanding operations to Boston!
Then iladelphia. Then Chicago. Then London...
Then the moon!
But boss, we can barely hold on to the turf we got! Things is goin' too fast!
Bah!
Fortune favors the bold! We'll be stopped when we let them stop us!
I've taken out Spider-Man! Everyone--cops, criminals--they're all scared of me!
I'm unbeatable!
Everyone is...
Until someone beats them.

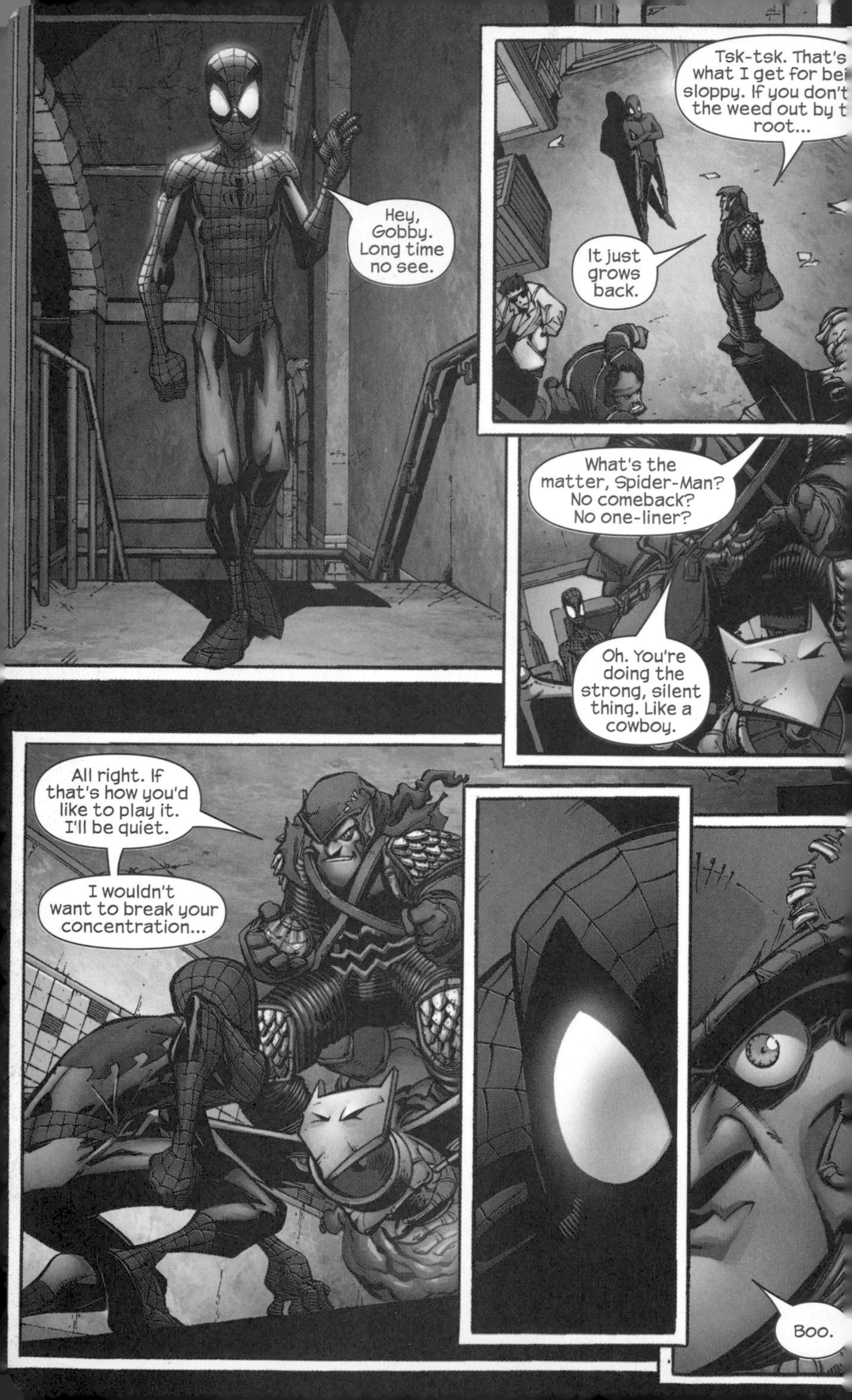
Hey, Gobby. Long time no see.
Tsk-tsk. That's what I get for bei sloppy. If you don't the weed out by t root...
It just grows back.
What's the matter, Spider-Man? No comeback? No one-liner?
Oh. You're doing the strong, silent thing. Like a cowboy.
All right. If that's how you'd like to play it. I'll be quiet.
I wouldn't want to break your concentration...
Boo.

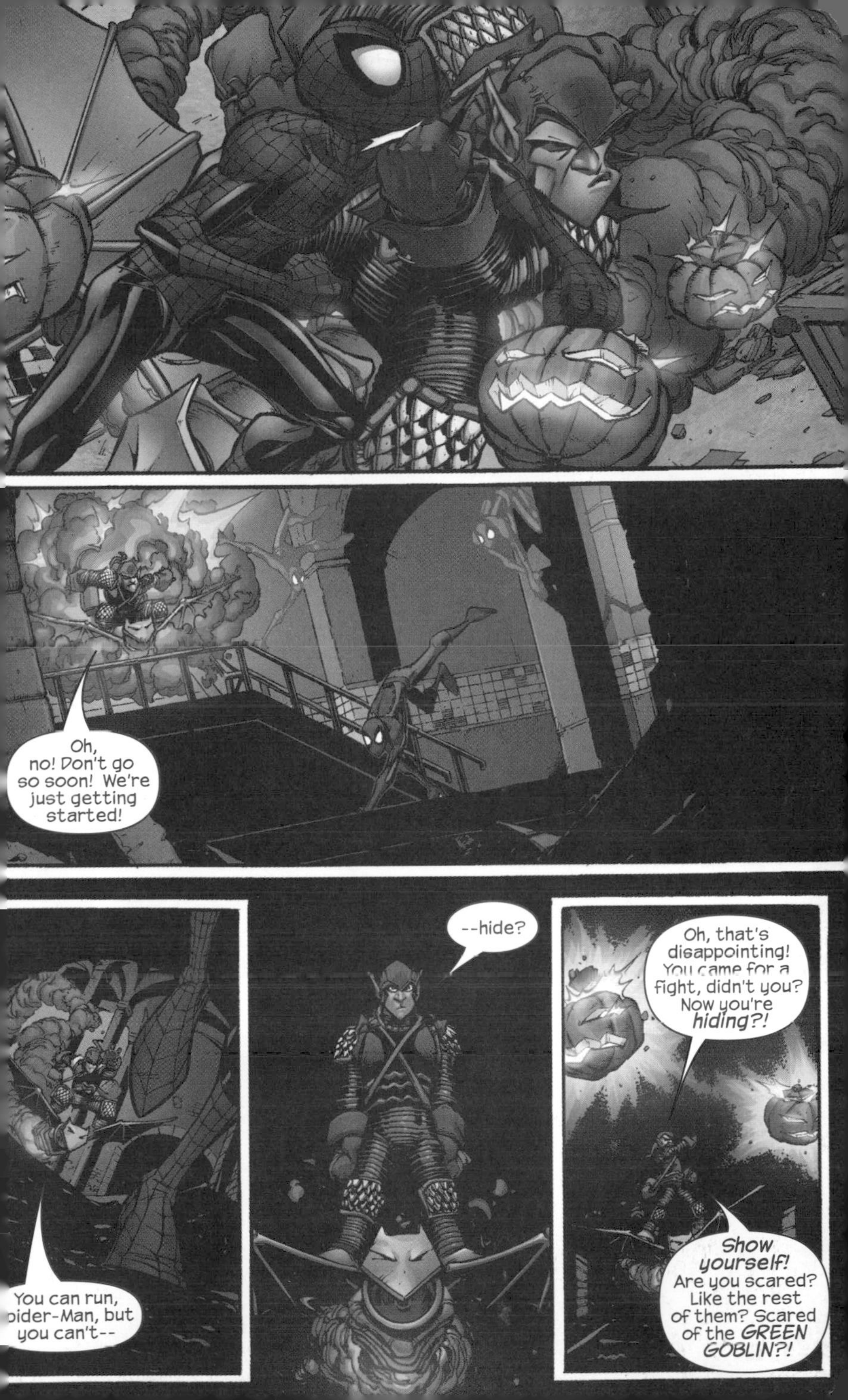
Oh, no! Don't go so soon! We're just getting started!
You can run, pider-Man, but you can't--
--hide?
Oh, that's disappointing! You came for a fight, didn't you? Now you're hiding?!
Show yourself! Are you scared? Like the rest of them? Scared of the GREEN GOBLIN?!

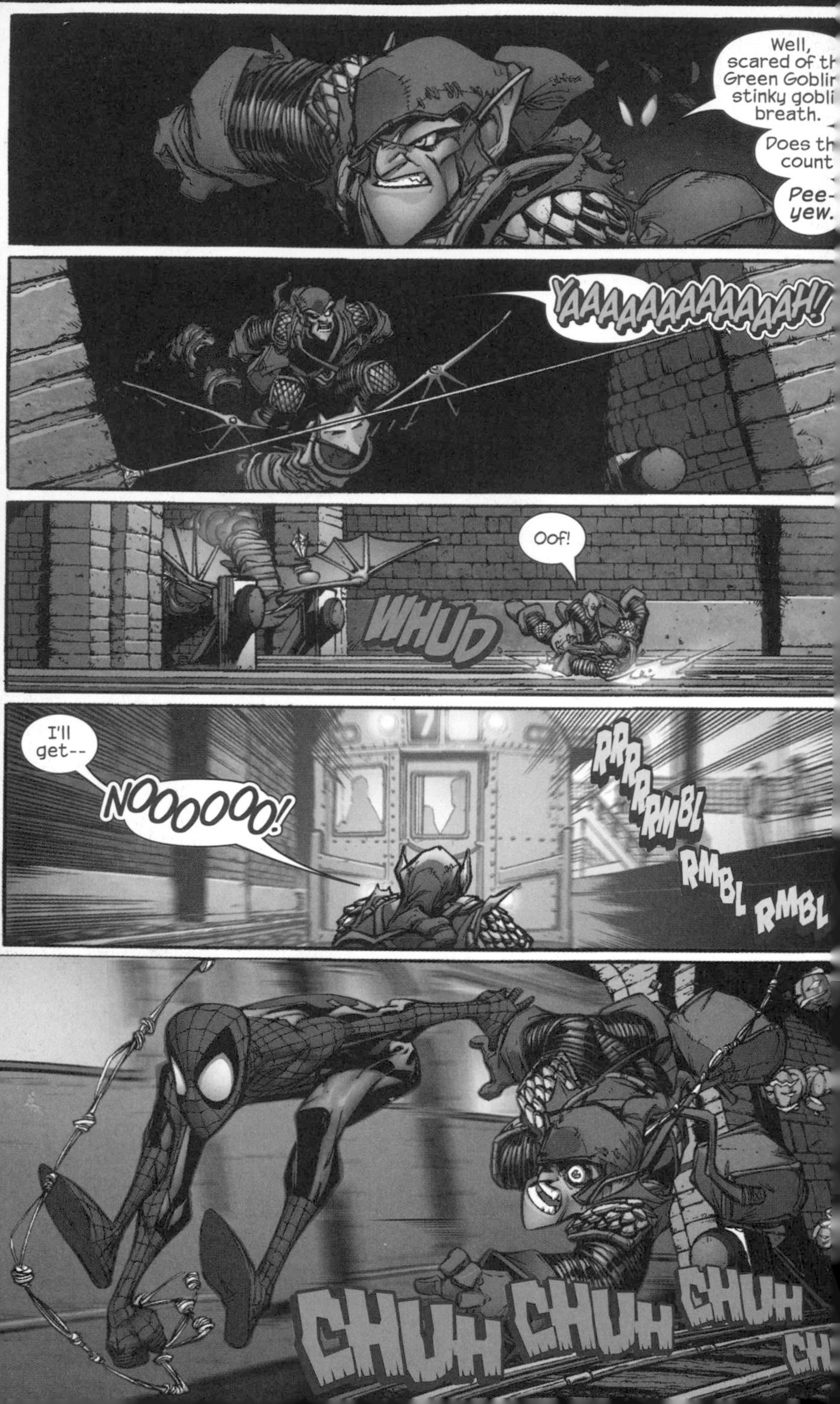
Well, scared of th Green Goblir stinky gobli breath.
Does th count
Pee-yew.
YAAAAAAAAAAAAH!!
Oof!
WHUD
I'll get--
NOOOOOO!
RRRRRMBL
RMBL RMBL
CHUH CHUH CHUH CH

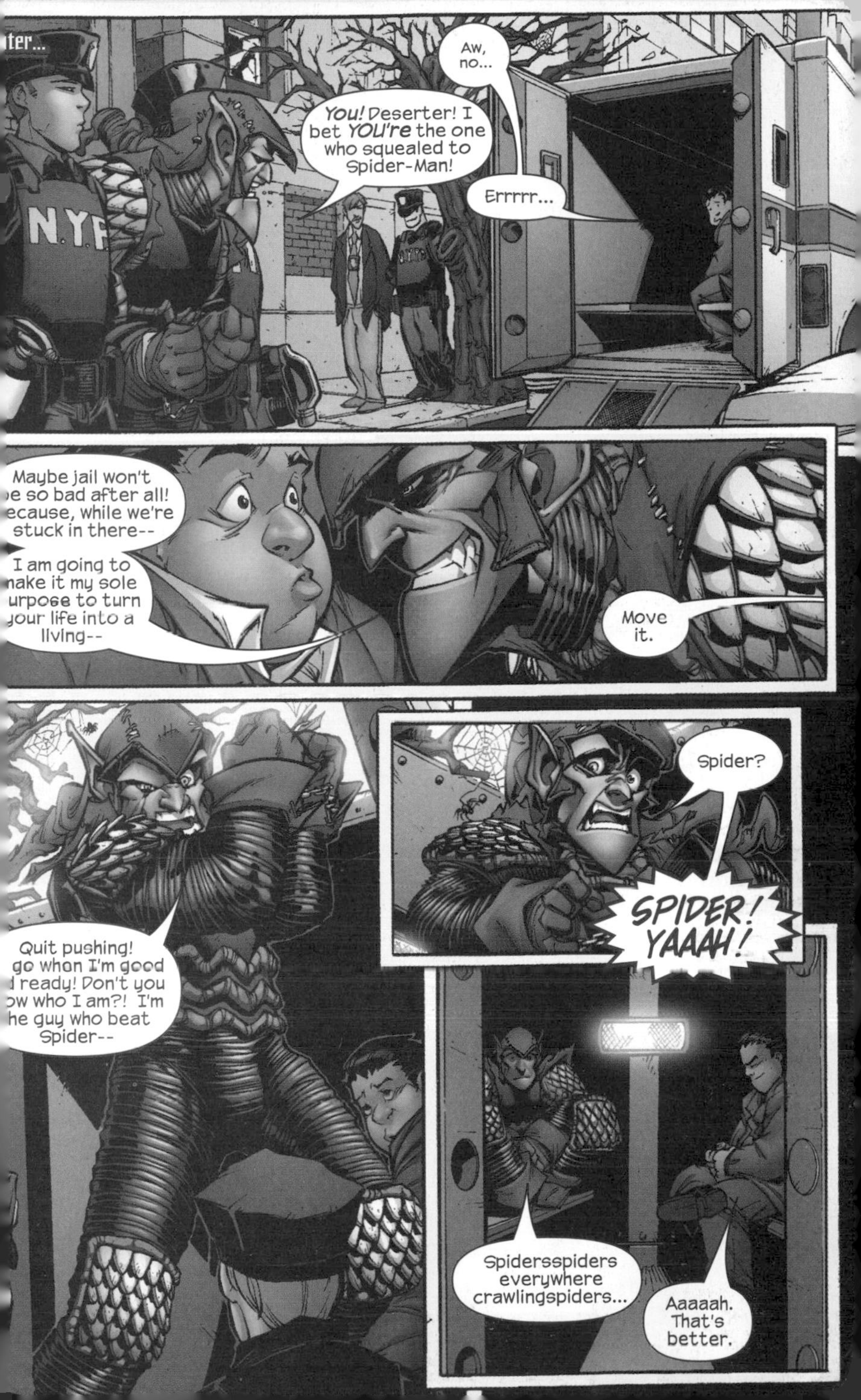
ter...
You! Deserter! I bet YOU're the one who squealed to Spider-Man!
Aw, no...
Errrrr...
Maybe jail won't e so bad after all! ecause, while we're stuck in there--
I am going to nake it my sole urpose to turn your life into a living--
Move it.
Quit pushing! go when I'm good d ready! Don't you ow who I am?! I'm he guy who beat Spider--
Spider?
SPIDER! YAAAH!
Spiderspiders everywhere crawlingspiders...
Aaaaah. That's better.

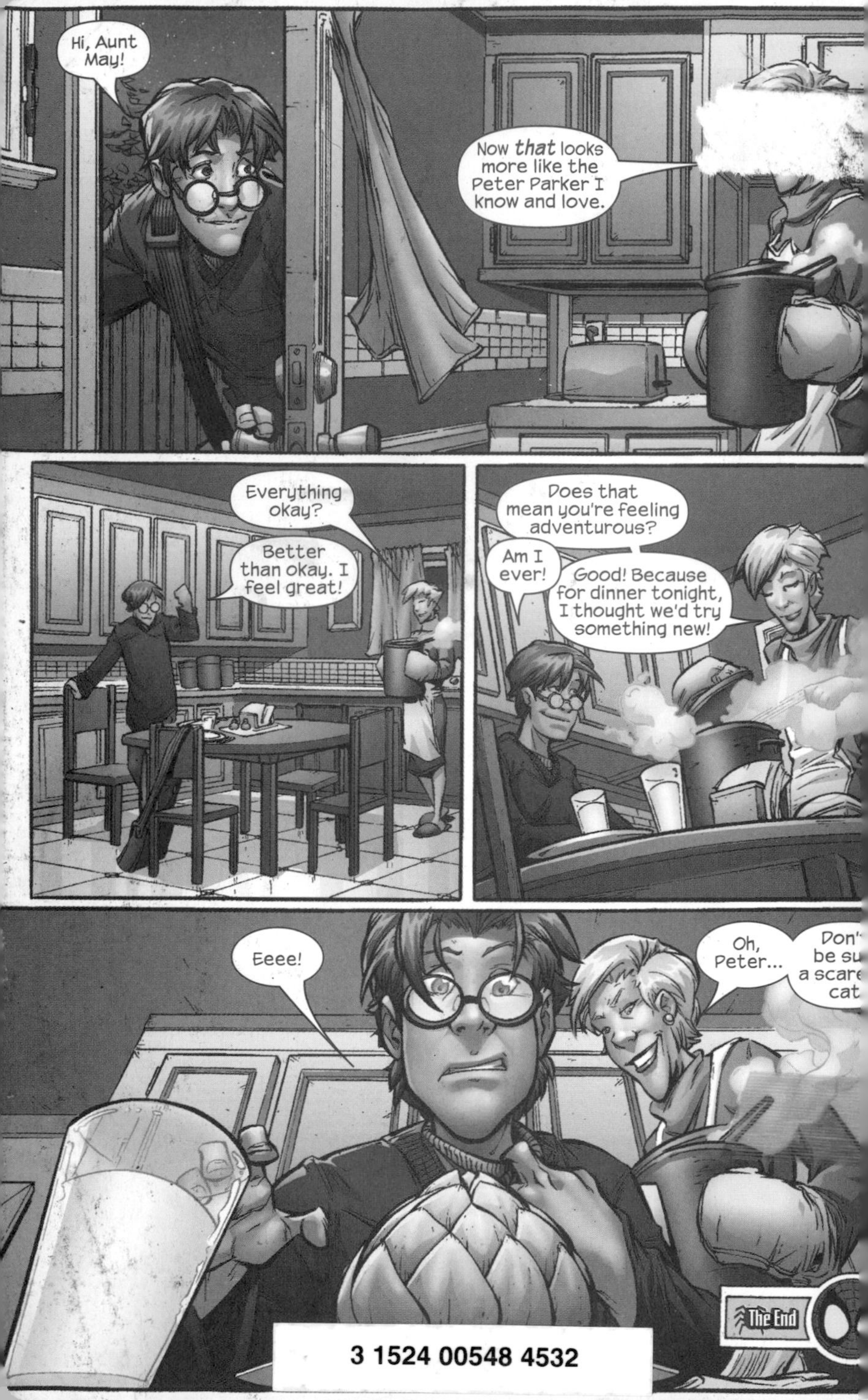
Hi, Aunt May!
Now *that* looks more like the Peter Parker I know and love.
Everything okay?
Better than okay. I feel great!
Does that mean you're feeling adventurous?
Am I ever!
Good! Because for dinner tonight, I thought we'd try something new!
Eeee!
Oh, Peter...
Don' be su a scare cat
The End